Dear Reader,

The Police Chief's Lady is the first of three books set in the imaginary but real (to me, at least!) town of Downhome, Tennessee. It's a place that needs doctors and offers them a second chance—with unexpected results.

People often ask where I get my ideas. In this case, the answer is easy: My father was, for a time, the only doctor in the small town of Menard, Texas. He rarely took a vacation because of the difficulty in finding another doctor to cover for him. Rather than have her babies at the nearest hospital, which was in another county, my mother gave birth at home, with Dad delivering my brother and me.

We eventually moved away, and I grew up mostly in Nashville, Tennessee, which is why I've chosen that state as the setting for these books. Although I live in California now, my mother still resides there.

I hope you'll enjoy the story of Jenni and Ethan, and look forward as I do to the next two books, to be published in February and April. My heroines will be Leah Morris, the teacher who's ready to spread her wings, and Karen Lowell, who's never entirely fallen out of love with Dr. Chris McRay, even though his testimony sent her brother to prison.

You can e-mail me at jdiamondfriends@aol.com, and check out my latest books at www.jacquelinediamond.com.

Happy reading!

Jacqueline Diamond

Jacqueline Diamond

The Police Chief's Lady

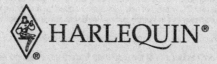

HARLEQUIN®

TORONTO • NEW YORK • LONDON
AMSTERDAM • PARIS • SYDNEY • HAMBURG
STOCKHOLM • ATHENS • TOKYO • MILAN • MADRID
PRAGUE • WARSAW • BUDAPEST • AUCKLAND

ISBN 0-373-75098-6

THE POLICE CHIEF'S LADY

www.eHarlequin.com

Printed in U.S.A.

In memory of my father

Books by Jacqueline Diamond

HARLEQUIN AMERICAN ROMANCE

Chapter One

"Nobody knows better than I do how badly this town needs a doctor," Police Chief Ethan Forrest told the crowd crammed into the Downhome, Tennessee, city council chambers. "But please, not Dr. Jenni Vine."

He hadn't meant to state his objection so bluntly, he mused as he registered the startled reaction of his audience. Six months ago, he'd been so alarmed by the abrupt departure of the town's two resident doctors, a married couple, that he'd probably have said yes to anyone with an M.D. after his or her name.

Worried about his five-year-old son, Nick, who was diabetic, Ethan had suggested that the town advertise for physicians to fill the vacated positions. He also recommended that they hire a long-needed obstetrician. In the meantime, patients who couldn't be helped by the nurse practitioner or staff nurse had to drive twelve miles to Mill Valley.

Applications hadn't exactly poured in. Only two had arrived from qualified family doctors, both of whom had toured Downhome recently by invitation. One was clearly superior, and as a member of the three-person search committee, Ethan felt it his duty to say so.

"Dr. Gregory is more experienced and, in my opinion, more stable," he said. "He's married with three kids, and I believe he's motivated to stick around for the long term." Although less than ideal in one respect, the Louisville physician took his duties seriously and, Ethan had no doubt, would fit into the community.

"Of course he's motivated!" snapped Olivia Rockwell, who stood beside Ethan just below the city council's dais. The tall African-American woman, who was the school principal, chaired the committee. "You told us yourself he's a recovering alcoholic."

"He volunteered the information, along with the fact that he's been sober for a couple of years," Ethan replied. "His references are excellent and he expressed interest in expanding our public health efforts. I think he'd be perfect to oversee the outreach program I've been advocating."

"So would Jenni—I mean, Dr. Vine," said the third committee member, Karen Lowell, director of the Tulip Tree Nursing Home. "She's energetic and enthusiastic. Everybody took to her."

"She certainly has an outgoing personality," he responded. On her visit, the California blonde had dazzled people with her expensive clothes and her good humor after being drenched in a thunderstorm, which she seemed to regard as a freak of nature. It probably didn't rain on her parade very often out in the land of perpetual sunshine, Ethan supposed. "But once the novelty wears off, she'll head for greener pastures and we'll need another doctor."

"So you aren't convinced she'll stay. None of us is in the mind-reading business," Olivia opined. "Is that the extent of your objections? This isn't typical of you, Chief. I'll bet you've got something else up that tailored sleeve of yours."

Ethan was about to pass off her comment as a joke, when he noticed some of the townsfolk leaning forward in their seats with anticipation. Despite being a quiet town best known for dairy farmers and a factory that made imitation antiques, Downhome had an appetite for gossip.

Although Ethan had hoped to avoid going into detail, the audience awaited his explanation. Was he being unfair to the applicant? he asked himself. True, he'd taken a mild dislike to Dr. Vine's surfer-girl demeanor, but he could get over that. What troubled him was the reason she wanted to leave L.A. in the first place.

"You all know I conducted background checks on the candidates," he began. "Credit records, convictions, that sort of thing."

"And found no criminal activities, right?" Karen tucked a curly strand of reddish brown hair behind one ear.

"That's correct. I also double-checked with the medical directors at their hospitals."

"You didn't mention that," Olivia murmured.

"I hoped I wouldn't have to bring it up."

"I wasn't criticizing," the principal said. "I admire your thoroughness."

Around the room, heads bobbed. Ethan felt glad the townspeople respected his approach. Four years ago, when he left the Nashville Metropolitan Police Department and returned home after his wife's death, he had believed his professionalism was the reason they'd chosen him as chief over several other candidates.

Well, he had a bombshell to drop, so he'd better get it over with. "A few months ago, Dr. Vine became enmeshed in a controversy." He tried to ignore the impatient way Karen twirled a pencil between her fingers. "Dr. Vine was counseling one of her patients about marital problems. She met with the woman and her husband outside of work."

"What's wrong with that?" demanded the nursing home director.

"Nothing, on the face of it," Ethan replied. "However, a

short time later, the patient filed a complaint. She told the medical director that her husband had confessed to becoming involved in an affair with Dr. Vine."

Karen's pencil went flying. In the audience, a couple of exclamations broke the stillness and some faces registered disapproval.

Olivia raised one eyebrow. "From this you conclude that she's a husband-stealing tart who would sully the moral fiber of our community?"

"If we hire her, we're placing her in a position of trust," Ethan responded. "If she's the type of person to exploit a situation, it makes me uncomfortable."

"Jenni has a right to defend herself," Karen said. "Did you speak to her about this?"

"Not directly, but I did look further." Ethan checked his notes. "In response to the hospital board's inquiry, Dr. Vine denied the allegation. She claimed the husband had been antagonistic and lied to get her out of the picture." It struck him as a weak excuse, but he was here to present the facts.

"What action did the board take?" Olivia asked.

He folded the notes into his pocket. "They concluded there wasn't enough evidence to take action. However, word got out, and the medical director says Dr. Vine's presence on the staff has become awkward. Even assuming she's innocent, that reinforces my concern as to whether she intends to stay here or is simply grasping at the first chance to escape an unpleasant situation."

Council member Mae Anne McRay, a retired principal whose wheelchair barely permitted her to see above the council's raised counter, piped up. "We advertised that we were offering doctors a second chance, didn't we?"

"A second chance to live in a friendly, affordable town and escape from practicing corporate medicine," said the mayor, Olivia's husband, Archie Rockwell, who owned the feed store. "Not a second chance to seduce someone's husband."

"How about a second chance to prove she cares about patients and isn't afraid to stick her neck out?" Mae Anne retorted.

"A recovering alcoholic needs a second chance, too," Ethan observed. "And he's been clean for a couple of years."

Archie frowned. "I'm with Ethan on this one. Seducing a patient's husband—that's a serious allegation."

"Maybe she was conducting sex therapy," cracked Gwen Martin. The peppery café owner lived by the dictum that nobody over fifty should hesitate to speak her mind. "For Pete's sake, the hospital board cleared her."

"We didn't advertise for no sex therapist," grumbled 79-year-old Beau Johnson, who maintained a colloquial way of speaking despite his stature as grocery store owner and a descendant of the town's founder.

"It's not a matter of yea or nay on Dr. Vine. We have an excellent choice in Dr. Gregory," observed Mayor Rockwell, keeping a wary eye on his wife. Olivia ruled her family as firmly as she ruled the town's elementary and high school in her consolidated role as the town's principal.

"We have to be careful. A controversy like this could tear our town apart!" cried the council's fifth member, Rosie O'Bannon, owner of the Snip 'N' Curl salon. Since she was given to making dire pronouncements that hardly ever came true, no one bothered to answer.

"Let's put it to a vote," the mayor said. "I know some folks in the audience have to get up early in the morning to tend to their farms, so do I hear a motion?"

"I move we hire Dr. Jenni Vine," Gwen said.

"Second," said Mae Anne.

"Discussion?" the mayor asked, following the formalities.

"We already had one," Beau snipped.

The vote split three-to-two, women against men. That surprised Ethan, who'd expected Downhome's ladies to reject a potential predator in their midst.

In any case, the decision had been made. Dr. Vine would be offered the position.

As the meeting broke up, he tried not to show his disappointment. Although the physician might have been falsely accused, Ethan had always had a knack for sizing people up, and his instincts told him that their new doctor was materialistic, spoiled and accustomed to charming her way out of difficulties.

"Well, Ethan?" Olivia asked as she collected her purse. "Think you can get used to a liberated lady in a white coat?"

"I'd hoped whoever we hired would work on the outreach program, but she didn't show much interest when I mentioned it." He shrugged. "As for my son…Nick's medical team is in Nashville. We only contact the local doctor if there's an emergency."

"That's your answer? That you're going to avoid her?" the principal challenged.

"Quite the opposite. I keep my eye on everything that happens in Downhome. But I expect she'll soon get tired of playing Marcus Welby and find a job closer to a shopping mall."

Nearby, Karen straightened after retrieving her pencil. She bestowed a brief glare on Ethan before heading off.

He wished he hadn't made such a tactless remark in Karen's hearing. She apparently identified with Dr. Vine, perhaps because both were single women in their early thirties…or because her family was no stranger to questionable accusations.

Well, the time had come to switch from cop to daddy and collect Nick from his grandma's house. At this hour, Ethan could expect only a sleepy hug as he tucked Nick into bed, but maybe he'd get lucky and hear a five-year-old's recap of the day's events.

He decided not to worry about Karen's reaction. By the time Dr. Vine arrived, his comments would be old news.

THE WHIRR OF THE SEWING MACHINE masked the ring of Jenni's cell phone. Attuned to being on call, however, she stopped in mid-seam and made a dive for her purse, which she'd dropped on the sofa bed after work.

She extracted the instrument and said breathlessly, "Dr. Vine."

"Jenni? It's Karen." The Tulip Tree director's excitement pulsed across the two-thousand-mile distance. "They voted! You'll be getting a call from the mayor tomorrow."

She could hardly breathe. "Do you mean…?"

"You got it!" Karen crowed. "Congratulations! When Archie calls, act surprised, okay?"

"You bet. That's wonderful!" Jenni performed a little dance across the worn carpet of her tiny East L.A. apartment, which was all she could afford while paying off medical school loans.

No more commuting forty-five minutes each way in heavy traffic! No more worries about a possible threat from the abusive man whose wife she'd tried to rescue, and no more dubious looks from colleagues because of his lies. And since she'd written her last student loan check the previous month—which she'd celebrated by bringing doughnuts for everyone at work—she could afford to take a small-town position.

She felt ready for a change and for a second chance, as the ad had suggested. The friendliness of the people she'd met on her visit—most of them, anyway—had clinched her decision to take the position if it was offered.

"How soon can you come?" Karen asked. She and Jenni

had clicked instantly, a fact that made the town all the more inviting.

"I have to give two weeks' notice." Jenni's mind raced ahead. There wasn't much to pack, and the only person she felt close to, the physician who'd mentored her, had retired the previous year and moved with her husband to Arizona. "I'll need to find an apartment. Or is there a residential hotel?"

"No, but I'll watch for vacancies," Karen said. "You can stay with me till you locate a place. I'm sure my brother won't mind. We've got plenty of room in the house."

"That's really kind, but it seems like an imposition," Jenni replied.

"Actually, I'd enjoy it," her new friend responded. "Besides, you'll find a place before long."

"That sounds wonderful, then! Thank you." Things were meshing so easily that Jenni instinctively wondered what might go wrong. In her experience, you had to prove yourself wherever you went. "Some people must have preferred the other candidate." She'd heard he was a middle-aged guy with a family. "If there are reservations about me, I'd like to know in advance. Especially since I'm on three months' probation."

"That's true," Karen said. "Well…"

"You won't hurt my feelings." Living for years with relatives who didn't really want her had toughened Jenni to rejection, and taught her to deal with it up front. "Frankly, I figured the council would prefer someone older."

"Some of them did," Karen admitted. "It was a three-two vote. The women wanted you and the men preferred Dr. Gregory. Come to think of it, that was true for the search committee, too. It's funny how that worked out."

Jenni remembered the other two members of the committee quite clearly. "I'm glad I won Olivia's approval. So the

police chief disagreed. What was his name again?" She'd
done her best to put it out of her head.

"Ethan Forrest."

"Right." She'd first seen him as she pulled her rental car
into the clinic's parking lot, twenty minutes late after a long
drive from Nashville. He'd been scowling as he paced the
walkway.

Even at a distance, Chief Forrest's solid build and dark,
masculine good looks had struck her. When she emerged
from the car, Jenni had experienced what she called a go-back
moment, an abrupt mood shift; suddenly she felt like a fif-
teen-year-old about to be chewed out by an adult. As a teenager, she'd often landed in trouble because she defied anyone
who tried to put her down.

Ethan Forrest hadn't scolded Jenni for tardiness. He'd
even managed a smile, but not a warm one. She'd felt his
brooding gaze following her the whole day as she toured the
medical facilities and the town. Apparently, he'd taken a dislike to her, although she had no idea why.

"What exactly were his objections?" she asked.

After a moment's hesitation, Karen said, "He brought up
some accusation—which I'm sure isn't true—about you and
a patient's husband."

Jenni's hands clenched. How dare he embarrass her publicly without even hearing her side of the story! She had to
remind herself that the council had voted in her favor anyway.

"I hope nobody believed it," she responded. "Because it
isn't true."

"I know that!"

"Apparently, Chief Forrest doesn't." She decided imme-
diately to call him by his first name as if they were equals.
In some ways, they were, although she still faced probation.
"What else did Ethan say?"

"Something about keeping an eye on you," Karen admitted.

What did he think she planned to do—spend her days targeting other women's husbands? But Jenni refused to vent her anger while talking to her new friend.

With an exercise of will, she kept her voice level as she assured Karen that she felt certain Ethan would come around. "And I promise to sound totally shocked when Mr. Rockwell calls tomorrow," she added.

"I'm so thrilled! My friend Leah Morris—she's a teacher—suggested we single women hold a potluck in your honor when you get here. Maybe you can share some stories about L.A. and we can clue you in about the local guys. Not that there are many worth talking about."

"That would be great." Jenni looked forward to meeting a supportive group of women. In L.A., she'd barely had time to keep up with her professional reading and affiliations, let alone socialize.

Her good mood lasted until she and Karen hung up. Then the information about Ethan Forrest came back to her. What was the man's problem?

Grabbing a pillow, she whacked the arm of the couch. "Why?" Jenni demanded of this imaginary target. "Why did you try to screw things up for me? What did I ever do to you?"

She stood there, pillow in hand, overcome by another go-back moment. Ethan Forrest was a big man in Downhome and she'd be an outsider. She could picture him forever finding fault, searching for ways to turn others against her as Cousin Laura had done when Jenni, as a high school freshman, had to stay at her aunt's house after one of her mother's drug-related arrests.

Laura, a junior who resented having to share her home and her mother's attention, had made life miserable for months by taunting Jenni at school. Jenni had initially tried to please her, but finally decided she'd turned the other cheek long enough.

One day, she'd responded to a gibe in kind, in front of other kids, tossing out embarrassing details until Laura fled in tears. Following her, Jenni had threatened worse if she reported the incident, and after that, Laura had left her alone.

Jenni wasn't proud of what she'd done, but she'd felt desperate. She'd learned a lesson that day about standing up for herself.

Confronting the police chief might not be the wisest policy. However it went against Jenni's nature to let him run her down behind her back. If he had anything to say, he had better be prepared to say it to her face.

Still stewing, she returned to her machine. Thank goodness for her flair with the needle, because she could never afford to buy a designer suit like this.

That was another life lesson she'd learned: no matter how poor you were, dressing badly made you the object of scorn. Survival had its rules, and Jenni was a survivor.

She intended to get that message across to Ethan in a manner he wouldn't forget.

Chapter Two

From his office window, Ethan glanced across Tulip Tree Avenue at a couple of dog walkers making their way through the central square known as The Green. On a Monday morning, the center of Downhome spread placidly before him. To his left, a dairy truck turned south at the intersection of Tulip Tree and Home Boulevard; across the street next to The Green, a couple of workmen emerged from Pepe's Italian Diner with cups of steaming coffee.

The town didn't appear a likely setting for a crime wave. And by city standards, the recent reports of petty thefts seemed tame. Still, Ethan found something disturbing about the reports on his desk.

"You wanted to see me?" Captain Ben Fellows, the top-ranking officer below Ethan, appeared in his doorway. Unofficially, Ben filled the role of assistant chief. A few years older than Ethan and with fifteen years on the force, he'd been in the running for the top job four years ago, but didn't seem to resent having been passed over.

"Yes. Is Mark with you?"

"Right here" came the voice of Lieutenant Mark O'Bannon, who supervised detectives and traffic in the small department.

Ethan gestured them into seats. His office provided enough

space for a few visitors as well as a bookcase, file cabinet and computer station. As for the decor, his mother, Annette, a part-time interior designer and part-time baby-sitter, had picked out the cream paint and subtle green-and-cream print curtains. He'd retained the former chief's oversize desk, with its accumulated scars, as a tribute to departmental tradition.

"This latest report—that makes three cases," Ethan noted. "I'd say it rules out family and friends of the victims, which means we could be dealing with a serial criminal. The fact that no one's been hurt and property loss is minimal doesn't change the reality that these crimes are invasive and threatening by their very nature. What do you think?"

Mark, the twenty-eight-year-old son of council member Rosie O'Bannon, deferred instinctively to Captain Fellows. Ethan was also eager to hear Ben's insight, since the man served as pastor at the Community Church and knew the citizenry better than anyone.

"Frankly, it's a new one on me." Ben scratched his head. "Someone slipping into houses and stealing family portraits off the wall is weird. And I agree, somewhat scary because it seems like a hostile thing to do. The guy might have the potential for violence, especially if someone stumbles across him."

"At first, I figured it was a prank," Mark noted. "I assumed the photos would turn up soon."

"We can rule that out at this point," Ethan said. "The stories in the paper have made it clear how distressed the victims are."

The first case had been reported a month ago. A woman returning from a shopping trip had noticed a family photo missing from her living room wall but assumed her husband had taken it down. Only when she'd asked him about it that night and learned otherwise had she remembered leaving a side door unlocked. When she'd called the cops, they'd found a couple of leaves tracked inside but no real evidence.

In the second theft, two weeks later, a retired couple had been puzzled by the absence of their favorite photo and distressed a few days later when they realized it hadn't simply been mislaid by the cleaning lady. The group portrait, which was irreplaceable, included a son who'd been killed in military action.

The latest case involved Pepe Otero, who owned Pepe's Italian Diner, although his family had immigrated from Argentina. Since he lived over the restaurant, he frequently left his apartment unlocked. The previous night, he'd lost a picture of himself and his three kids in their younger years, a scene from which he'd had the image of his ex-wife digitally removed.

"Maybe Connie took it," he'd told Ethan that morning when he filed the report. "She's still mad at me, even though it was her who got tired of living in a small town. Maybe she sneaked in and swiped it."

"Why would she?" Ethan asked. "She's been gone for years."

"Who else would take it?" Pepe had replied, and had been surprised to learn his was the third such theft. He admitted he rarely had time to read the weekly *Downhome Gazette.*

"We're already pursuing the investigation," Mark said. "What else should we do?"

"I'll ask the paper to issue a warning," Ethan answered. "I don't want to make people panic, but they need to take this seriously and keep their doors and windows locked."

"You want me to call Barry?" Ben was referring to the editor of the *Gazette,* Karen Lowell's brother.

"I'll handle it," Ethan said. "However, I want to get your feedback first. You've both lived here longer than I have. Does anyone come to mind as a possible suspect? I'd like your gut feelings."

Mark cleared his throat. "This probably isn't relevant."

"Let's hear it."

The young lieutenant folded his arms. "I stopped by the beauty shop to see Mom maybe six weeks ago and this guy named Arturo dropped by. He's dating Helen, the manicurist."

"Arturo Mendez?" Ben asked. "We've had some trouble with him. Minor stuff—mutual combat with other kids, graffiti, that kind of thing. He's about nineteen." Without being asked, he filled in. "Barely made it through high school, although he's a talented artist. Does odd jobs around town and tries to sell his paintings where he can."

"He seemed ticked off about this picture my mom has on the wall of her, me and Dad." Mark's father had died when he was young. "He made a crack about smug people who think they're better than everybody else. Mom started clicking her scissors like she wanted to give him a haircut he'd never forget. Helen shooed him out of there in a hurry."

"Does Arturo have a history of breaking and entering?" Ethan inquired.

Ben shook his head. "No, but he can be destructive. We made him repaint the back of the feed store after he covered it with graffiti. Archie said he liked the bright colors. Still, he couldn't leave those four-letter words out there."

"What about a search warrant," Mark suggested. "We might find those photos at his apartment."

"All we have are suspicions, not evidence," Ethan said. "You can't get a search warrant with that."

"And if he's not our culprit, seeing his house turned upside-down might push a mildly antisocial young man over the edge," Ben pointed out.

"Agreed." Ethan considered the matter. "Let's do a little low-key sniffing around. Mark, drop into the beauty shop and encourage Helen to talk about her boyfriend. Ben, if Arturo tries any other funny stuff, that might give us a reason to check his place."

Heads nodded. Ethan made a mental note to take stock of Arturo as soon as he found an unobtrusive way to do so. He wanted to assess the fellow for himself.

The two men left. Ethan would have preferred to spend the rest of this sunny June morning cruising the area to identify potential problems and become better acquainted with the citizenry. However, paperwork kept him behind his desk.

Half an hour later, he was contemplating fixing a third cup of coffee, when Amy Arroyo, who doubled as his secretary and as records clerk, wandered in wearing a puzzled expression. "Chief, Dr. Vine is here to see you. She's in the lobby."

Although he knew the doctor was scheduled to arrive today, Ethan hadn't expected a visit. "This is a surprise."

"Shall I show her in?"

"I'll do it, thanks." He got to his feet.

"I thought they were going to hire that doctor with the three kids," the secretary said as she ambled into the hall. Although much of the town buzzed over every morsel of gossip, Amy lived in a world of her own.

"You didn't read the article last week?" Barry Lowell had described Jenni in glowing terms, omitting any mention of her questionable past. Having once been convicted of a crime he swore he hadn't committed, Barry—no doubt with Karen's encouragement—obviously intended to give the newcomer plenty of leeway.

"My copy of *Scientific American* arrived last week. I didn't have time to read anything else," Amy admitted as she wandered off.

Ethan passed Ben's office and the detective bureau, then opened the lobby door and saw Jenni. Against the tinted windows, she resembled a ray of sunshine with her short blond hair.

"Dr. Vine." He thrust out his hand as he strode forward. "Welcome to Downhome."

"Thank you." She shook firmly.

She'd seemed giddier the last time they met. Today her chin had a resolute set and she held herself with military straightness.

"What can I do for you?" Ethan asked.

"May I speak to you alone?"

"Of course." He held the door, noticing a light citrus scent as she breezed by. The desk officer gave her a big smile. When Jenni returned it, the fellow brightened as if she'd just made his day. Ethan suspected she had that effect on a lot of men.

For some reason, he remembered the night more than ten years ago in a Nashville country music bar when he'd first seen Martha perform. With her long chestnut hair, vivid face and soulful voice, she'd seemed utterly enchanting and unattainable. He would never have believed she could become his wife. Or that once he had her, he could lose her to cancer.

He shook his head, annoyed at the memory for intruding at this inappropriate moment. "My office is around to the left." He wasn't sure what made him add, "Ever been in a police station before?"

"I try to avoid them," the doctor replied.

Her flame-colored suit smoldered against the subdued hues of his office. Instead of sitting, Jenni walked to the window and surveyed the downtown. "Great view."

"I like it." He remained standing. This was not, Ethan gathered, a social visit.

She turned. "I prefer to get things out in the open. I can't stand when people talk behind my back, and I'm sure you would feel the same way."

"If something's bugging you, shoot." He had a suspicion this outburst stemmed from the insulting remark Karen had overheard. Although he was willing to apologize, Ethan decided to let Jenni make the first move.

"First of all, I perfectly understand why you might prefer the other candidate. In your position, I'd probably have supported him myself," she said.

Ethan kept silent.

"As for the slander that was spread about me in L.A., you should have asked for my side of the story."

"The medical director told me you'd denied it and that the board took no action against you. I conveyed that information to the council," Ethan explained.

She released a sharp breath. "But first you repeated that whole ugly business. Why?"

"It was my job. If I mishandled the situation, I apologize."

"You don't approve of me, do you?" she said coolly.

Ethan was caught off guard, perhaps because she'd hit on the truth. "I don't know you."

"You're being evasive." A death grip on her purse strap revealed her tension.

"You didn't make a very favorable impression last month," he conceded. "Perhaps I judged too quickly."

"You don't have to like me." Jenni faced him squarely. "But you're part of the establishment in Downhome and I don't want to feel as if I have to watch my back whenever you're around. I especially don't want to have to watch it when you're *not* around."

Ethan found the implication insulting. "If you're paranoid about authority figures, don't take that out on me."

"When someone objects to your high-handed behavior, do you always dismiss it as paranoia?" she returned.

They glared at each other across the office. Unwillingly, Ethan found himself admiring the woman's gumption.

She'd originally struck him as a fluffy California blonde. Now he'd have to describe her as a *fierce,* fluffy California blonde, if such a creature existed.

Ethan wondered what it took to warm up those blue-gray

eyes and why none of the millions of men in L.A. had given her a reason to stay. Suddenly, Downhome had become a more interesting place to live. But not necessarily a more comfortable one.

He needed to defuse the situation. Mildly, he said, "I should know better than to argue with a doctor. Particularly using a medical term like *paranoia*. I take that back."

"Do you ever smile?" Jenni asked. "I mean really smile, not just twitch the corners of your mouth?"

He blinked in surprise. "All the time. At home, anyway."

"I admire your wife if she has that effect on you."

Ethan didn't care to discuss Martha with Jenni. "I have a five-year-old son," he said. "Naturally, he's a brilliant wit." Simply mentioning Nick lightened his mood. "He has a gift for making me laugh."

"That's better." She relaxed her grip on her purse strap.

"What is?"

"When you mentioned your little boy, you gave evidence of containing actual human DNA," she quipped.

A strange thing happened to Ethan then. He chuckled. Until this moment, he hadn't realized how rarely he did that around anyone aside from Nick. "I'll have to be careful around you."

"Why?" Jenni asked.

"You're smarter than you—" He stopped.

"Smarter than I look?" Her voice held a challenge. "Believe me, I've heard that before." She seemed rueful rather than angry. "It's amazing the way some students assume a medical school must have accepted a blonde based on her sex appeal."

"What did you do about it?"

"I kicked their gluteus maximus on exams," Jenni returned. "It wasn't easy, since I'm no genius. You can accomplish miracles if you study like a maniac and forgo a social life."

She hadn't mentioned needing to work. Perhaps her parents had paid the bills, but Ethan could hardly hold that against her. "I'd say you just kicked my gluteus maximus, figuratively speaking," he said. "Coming here took guts."

It was her turn to smile. "You're a good sport."

"How about a truce?"

Jenni released a long breath. Apparently, she'd been prepared for a rougher reception. "Fine. Live and let live."

Ethan became aware that he'd instinctively shifted toward her. If he wasn't careful, he might start flirting, he realized with a jolt.

He eased back, trying not to be obvious. Although he didn't completely dismiss the possibility that Jenni had had an affair with her patient's husband, he could see why Karen and Olivia believed her.

"There is one matter I wanted to mention," he said.

"Oh?" She withdrew into caution again.

Being rich and gorgeous must be tougher than he'd thought if it produced such a strong defensive mechanism.

"Have a seat." Ethan wanted to put their meeting on a more neighborly basis. "Coffee?"

"No, thanks." She perched on the edge of a chair.

He helped himself to a mugful from the pot atop a low file cabinet. "When did you get into town?"

"This morning."

"You came to my office first thing? You must really have been steamed."

Her cheeks flushed. "I'm not sure my wheels touched the ground on the way from Nashville. I don't like the idea of being put under a microscope."

"Fair enough. In fact, from now on, you have leave to put me under a microscope. Turnabout's fair play, right?"

Her expression turned to one of mingled amusement and embarrassment.

"What did I say?" he inquired. "You have the funniest look on your face."

This time she blushed deep red. "I was wondering who you use as your personal physician."

Now he understood. If he became one of her patients, that would mean getting examined in a very intimate manner.

Ethan hoped his discomfort didn't show as clearly as hers. "Fortunately for both of us, I have a doctor in Nashville. I make appointments when I take my son in. He's diabetic," he added.

"I see. Please let me know if there's anything I can do to help." She folded her hands in her lap.

"There is, but not with Nick." Ethan finished stirring his coffee and settled behind the desk. "There's a public health project I've been trying to get under way for the past year, but it ran into some snags." He'd mentioned this during her visit, but since she hadn't responded, he chose to try again.

"Why is a police chief concerned with public health?" Jenni asked.

"It's outreach—a form of crime prevention." Inside a drawer, Ethan found the folder full of reference articles he'd saved, along with his comments. "I've been trying to talk the city council into funding a pilot project, but they don't see the benefits. So I figured you and I could prove to them how great the need is."

"There's no funding?" She frowned.

He bit back the urge to point out that investing some un-reimbursed time in her new community wouldn't kill her, especially considering that she could obviously afford a small fortune for designer clothes. "Not yet," he admitted.

"You realize we'd require materials?" Jenni probed. "I presume we're talking about vaccinations and so forth?"

"Right now, I'm more interested in assessing medical needs and educating people about everything from child development to gun safety." Ethan had been mulling the sub-

ject over since he'd returned to Downhome. "We'd make re-
ferrals rather than provide on-the-spot care."

"'We'?" she said.

"I'd need to accompany you, since we'd be visiting the less
savory part of town." He hadn't viewed that part of the project as problematic until now.

"You could use this as a chance to snoop into people's
homes," Jenni noted none too happily

"That's not my motive." Still, since she'd mentioned it, he
wouldn't mind paying Arturo Mendez a visit.

"Listen, Chief…"

"Ethan," he corrected.

"Okay, Ethan," Jenni said.

"May I call you by your first name?"

"Would you let me finish, please?"

He sat back, properly chastened. "Shoot."

"First of all, I just got here. I haven't even talked to my
nursing staff or met my patients. It's way too soon to con-
template a new project."

"We could wait a few weeks. I realize I'm pushing hard,
but I've run into delay after delay and I'm growing impatient."
Ethan could see that this approach wasn't working, so he
switched to a different one. "I'd like to get rolling this summer so kids don't enter kindergarten and first grade with untreated health problems."

"In addition," Jenni continued as if he hadn't spoken, "I
ran into trouble at my last position because I tried to help a
patient outside a clinical setting. Which reminds me that,
considering my reputation as a home wrecker, I wouldn't
want to spend too much time alone with a married man."

"A married man?" He recalled her comment about his
wife. "Oh, I'm single."

She thought it over. "Still, gossips can make mountains out
of molehills."

He pretended to be perplexed. "Meaning?"

"You and me. Some people could read implications into it. Heaven knows why."

"Yes, heaven knows why." *Aside from the fact that the air between us hums like a tuning fork.*

"You're smiling," Jenni said. "That was an attempt at humor, right?"

Ethan drew himself up as if offended. "I was *not* smiling. That was my poker face."

"Take my advice, Chief. If you want to play cards, stick to Go Fish." She rose. "Sorry to disappoint you about the outreach, but I can't handle it right now. If you'll excuse me, my staff is expecting me."

He didn't press the point. As matters stood, they'd simply opened negotiations. He could wait a while and try again.

When they shook hands again, Ethan found himself enjoying the contact much more than he should have. "I'll say one thing for you. You make a good sparring partner."

"Since you oppose violence, I'm sure you'll want to give me a wide berth," Jenni retorted.

"That would be my preference. However, it's a small town," he teased.

She shot him a look. "I'm sure we can manage to keep our distance."

Ethan felt a twinge of disappointment. "Of course. But they say distance is relative."

He escorted her to the lobby. A weathered farmer filling out an accident form at the front desk spotted the newcomer. "Ma'am." He swept the baseball cap off his head.

"Good morning. I'm Dr. Vine," she replied cheerfully.

"You're the new doctor? I feel better already," the old fellow replied gallantly. "I mean, I feel sick. How about an appointment?"

She laughed. "I never realized Southern men were so courteous. Men in L.A. don't remove their hats and they hardly ever pay compliments."

"They're durn fools," the farmer observed. "Guess I'll be visiting you about my arthritis soon. Just remembered my wife's been nagging me to get some medicine."

"I'll be glad to help."

When she went out, the man gripped the edge of the desk as if his knees had gone weak. To Ethan, he said, "She's really the doctor?"

"Yes, she is."

"And you wanted to hire some fella, instead? You ain't as smart as I thought you were, Chief." The farmer returned to his form.

Ethan felt as if he'd just lost a battle. He wasn't entirely sorry, either.

Chapter Three

Ethan made frequent uninvited appearances in Jenni's mind over the next few days. As if she didn't have enough to do with getting to know her staff, meeting patients and searching for an apartment. Now she also had to deal with the shiver of excitement that ran through her every time she thought about that annoying man.

Until recently, she hadn't understood what people meant when they talked about chemistry. Jenni had dated plenty of guys and had been intimately involved with several, yet they'd vanished from her awareness when they were out of sight. She certainly hadn't anticipated running into them on the street, imagining she saw their broad shoulders and feeling disappointed if the man turned out to be someone else.

The good thing about chemistry, she discovered, was that it waned over time. By Friday, she hardly thought of Ethan at all, except once in the dry goods store when she caught a whiff of the same aftershave lotion and had to fight the impulse to invent a pretext to drop by the police station.

Why his wife had left him wasn't hard to imagine. Despite his bluff appeal, the man was bullheaded and judgmental. He'd made no bones about the fact that he was seeking an excuse to pry into poor people's lives, either, although she was willing to give him credit for caring about the children. As a father himself, he'd need to be a total monster not to have a soft spot for kids.

She still believed he'd been wrong to bring up her past in front of the city council. Ethan might claim he was doing his duty, but she doubted he'd have behaved the same way if he'd come across negative information regarding her competitor.

Thank goodness most people she met that first week didn't appear to share his reservations about her. The clinic staff, far from clinging to some other candidate or the memory of the two departed doctors, greeted Jenni with enthusiasm, although perhaps that was due to their having lacked an MD on staff for months.

"You can't believe what a load I've been carrying," Estelle Fellows, the nurse practitioner and business manager, told Jenni. "I'm qualified to handle basic family care and the state of Tennessee allows me to write prescriptions, but without a doctor around, I feel like I'm walking a tightrope without a net."

"You must be exhausted." Jenni had sympathized after learning that Estelle had four kids. The eldest, nineteen-year-old Patsy, worked as office receptionist.

"And the hours!" Estelle went on, ruffling her short dark hair in frustration. "People think that because I'm the pastor's wife, I'm at their beck and call any old time. I hope they treat you with more respect!" Her husband, Ben, Jenni had learned, worked two jobs, as police captain and as minister, so theirs was indeed a busy household.

"I just hope they accept me."

"I'd say they already have."

Sure enough, a steady stream of patients dropped in once word spread that the new doctor was on board. Some people must have saved up their ailments, while others, Jenni got the feeling, mostly wanted to take a look at the new girl in town.

She handled a couple of evening emergencies that week,

one involving a broken arm and the other a baby with asthma. The on-call arrangement included her, Estelle and a Mill Valley doctor who lived halfway between the towns.

Estelle continued to treat those patients who requested her services, brought Jenni up to speed on the remaining clients and, at her request, gleefully left early a couple of afternoons to be with her younger children, who were on vacation. Later, she promised, she'd gear up to handle vaccinations and back-to-school exams.

A younger nurse, Yvonne Johnson, assisted Jenni in the office. If Estelle had been welcoming, Yvonne was downright effusive.

"I am *so* glad they hired a woman!" she said as the two of them ate sandwiches together in the clinic's lunchroom on Friday. Yvonne was a striking young woman with long silver hair and violet eyes, the hue of which was probably boosted by contact lenses. "I can't afford to move away, especially now that I've got a little girl," she explained "but you wouldn't believe how prissy folks can be about single moms."

"It must be tough on you," Jenni responded. During the past few days, she had heard Yvonne mention her year-old daughter, Bethany, several times. However, she'd said nothing about the father. According to Estelle, his identity remained a secret.

"That's putting it mildly. I went to Mill Valley to give birth. I just couldn't bear…" She stopped. "Well, never mind. Tell me about L.A. Did you go to clubs a lot? I'll bet that would be fun."

Jenni hated to admit how boring her life had been. "Once in a while I'd go dancing with some other women from the hospital." They'd had to drag her, because she hated loud music and rude men.

"Are the guys gorgeous?" Yvonne sighed at the prospect.

"Gorgeous and full of themselves," Jenni replied.

"You mean they expect sex on the first date?"

"I mean they expect sex before they decide whether there's going to be a first date."

The nurse made a face. "That almost makes Downhome sound appealing."

The fourth member of the clinic staff was a technician, a fellow with the confusing name of Lee Li, who commuted from Mill Valley twice a week to handle sonograms, X rays and routine lab work. Anything complicated had to be sent out by courier, and anyone needing advanced diagnostic treatment such as an MRI had to travel to another town. For major emergencies, Jenni learned, she could call on Vanderbilt University Medical Center's LifeFlight helicopter to transport the victim to Nashville.

To be so isolated after working in a metropolitan area where medical centers sprouted on every corner felt strange. In L.A., the question had been not where to find a cancer specialist or a neonatal intensive care unit, but which one to use.

Jenni hoped she wouldn't have to deal with many such cases. No town was immune to tragedy, though.

After lunch on Friday, the influx of patients dwindled. Jenni felt tempted to slip out early to search for an apartment, but her sense of responsibility kept her around.

She enjoyed staying with Karen. However, the house was noisy, since Barry had a stream of newspaper subscribers and advertisers ringing the doorbell and the phone in the early mornings and evenings. Most could have contacted him during work hours, he grumbled. Still, he couldn't afford to turn away business.

So far, most of the rentals Jenni had found were houses too large for her needs or rooms where she would have to share a kitchen and bathroom with strangers. Other than that, she'd visited one duplex apartment next to another occupied by a large family who screamed at one another while the TV blared.

There had to be something better.

"Dr. Vine?" Patsy, the receptionist, appeared in the doorway to Jenni's office, where she'd retreated to write up the day's reports. "Mrs. Forrest just brought Nick in. He scraped his shin and he's diabetic, so she wanted you to check him out. They're in examining room two."

The young woman seemed to assume that Jenni would recognize the names. And of course she did. Nick must be Ethan's son and Mrs. Forrest, she assumed, was the ex-wife.

Unexpectedly, her throat clogged. What was this woman like who'd managed to tame the glowering beast? And why, Jenni wondered, did she feel a curious reluctance to meet her?

"Is Yvonne with them?" she asked. The nurse should be taking the boy's vital signs.

"She just finished. She's in the nurses' lounge, playing with her baby." Seeing her perplexed expression, Patsy explained. "Usually, Yvonne's cousin babysits, but Mrs. Forrest helps out sometimes. Today she brought Bethany with her."

"I see." In Downhome, everyone seemed to be connected to everyone else, Jenni reflected as she rose. It was a little disconcerting, but a welcome change from the lack of connections she'd experienced during her own fractured childhood.

Outside the examining room, she read the clipboard containing the boy's medical history. Now five years old, he'd been diagnosed with type 1 diabetes at age three. A year later, he'd been fitted with a pump to provide the insulin his pancreas couldn't make.

Like most children, he had some problems complying with the strict diet and the frequent finger pricks to make sure his blood-sugar level held steady. However, the chart indicated he was generally healthy.

Still, the injury concerned Jenni. Due to reduced circulation, diabetics were vulnerable to infections, particularly in their lower extremities.

Taking a deep breath, she tapped on the door, then went in.

Two earnest faces tilted toward hers. On the examining table, a little boy with huge dark eyes and chestnut hair regarded her anxiously. From his slightly dirty shorts and the smudge on his nose, she could tell he'd been playing outdoors.

In the chair beside him sat a woman of around sixty. Her worried air softened as she smiled at Jenni. From the stylishly cut hair to the trim pantsuit, she gave the impression of a retired professional. A scan of Yvonne's notes revealed that the woman's first name was Annette.

This had to be Ethan's mother, not his ex, Jenni realized with an odd sense of relief. At the same time, she wondered why the grandmother, instead of Nick's mother, cared for the boy.

"Mrs. Forrest? I'm Dr. Vine." Jenni shook hands with her. Although she wanted to get to know the woman, she wished to establish a rapport immediately with the patient, so she turned to him. "It's nice to meet you, Nick."

"Are you going to stick me with a needle?" the boy asked.

"I don't plan to." She glanced at his chart again. "I see you've had a tetanus shot, so you won't need one of those. Can you show me where you hurt yourself?"

Biting his lip, he stuck out his leg. The scrape, midway between knee and ankle, was about two inches long, wide but shallow.

"I cleaned it right away and applied an antiseptic," Mrs. Forrest explained. "It doesn't seem like a big deal, but Dr. Luther always insisted I bring him in for antibiotics if he got hurt." By Dr. Luther she must mean Luther Allen, Jenni thought. Mrs. Forrest had probably referred to him this way to distinguish him from his wife. He'd been the pediatrician and she the family doctor.

"I don't see any signs of infection," Jenni was saying when the door opened.

With his muscular frame and restless energy, Ethan Forrest dominated the room even before entering it. Scarcely nodding to the two adults, he rushed to Nick's side. "Are you okay, little guy?"

"I have a boo-boo, Daddy." The boy wiggled his leg.

With a grim shake of the head, Ethan glanced at Jenni. There was no sign of lightheartedness about him now. "Well?"

She hoped he wasn't going to overreact to a minor childhood mishap. In her experience, take-charge fathers who hated losing control often demanded unnecessary treatments. Still, she knew his response stemmed from love. "I was just beginning my examination."

Reluctantly, Ethan stepped back. "Go ahead."

Jenni washed her hands at the sink, then bent over the boy. "Tell me how it happened," she said as she examined the wound more closely.

"I was riding my bike on the sidewalk."

"In shorts?" Ethan demanded of his mother.

"I didn't realize he'd gone outside," she answered without sounding defensive. "Ethan, he's not made of eggshells."

"He got hurt, didn't he?" The chief waved one hand apologetically. "I'm sorry, Mom. It's just that when they gave me your message, I thought the injury might be serious."

"I understand," she replied.

Jenni asked more questions, establishing that the sidewalk recently had been washed and that Mrs. Forrest hadn't found any dirt or bike oil in the wound. "It's not necessarily bad that he was wearing shorts," she said. "Fabric can harbor bacteria, and if it gets pushed into a cut, it's bad news. Puncture wounds through sneakers are particularly nasty. You wouldn't believe what grows in some people's shoes." For Nick's sake, she added, "It makes them stink, too. Peeuw."

He wrinkled his nose and grinned. The sweetness in his face touched her.

Jenni cleaned the wound again. Normally, the nurse would have done this. However, Jenni saw no reason to interrupt Yvonne's time with her baby, and besides, she wanted to make it clear she took a personal interest in her patients.

"I can apply an ointment if you like, but frankly, it might delay healing," she told her audience. "I don't recommend stitches for a scrape like this, since it's so shallow."

"Aren't you going to cover it?" Ethan inquired.

"I will if he'll be playing outside again," Jenni answered. "Otherwise, it's best to expose it to air."

"I'll keep him inside," Mrs. Forrest said.

"Does it hurt?" Jenni asked Nick.

He straightened like a miniature version of his tough-guy Dad. "I can take it."

"That bad?" she queried.

"Not really," the boy admitted. "It used to sting, but it's okay now."

"You're a very brave young man. I think you're going to be fine."

"Whoa." Ethan gave her a disbelieving stare. "What about a prescription?"

She remembered his mother's statement about Dr. Allen. "Antibiotics aren't recommended in a case like this. Overuse causes them to lose their effectiveness and there can be side effects. But if he develops any pus or the skin becomes red, warm or swollen, or it starts hurting badly, I'll be glad to prescribe some."

"That's it?" the chief asked. "I could have treated him this well myself!"

"I know you're used to a different approach with Dr. Luther," she responded. "Times change and so does medical care. We've learned that in minor cases like this, sometimes nature is the best healer."

"I like you better than Dr. Luther," Nick announced.

"You do? And I haven't even offered you a sugar-free lollipop yet!" Jenni joked.

"Why do you like Dr. Vine better?" Ethan regarded his son.

"She talks to me and not just the grown-ups." To Jenni, Nick said, "Do you have any lemon pops?"

"Let me see." She searched in a drawer. "Sure thing." After handing him one, she offered a sampling of flavors to Ethan and his mother.

"I don't mind if I do." Annette chose cherry.

Ethan tried to keep a straight face, but he couldn't. "I haven't had one of these in years," he admitted, and selected lime.

Jenni relaxed. Apparently, the chief had decided to bow to her expertise. Considering his obvious worry over his son, that meant a lot. "We've got coloring books, too." She gave Nick one about healthy foods.

"You're good with children," Annette commented.

"I love kids." Jenni enjoyed treating them as part of her practice. She hoped the next doctor to be hired would be an obstetrician rather than a pediatrician, although she did want the kids to get the best possible care.

"According to the grapevine, you're looking for an apartment," the woman went on.

"Mom!" Ethan's voice sank to a growl.

Jenni didn't know what was going on here. Still, she figured she ought to stay out of it. "I'm sure I'll find one eventually," she replied, and turned to the chart. "In case of emergency, I need to be sure we have up-to-date contact information." The Allens hadn't double-checked phone numbers and addresses for years, she'd discovered earlier. "Is this correct?" She read off the phone numbers for Ethan and Annette.

Both nodded.

"Is there anyone else?" Jenni didn't want to be too blunt, but omitting one parent seemed strange. "A child's whole family is important."

"There isn't anyone." Annette glanced at her grandson. However, he was absorbed in looking through his coloring book. "My husband and daughter-in-law both passed away some time ago."

"I'm sorry." So Ethan was a widower. Jenni felt a wave of sympathy for the man and child who'd lost so much.

This didn't make her like him any better, though. In fact, it made her wary, because with his judgmental nature, he probably compared every woman he met with his deceased spouse.

"Speaking of families, didn't your parents object to your moving so far away?" Annette asked. "They must worry about you."

"My parents?" That was almost funny, although Jenni didn't suppose it would strike anyone else that way. "They're not the sort of people who worry about others, I'm afraid."

"You'd be surprised," the older woman said. "Maybe they're afraid you'd resent it if they showed how much they cared."

"If they cared, they could have stuck around when I was a kid." Hearing her edgy tone, she added, "Sorry. That was inappropriate."

Ethan looked puzzled. His mother wore a determined expression. "I knew you were the right person to rent the flat over my garage! If you haven't got a family, you should at least live close to one."

So that was what the two had been clashing about earlier. Jenni peeked at Ethan, but he was studying his son. "That might be awkward, since your grandson is my patient."

"Awkward? Having a doctor on the premises would be reassuring," Annette countered. "Besides, everyone in town is likely to be your patient at one time or another. And it's furnished, which I believe you need, since you didn't ship any furniture."

"How do you know that?" Jenni asked in amazement.

"My mother is friends with Gwen Martin, who owns the café, and half the town shows up there to gab." Ethan's gruffness couldn't disguise his affection. "Between the two of them, they know almost everything that happens around here."

"That's a little scary." Anonymity had become Jenni's friend over the years. The fewer people who learned about her family, the better, and getting away from vicious rumors had been one of her reasons for moving to Downhome.

"If you're my renter, I promise we won't gossip about you," Mrs. Forrest said. "I only live three blocks from the Lowells, so you can stop by anytime. The house faces Jackson Park."

Jenni had walked by the park several times and enjoyed the relaxed, old-fashioned setting. The lush greenery, like much of the Tennessee landscape, soothed her after the hard urban surfaces of L.A. "It isn't the beautiful Victorian with the window boxes, is it?"

Annette nodded. Ethan shook his head, but he was obviously joking. "She failed to mention that the apartment overlooks my backyard."

Uh-oh. She'd have the police chief for a neighbor? Not good.

"Can I get back to you on that?" she asked Annette.

"Of course."

"Take your time," the police chief said. "Months, if necessary."

"Ethan, where are your manners?" demanded his mother. "You've hurt Dr. Vine's feelings."

"No, he hasn't," she assured them.

"I know how it feels to be an outsider," Annette persisted. "When my husband and I moved to Nashville—he worked for a religious publishing company—it took the longest time for me to make friends. Jenni, the least you can do is look at the place."

"I can't…"

"Surely you're curious about the house!" Mrs. Forrest teased. "You've acknowledged that you noticed it."

Jenni smiled. "Yes, but I really can't come tonight. Karen Lowell is having some friends over for a potluck. Kind of a welcome party for me."

Apparently satisfied that he'd won the day, Ethan lifted a radiant Nick onto his shoulders. "We men are going to go take care of the bill," he told his mother. "See you in a few minutes."

"Giddyap!" the little boy cried, then looked self-conscious.

At age five, he was already feeling too grown up to act like a toddler, Jenni realized.

Annette beamed at the pair as they exited, both ducking to clear the doorway. "I can't believe my grandbaby's going to start first grade in September."

Instinctively wanting to keep her hands occupied, Jenni straightened the examining room. If there'd been patients waiting, Yvonne would have alerted her, so she could afford to linger. "I'm sorry to hear his mother's deceased."

"Martha was a beautiful girl and a wonderful singer. She bowled Ethan over," Annette said. "Nick was only a few months old when she died."

"That must have been terrible." Not wanting to pry into

Ethan's personal life, Jenni veered from that subject by focusing on Annette. "You probably weren't expecting to take on child-raising duties again."

"No, but it's worth it," she said. "I'd do the same to help my daughter, Brianna, Ethan's younger sister. She just went through a nasty divorce and I'd love for her to move here."

"I'm sorry about the divorce." Jenni hadn't expected so many confidences. "If she does come back, she might need the apartment."

"I don't see it happening anytime soon. I'd like you to take a look at the place."

Annette obviously wasn't an easy woman to dissuade.

"The offer's open. Drop by any time."

"Thanks," she replied.

After Annette left, a glance at the clock showed it was after five o'clock. Jenni gathered her purse, helped Yvonne close the office and went out to the compact car she'd leased.

Tonight ought to be fun, a chance to let down her hair and get to know some other women. Karen had promised that they'd give her the lowdown on the singles' scene.

Jenni didn't want to start dating anytime soon, though. Ethan already considered her a husband-stealing flirt, and for some reason, she wanted to disprove his low opinion.

The prospect of living next door to him made her shudder. No one could stand up to that kind of scrutiny, especially if she was being compared with an idealized wife.

Yet an image lingered of him carrying the little boy on his shoulders, two pairs of dark eyes shining and two sets of white teeth flashing. It made Jenni long for something she'd never had and probably never would have.

Pushing away the thought, she headed for the Lowells' house.

Chapter Four

Shortly after six p.m., Ethan found the outdoor terrace already filled at the Café Montreal, Gwen Martin's establishment at the south end of The Green. Once in a while, he stopped in for lunch or dinner, as much to keep his ear to the ground as for the exceptional food. He preferred to dine with his mother and Nick, but tonight they were attending a kids' birthday party.

On this warm June evening, customers sat enjoying their meals as colored globes glowed in the twilight. Ethan identified the scents of garlic, sausages and orange crepes, reminding him that he hadn't eaten since lunchtime. He paused briefly to exchange greetings with Archie and Olivia Rockwell before making his way inside.

A waitress showed him to a table near the glass-fronted pastry display. Although picking out a dessert was hard to resist, he ordered only his usual bowl of onion soup and a patty melt on rye.

Ethan had no idea what a real French café looked like, whether in Paris or Montreal, but he enjoyed the ambience created by Impressionist prints on the walls and striped awnings above the service counters. He also appreciated that between this cafe and Pepe's Italian Diner, Downhome offered international cuisine in addition to the Southern fried chicken, hush puppies and grits available at the local coffee shop.

His fellow diners were a mix of workers, farmers and re-tired folks. The strangers sprinkled among them must be travelers passing through. The town didn't attract tourists except the one weekend a month when Gwen organized a Farmers Market and Crafts Fair on The Green.

The owner, in a red-and-white checked apron, stopped by his table. Although she wore her steely gray-on-black hair in the usual bun, tendrils curling from the sides softened the contours of her face. "So what do you think of our lady doctor? I heard Nick went to see her."

"She seems competent." Ethan had been impressed by Jenni's assurance and by the rapport she'd struck with Nick, whatever his other reservations about her. Despite his impulse to demand further treatment, he'd recognized that she was probably right to avoid antibiotics. "What's the consensus?"

"The women love her. They say their husbands are suddenly deciding they need the physicals they've been putting off for years."

"They're not jealous?" he asked.

Gwen shook her head. "Any woman can tell Jenni's not on the prowl."

"I don't see how."

"She isn't needy. Or greedy, either." Gwen swung toward the pastry counter and addressed the young man behind it. "Box me up a dozen of those tarts, a couple of pounds of cookies and a lemon pie, would you, Jimmy?"

"Sure thing," he called back.

"What's that for?" Ethan inquired.

"Potluck at Karen's."

"Oh, right." He remembered Jenni mentioning it. Too bad he wasn't invited. The food would be great, and always curious, he'd love to know the topics of conversation.

"Still think we made the wrong choice of physician?" Gwen challenged.

"Too soon to tell."

"According to the grapevine, she paid you a visit Monday morning." The café owner watched her employee box the desserts. "Must have been an interesting discussion."

"Very." He let it go at that. No point in feeding the gossip mill, which was obviously working overtime.

Gwen shook her head at him. "One of these days, Ethan Forrest, some woman is going to get under your skin. You'll open that gorgeous mouth of yours and poetry will flow out."

He raised his water glass in a toast. "I live for that day, *chérie*."

She gave an exaggerated sigh. "If I weren't old enough to be your mother, I'd take a stab at it myself." Across the counter, she accepted a stack of pastry boxes. "Well, I'm off. I'll give the ladies your regards."

"Please do."

His onion soup arrived, encrusted with melted cheese. Savoring the taste, Ethan let his thoughts wander back to that afternoon.

He wondered what Jenni had meant about her parents not being around much during her younger years. Perhaps they'd shuffled their child off to boarding schools.

Having worked summers and weekends since he was a teenager, Ethan found it hard to sympathize with a poor little rich kid, but he had to admit Jenni had turned out squarely grounded. She must have worked hard in medical school, and he assumed she put in long hours at her profession.

That she'd chosen to relocate to Downhome puzzled him. Even in light of the scandal in L.A., she must have had other options. Perhaps she'd decided to play at being a country doctor.

What had Mom been thinking when she offered to rent to Jenni? The last thing Nick needed was to grow attached to a short-term renter.

More people entered the restaurant, and Ethan forgot about Jenni as acquaintances stopped to say hello. One expressed concern about the portrait thefts. A couple of people asked if he'd heard the talk of a proposed new shopping center on the west side of Downhome. He had, of course. Rumors had swirled for months over the sale of several hundred acres in that area, but so far a proposal had not come before the city council. Ethan knew no more than anyone else.

He was digging into his patty melt when Barry Lowell slid into the chair across from him. "Mind if I join you?" The editor had picked up a Reuben sandwich at the take-out counter.

"Be my guest. Did your sister ban you from the premises tonight?"

"What? No." He pulled the plastic lid from his soda cup and took a swallow. A few years younger than Ethan, Barry had thick brown hair that perpetually flopped on to his forehead, almost covering the scar he'd received in prison. Although he worked next door to the Snip 'N' Curl, he rarely found time to pay it a visit. "I just finished putting the paper to bed."

The *Gazette,* which came out on Tuesdays, was printed in Mill Valley. Ethan assumed Barry sent his pages over there electronically. "Competing with other media must be hard when you only publish once a week."

"It's not hard at all," Barry said between bites. "You think CNN's going to cover the disappearance of Pepe Otero's family photo?"

"I suppose not." Hearing a touch of bitterness in the editor's voice, Ethan avoided making further comments about the national media and turned to the need for people to lock their doors until the wave of break-ins was solved.

Barry readily agreed. It was a far cry from the kind of journalism he longed to practice, though, Ethan knew.

By all accounts, Barry had been an ambitious teenager, editing the school paper and working part time for his parents' *Gazette*. He'd made no secret of his plans to write for a major newspaper someday.

When he was seventeen, he was accused of killing a farmer during a prank. Based on the testimony of his best friend, Barry had been convicted of manslaughter, despite his claim that he'd only struck a glancing blow in self-defense.

Although Ethan's family had moved away by then, he'd read the police reports since his return. The case was a tragedy all around, since it seemed obvious Barry hadn't intended to harm anyone. Still, he must have struck harder than he realized, because the farmer died of his injuries.

In prison, Barry had taken college courses and, following his release, earned a journalism degree from the University of Tennessee. His murder conviction had ended his dreams of making it in the big league, however, and he'd eventually returned to Downhome to take over the *Gazette* from his parents.

"So you get to relax for the weekend?" Ethan asked, making conversation.

"No. I've got an advertising publication to put together." Barry downed a handful of french fries before continuing. "And I'm working on a story of my own, kind of a long-term thing. That's what I wanted to talk to you about."

"I'll be in my office for a few hours tomorrow," Ethan said. "If you want to access records, though, you'll need to wait till Monday, when Amy's on duty."

"No, no, I'd just like to show you what I've put together. I'd appreciate your opinion," Barry explained.

"It's a crime story?" This aroused Ethan's interest. If the newspaper planned to run an exposé, he wanted advance notice. "I'd be glad to read it."

Barry swept aside the remains of his meal. "Are you free tonight?"

It occurred to Ethan that his colleagues in Nashville would have found it odd to see a police chief eating dinner with a convicted murderer, and even odder to find him treating the man as a friend. But Barry Lowell had reclaimed his place in society, and besides, Ethan liked him.

"Sure. We can walk over to your office right now."

"It's not at the office. It's at my house," Barry said. "I was hoping you could stop in on your way home."

Now, that was a tough one, Ethan thought ironically. He'd just been invited to the very place where Jenni, Karen et al were probably dissecting him and the town's other single men.

Discretion urged him to schedule a visit some other time. But he'd like to get his outreach program started this summer, and if he had a chance to join the conversation, he might be able to enlist the support of the other ladies.

He supposed the tactic might irritate Jenni. On the other hand, she could hold her own, and Ethan was in the mood for a round of sparring.

"That would be fine," he replied.

Barry crumpled his paper napkin. "Let's go."

THE LOWELLS' TWO-STORY BRICK HOUSE on Heritage Avenue rang with lively voices and good fellowship. Jenni found it hard to believe she was the center of attention, accepted by the other women as if she belonged here.

She wasn't accustomed to belonging. They almost seemed to have mistaken her for someone else—although she knew that wasn't true.

Karen had set out her best patterned china on the cloth-covered dining table, along with a plate of deviled eggs and platters of cold cuts and sliced bread. She'd waved away Jenni's offer to cook something, as well—a relief to Jenni, since her chief culinary skill was reheating pizza.

Jenni was surprised to discover that Karen's women friends ranged in age from their thirties all the way up to 80, but in a town this small, she learned, people didn't segregate along age lines—and the menu proved the big winner. Gwen Martin had brought incredible pastries from her café. Rosie O'Bannon, the forty-something owner of the beauty parlor, produced a multilayered taco dip with sour cream, guacamole and refried beans. She proudly offered it as a California recipe in Jenni's honor.

Rosie's niece, Leah, a first-grade teacher, was introduced as Karen's best pal since childhood. She'd prepared not one but two dishes—a green bean casserole and a Jell-O mold. Leah radiated goodwill, appearing not the least threatened that her closest pal had acquired a new friend.

From the nursing home, Karen had fetched Mae Anne McRay, the liveliest octogenarian Jenni had ever met, who'd prepared a fruit salad. Despite being confined to a wheelchair due to osteoporosis, she served on the city council.

Two people were missing. Renée Lowell, Karen and Barry's mother, whom Jenni had met previously, had stayed at the convalescent home because of a headache. A quadriplegic since a tractor hit her car years earlier, Renée had inspired Karen to apply her business administration training to running the convalescent center.

In addition, Amy Arroyo, the police chief's notoriously absentminded secretary, hadn't shown up by the time the women began taking their places around the table. Karen went into the kitchen to call her and returned a few minutes later.

"She forgot," she reported.

"No surprise there," Gwen responded.

"She said she's taking a bubble bath and reading a book. Naturally, she didn't remember to fix any food, either." Karen shook her head indulgently. "I urged her to come anyway, but she declined. I think she was embarrassed."

"She should be," Mae Anne observed.

"I hope it's a good book. Still I doubt it's worth missing this feast," Jenni said.

"Amy ought to pay more attention to real life," the hostess replied. "I hope you aren't offended."

"Not at all," Jenni responded. "I learned a long time ago that it's healthier to forgive and forget."

"Does that include Ethan Forrest?" Karen teased as she took a seat.

Across the table from Jenni, Leah let out a low whistle. "Getting a little personal, aren't we?"

"He didn't mean to attack her in front of the council!" cried Rosie, who, Jenni was learning, tended toward the dramatic. "Surely she doesn't hold it against him."

"Of course not. The woman isn't blind." Mae Anne helped herself to the Jell-O mold. She'd positioned her wheelchair at the foot of the table, where the food gravitated toward her. "He's the best-looking single man in Downhome. How could anyone hold a grudge against Ethan?"

"He was at the café earlier." Gwen tilted her head, apparently visualizing him. "It's a darn shame he's still carrying the torch for his late wife. That man's too good to waste."

"There are other desirable men around here," Jenni protested. "Like your brother, Karen."

"Not in his current state," her hostess replied promptly. "He's got too much to prove before he can even consider getting involved with anyone."

She'd explained earlier about her brother's murder conviction. Sharing a house with a killer had made Jenni uneasy at first, but Barry had reassured her with his openness and his intellectual curiosity about almost everything. She'd come to believe he really was innocent.

"Rosie's son Mark is cute," volunteered Gwen. "He's a lieutenant at the police department."

"Too young for me, even if he wasn't my cousin," Leah noted. "He's only twenty-eight. I'm surprised he doesn't have a girlfriend, though."

"He went to the senior prom with Amy, but he doesn't have a girlfriend now," responded her aunt. "He'll probably die a bachelor and I'll never have grandchildren!"

"Aren't there any other cute guys over thirty?" Jenni asked.

"Pepe Otero." Rosie clapped her hand to her mouth. "I didn't mean to say that! He likes Gwen."

"He does not," said the café owner. "Besides, he wouldn't dare ask me out. It's kind of a long story, Jenni. See, he gets food at a discount from Beau Johnson, who's mad as a wet hen because I organize a once-a-month Farmers Market that he considers competition for his grocery store. Beau ups the prices anytime I walk in the door, so I buy my supplies out of town."

Rosie nodded. "When she needs milk, I pick it up for her."

Jenni wondered if they were joking. "You don't mean the grocery store changes prices for different customers!"

"Just Pepe and me," Gwen explained. Heads nodded. "Pepe gets a discount—because Beau figures his restaurant is my competition."

"Well, if Pepe won't ask out the woman of his dreams because he might have to pay more for milk, he's a pretty poor prospect," Jenni said.

"I agree," Gwen volunteered. "A man ought to have the courage of his convictions. A woman, too. If I were young enough, I wouldn't give up a chance at Ethan Forrest, even if it meant paying triple for everything."

"Could we *not* talk about the chief?" Jenni asked, and then realized she'd probably revealed more than she meant to about the state of her thoughts.

Tactfully, no one pointed out that she wouldn't mind if they were discussing, say, Beau Johnson's romantic attributes. Or anyone else's.

"Okay," responded Karen. "Who has news to share?"

During the brief silence that followed, Gwen handed around a plate of cookies. At last Leah spoke. "I guess this is as good a time as any to make a confession."

Karen paused with a gingersnap in one hand. "About a man?"

"No! About myself." The teacher steepled her hands on the table. "I suppose I should have discussed it with you before, Karen, but I came to this decision on my own. I'm going to leave Downhome."

A flurry of shocked responses filled the air. "Why?" and "Since when?" and "Where would you go?"

Jenni listened with a trace of envy. She couldn't help recalling that no one at the hospital in L.A. had seemed distressed upon hearing of her impending departure.

"I'm not sure where," Leah explained. "Next month, I'm going to visit my cousin in Austin, Texas, and then an old friend in Seattle to apply for teaching jobs. It could take a while to land one, so my departure isn't imminent."

"What brought this on?" Karen looked the most stunned of anyone.

Leah gazed around the table. "Certainly not a desire to leave my old friends. Still, except for college, I've lived my whole life in Downhome. If I don't leave, I'll grow old here without ever having an adventure. I guess that sounds kind of naive, but it's what I want. And I'd like to have children, too."

"I can relate to that," Karen admitted. She and Leah were both thirty-two, a year younger than Jenni.

She understood their feelings. Sometimes when she held a baby or examined a child, she was overcome by a longing to have one of her own. However, her parents had set such a poor example that she wasn't sure how well she would handle motherhood. She might risk it if she met the perfect guy, but how likely was that?

"You were always such a shy child," Rosie said. "Then you turned from a duckling into a swan in high school and scared off the guys."

"Is that what happened?" Leah asked ruefully. "They sure steered clear of me. It was painful."

"Is finding Mr. Right part of your plan?" Karen asked.

"Not really." Her friend gave her an apologetic smile. "I want to do exciting things, get to know new places, do something wild. I can't act that way here. A guy—well, he might hold me back. I've been thinking about adopting a baby from a foreign orphanage."

"I had a brief spell of wanting kids when I was in my thirties, but I got over it," said Gwen. She'd never married, Karen had mentioned.

"Congratulations, Leah," Mae Anne said.

"Because I'm taking a risk?" the teacher inquired.

"No. Because you got our minds off Ethan Forrest for about five minutes."

Chuckles sounded around the table, then broke off as, in the next room, the front doorknob turned. Jenni still hadn't grown accustomed to the Lowells' habit of leaving their house unlocked during waking hours.

Barry entered. Peering through the archway between dining and living rooms, Jenni was startled when she glimpsed his companion.

"Uh-oh," Rosie muttered.

"Well, now, that just blows the whole thing, doesn't it?" commented Mae Anne, sending them into gales of laughter.

In the living room, Ethan wore such an endearingly baffled expression at their mirth that Jenni almost sympathized with him. Then she remembered telling him that she'd planned to attend this party tonight. He'd accompanied Barry knowing full well she would be here.

She reminded herself not to make assumptions. Maybe he

had business to conduct. Besides, the warmth with which some of the other women greeted him made her realize how much female attention he must attract wherever he went.

Determined not to reveal her mixed feelings, Jenni gave the men a lazy grin and stretched like a cat. "Hi, Barry. Good to see you, Chief."

Ethan's appreciative gaze made Jenni blushingly aware that the movement had drawn her knit top tightly across her breasts. Darn it, she'd been trying to act casual, she thought as she shifted to a more modest position.

"Good to see all of you," Ethan said. "Carry on, ladies. We have a few things to discuss."

With a nod, Barry headed for the stairs. "Want to take some food with you?" Karen offered.

"No, thanks." As usual, her brother was in a hurry.

"Don't mind if I do." Ethan strolled to the table, his powerful build inside the tailored suit drawing more than a few pairs of admiring eyes. As he claimed a cookie, he graced them all with a knowing wink that brought a round of smiles. Then he followed Barry up the stairs, leaving behind the sophisticated scent that had plagued Jenni's senses all week.

Nobody spoke until, upstairs, a door closed. "That man," Gwen said at last, "has charisma."

Jenni didn't bother to argue.

Chapter Five

For one inexplicable instant downstairs, the entire room had vanished except for Jenni Vine. Ethan didn't understand it. He'd never been drawn to blondes, and he considered this one an ill fit to the community. Yet he'd battled the urge to stand there drinking her in, as if she cast a sunny spell over him.

She'd been perfectly aware of the effect she created. She'd stretched provocatively, while he, who made a point of keeping a friendly distance between himself and anything resembling male vulnerability, had stood there verging on meltdown.

This wasn't entirely her fault, he conceded. As Gwen had said earlier, men all over town were scheduling their long-delayed physicals for a chance to be around her. Reducing adult males to the level of lusty adolescents had probably become second nature to her.

He almost wished he weren't so scrupulous, or so cognizant of his position. If circumstances had been different, Ethan might have enjoyed a fling with the lady before she decamped for more interesting surroundings. Assuming she wanted a fling, of course.

No, he thought, he wasn't the love 'em and leave 'em type, or the love 'em and be left by 'em type, either. When he'd fallen in love with Martha, he'd stayed in love. Heaven help him if he ever made that mistake with Jenni.

"What've you got for me?" he asked, following Barry into an upstairs rec room converted to a large office. Amid the file cabinets, desk and computer equipment was a bulletin board covered with old clippings and hand-drawn charts.

"Although nobody seems aware of it, Ethan, you've got an unsolved murder in this town," Barry replied.

That caught his attention, all right. "Who's the victim?"

"Norbert Anglin."

Anglin was the farmer Barry had been convicted of killing. So this was about that case. "Go ahead."

"The coroner said the killer struck him three times. I only hit him once," Barry said.

"With a shovel," Ethan reminded him dryly.

"He attacked me with a pitchfork." Barry and his friend Chris McRay, Mae Anne's grandson, had aroused Anglin's wrath one night when he caught them freeing chickens at his farm. "Maybe I hit him harder than I thought, but I know I didn't land more than one blow."

"I've heard this before," Ethan reminded him, studying the piles of papers in dismay. To see such a talented man unable to move beyond the past bothered him. "They said you might have lashed out two or three times without realizing it."

"But I didn't. And the cops were so quick to finger me they never tried to figure out who really killed him." Barry selected a chart. "I've diagrammed his property and re-created the movements of everyone at the farm that night—Mrs. Anglin, the hired man, that transient who was supposedly sleeping in the barn—and, of course, Chris and me."

Ethan resisted the urge to dismiss the matter. The editor had invested too much work and too much emotion to let go that easily. "I reviewed the case at your request last year, as you'll recall. I can't say the police did as thorough a job as they might have, but they had an eyewitness."

"Chris." Barry's voice rang with resentment. "He's the one who put me in prison."

"He testified to the same thing you did—that you smacked Mr. Anglin with a shovel," Ethan noted.

"No, he didn't!" the editor replied. "He said I was yelling and flailing around, so he couldn't be sure the shovel didn't connect more than once."

Ethan saw no point in debating. Better to go right to the point. "Are you telling me you've identified another suspect?"

"Yes, I have."

That startled him. "Who? The transient?" He'd been ruled out because Chris had testified to seeing him some distance away as the two boys fled.

"Let me explain first so you'll understand." Barry selected a paper bearing a shaky signature. "I had to track Lou Bates—the transient—all the way to New Orleans, but I managed to interview him. I found the hired hand in Oklahoma six months ago."

Barry had attended a newspaper conference in Louisiana the previous month, Ethan recalled. He supposed the Oklahoma trip had involved work, as well. "So that's why you've been traveling so much."

Barry forged ahead. "They both said the same thing. They spotted two figures running, and then a few minutes later they saw one of them sneak back."

Ethan weighed the implications. "At the trial, the transient said he might have seen you head back."

"And the DA implied that if I didn't strike Norbert more than once the first time, I returned to finish the job," Barry added. "But both told me they only made those statements because the police asked leading questions. They really didn't think the man moved like me, only they were afraid to contradict the authorities."

"After so many years, they probably don't remember what

happened." Ethan had to play skeptic, no matter how much he sympathized with Barry. "Besides, Chris said he couldn't find you afterward."

"We split up while we were running, and I laid low for a while in case Anglin came after me. I was pretty scared."

Ethan could envision a number of possibilities, including the witnesses conspiring to lie for some reason of their own. Since neither had profited from the farmer's death and they'd had no criminal histories, however, such speculation couldn't clear Barry. "You said you have a suspect."

"It's Chris. He must have done it." The paper rattled in Barry's hand. "He was the one who'd had an argument with the farmer the week before. That was why we were picking on him."

"What did they quarrel about?" Ethan didn't recall the subject appearing in the trial documents. Probably it hadn't been relevant to the DA's case, and Barry's lawyer hadn't introduced it, either.

"The old coot accused him of flirting with his wife. Which is ridiculous, considering she was twenty years older than we were, but he embarrassed Chris in front of other people." Barry moved restlessly around the room.

"That explains the prank, but it's hardly a motive for him to go back and kill the guy, then pin it on you," Ethan observed.

"I don't think he intended to frame me," Barry conceded. "We focused on the fact that Anglin tried to stab us. But he also threatened to bring charges."

"I'm sure he did."

"It bothered me, but it must have upset Chris a lot more. I mean, he was planning to be a doctor. They're held to high standards." Barry pushed a wing of overgrown hair off his forehead. "An arrest record would have hurt his chances of getting into medical school. So I guess he wanted to shut Anglin up permanently."

"Didn't you have the same concern?" Ethan asked. "Or aren't journalists held to high standards?"

The editor paused in front of his computer screen, glanced at a couple of flashing instant messages and then clicked them shut. "Being an ex-con has shut off certain avenues, but it doesn't stop me from running the *Gazette,* because I inherited it. Chris wasn't going to inherit a medical practice."

"So he might have had a motive and opportunity," Ethan said. "That isn't evidence, Barry."

"You could reopen the case and dig some up." The editor's movements grew more agitated. "How do you think it makes me feel that he's gone on with his life, while mine has been torn apart? My dad never got over it. He died of a heart attack while I was in prison."

"While Chris went on to become a pediatrician." Ethan knew all about that, because McRay had applied for a position at the clinic. "But he left town. He must have felt bad."

"Of course! He was ashamed to face me and my family," Barry said. "Chief, he got away with murder. The evidence has to be there. The witnesses are still alive. Why not give it a chance?"

"Barry, this case is fifteen years old," Ethan told him regretfully. "What you've found isn't even close to enough evidence to persuade the DA to file charges. I'd be wasting the town's resources to reopen the case. I respect the work you've done, but the truth is likely to stay buried. You're only hurting yourself with this obsession."

"I'm going to clear my name. Whether you help me or not. It'll make a terrific story when I run it. Maybe I'll even get a chance at the big time, after all. Chris threw my whole life off track. I only went along that night to do him a favor. He has to pay for what he did."

"Make sure you stay on the right side of the law."

"I'm not stupid. The last thing I'd risk is being charged with another crime."

"Please keep me informed of what you find." Ethan wished he didn't have to leave it at that. However, he couldn't get involved in a personal vendetta.

Unfortunately, he could tell from Barry's narrowed eyes that the man wasn't likely to give up. And that he now considered Ethan an obstacle, if not an outright antagonist.

FOR A WHILE after Ethan went upstairs, the conversation centered on police matters. Jenni was puzzled to learn that someone had been stealing family portraits.

"Just the pictures?" she asked. "Nothing else?"

"Not that anyone has mentioned," Gwen told her. "Except the frames, of course."

"It might be just the first step," Rosie warned. "This man could be studying his victims and planning to murder them in their sleep."

"Some of us watch too much television," Mae Anne rebuked. "But I'll admit, it is unnerving. What a hostile act."

"Why would anyone get hostile about a family photograph?" Gwen said.

"I don't understand, either," Rosie agreed. "But I do know somebody who feels that way."

Around the table, the other women leaned forward. "Who?" Leah asked.

"There's a young fellow who's dating my manicurist," Rosie said. "Arturo Mendez. He's got a chip on his shoulder the size of Colorado."

"He's a darn good painter, but he's arrogant," Gwen remarked. "After he painted graffiti all over the back of Archie's store, I invited him to display his work at the crafts fair. He turned up his nose at the idea. Mumbled something about not wanting to be lumped in with a bunch of hacks."

"He saw that picture of me with Mark and Mark Senior in the Snip 'N' Curl," Rosie said. "He told me we looked so full of ourselves he wanted to slap us. What kind of man talks that way?"

"No one's stolen your picture, I hope." Jenni didn't dare admit that as an outsider, she understood why a kid might resent those he considered smug, even though she thought it unfair to Rosie.

During her teen years, one friend's mother, on learning that Jenni had a parent in jail on drug charges, had followed her around the house to make sure she didn't steal anything. And at school after someone had taken money from a teacher's purse, the principal had questioned Jenni, even though she'd been nowhere near that classroom.

"My picture's fine," Rosie replied. "I've got a burglar alarm on the shop. But I don't like that young man. And now Helen's in trouble… Oops. I didn't mean to mention that."

"In trouble how?" Karen, who'd been collecting plates, paused to listen.

"I was meaning to ask Jenni about it, although I'd prefer to keep this to ourselves." The salon owner released a long breath. "She's pregnant. I found out when I caught her throwing up in the bathroom. She hasn't seen a doctor and told me she plans to use an unlicensed midwife. Isn't that dangerous?"

It certainly was. "She needs proper prenatal care," Jenni answered.

"But she's young and healthy, and having babies is a natural process," Rosie said. "Not that I'm arguing with you. Those are her words, more or less."

"Natural or not, serious problems can arise," Jenni explained. "We tend to forget that before modern medicine, the rates of infant and maternal mortality were quite high."

"I don't suppose she has insurance, does she?" Leah asked thoughtfully.

Rosie shook her head. "She only works part time. And her family has a lot of pride. They won't accept charity."

"Aren't there social services? She ought to accept those for her baby's sake." Jenni remembered what Ethan had said about his plans for an outreach program, but he hadn't been talking about expectant mothers.

"This isn't what you're used to, Jenni," Mae Anne said. "Downhome didn't even have a doctor until this week, remember?"

"What about the county?" she inquired.

"A situation has to be really serious before the county intervenes," said Leah, who was helping Karen clear the table. "I get frustrated when I see how many of my students haven't had their vision or hearing checked. If the family can't pay, it takes forever to get it done."

"I'd be happy to donate my services to Helen," Jenni offered. "And surely the hospital has a policy about treating the indigent." Downhome patients usually delivered their babies in Mill Valley.

"Like I said, Helen's family won't accept charity," Rosie warned. "I doubt she'd let you help unless you were being paid. The problem is, she smokes, and her father's disabled from a stroke, so I'm a little worried."

"Has she had her blood pressure checked?" Jenni asked, concerned.

"Not as far as I know."

This patient couldn't be left to chance. If Helen suffered from high blood pressure, a possibly hereditary condition that could be aggravated by smoking, it might have serious repercussions.

Before Jenni could say anything further, masculine footsteps thumped down the stairs. A moment later, Ethan appeared, alone.

"Do I smell coffee?" he teased, although the answer was

obvious. "Now, don't tell me some of those cookies might be left over. It's a crime. I might have to arrest somebody."

"Sit down and finish them," Karen commanded.

Rosie pushed the pastries toward him. "Try the apple tarts."

"Marry me," Gwen said, and they all laughed.

Ethan positioned his chair between Jenni and Mae Anne. "That's a tempting offer, Gwen."

"Don't take it too seriously," the café owner warned. "I'd hate to disappoint all my admirers."

"And I'd hate for them to challenge me to a duel," he joked. "My sword-fighting skills are a little rusty."

Although he wasn't looking at Jenni, she caught her breath when their shoulders brushed, and hoped no one had noticed. But Ethan, she was beginning to believe, noticed almost everything

"Don't let me intrude on the conversation," he added. "You ladies continue."

"We were discussing the lack of social services," Gwen explained. "You know, Jenni, the chief's been pushing for an outreach program."

"So he tells me," she replied.

"The man moves fast," Mae Anne observed.

"Well?" A sidelong glance from Ethan's dark eyes sent Jenni's heart into overdrive.

"Well, what?" She took a sip of her decaf.

"Aren't you going to help?" The words, spoken almost into her ear, rumbled through her nervous system.

"I think you can manage without me," she said stubbornly.

"I wish that were true. But if something isn't done, that girl could die!" Rosie explained.

"What girl?" Ethan asked.

The other women told him about Helen and why she probably wouldn't accept Jenni's offer to provide free care. Ethan's expression sobered.

"We need to talk," he said to Jenni when they'd finished. "Why don't we go for a stroll, Doc."

She didn't relish the notion of being alone with this man, so she blurted the first excuse that came to mind. "I have to help Karen clean up."

"We'll take care of that," Leah offered.

"What we can't do is deliver a baby," Rosie told her.

"Go on, please." Their hostess refilled Mae Anne's cup. "This is important."

Ethan waited patiently, no doubt aware that she couldn't refuse. Although being cornered, Jenni adopted the tactic she'd learned to use under pressure: she assumed her cool medical persona.

"Very well, Chief," she said. "Let's discuss it."

He stood, then reached to help her up. Pretending not to notice, she scooted to her feet. She could feel everyone's gaze fixed on them as they went out the door. "We'll be right back," she called, grabbing her purse.

"No hurry," Karen responded.

Ethan closed the door behind them, shutting off the warmth and safety of the house.

Chapter Six

They descended the steps into a vivid nighttime scene. Brilliant stars dappled the blue-black expanse like a scene from a Van Gogh painting. Along the modest street, lamp glow spilled through the windows of the houses.

In place of a straight sidewalk, the pedestrian path meandered from property to property, its surface varying unpredictably. Although some homeowners had paved their sections, others had laid down gravel and some had left hard-packed dirt. The lack of curbs gave the whole neighborhood a rural feeling, which was heightened by the scattering of untrimmed trees.

Instinctively, Jenni turned left toward Jackson Park. She'd strolled there a couple of times without knowing that Ethan lived adjacent to it. Now, as that realization dawned, she broke stride and considered heading in a different direction.

"Cold?" he asked, misunderstanding.

"I'm fine." In L.A., Jenni would have needed a jacket to insulate her from the evening chill, but the Tennessee air remained warm at night.

"It's these darn sidewalks. They're hard to navigate in the dark." Ethan crooked his arm. "Please hold on. I wouldn't want you to stumble."

She didn't entirely trust his protective attitude. Still, to refuse would be awkward, particularly since she'd neglected to change from pumps into jogging shoes and really might trip.

When she took his arm, he felt solid and reassuring. As they strolled along, a vague memory stirred, of her hand enfolded inside a much larger one. Her father's, Jenni supposed, although since he'd left when she was five, she scarcely knew him.

It was time to broach the reason she and Ethan had come out, she decided after they'd walked half a block. "You know, I appreciate your concerns, but I don't believe our interests coincide."

"You mean about the outreach project?"

"Of course," she said. "Isn't that what we're discussing?"

"On a night as glorious as this, we could talk about any number of things." With his free hand, Ethan gestured toward the sky. "About whether the stars can predict the future. Or why no matter how good decaf tastes, it never beats a cup of the real stuff."

What a whimsical man he was. "For a police chief, you've got an original way of expressing yourself."

"I wasn't born a police chief," he murmured.

"Didn't you always want to be in law enforcement?" Jenni asked.

"I suppose I always wanted to make the world a better place." Ethan guided her across a rough stretch of earth in front of a clapboard house with a wraparound porch. "I considered social work at one time, but I lose patience with bureaucracies."

"A police department is a bureaucracy," she pointed out.

"In a sense," he conceded, "though at least I get to spend time in the field. I'm a hands-on kind of guy."

Hands-on. The phrase inspired an unwilling image of Ethan smoothing back her hair, caressing her shoulders... Enough of that, she told herself.

"How about you?" he asked. "Did you always want to be a doctor?"

In front of the next house rose an arched gateway entwined with roses. If Jenni had grown up in such a place, perhaps she would have been able to give him an easy answer. *Oh, yes, I just knew I'd grow up to be like those doctors on E.R.* Or perhaps, *No, I wasn't sure I could, but my parents encouraged me.*

The truth was that, if she had ever thought about the future, she'd have pictured herself waitressing like her mother. Wait—she'd forgotten something, Jenni realized. "No. Before that, I considered joining the military."

"You did?" Plainly, he hadn't expected that insight. "Don't tell me you caught a rerun of *Private Benjamin* and decided you liked the uniforms."

She'd enjoyed the comedy about a goofy young woman who enlists expecting to have fun, but Jenni had considered the military because she'd needed a place to go. Her relatives, who'd been paid through the foster-care program, had shown no interest in helping her once she finished high school.

She refused to tell Ethan that. Jenni didn't want anyone feeling sorry for her. "Is that how you see me?" she replied, instead. "As a silly California blonde?"

Ethan's hesitation gave him away, although he covered by saying, "Before I got to know you, perhaps. Still, I'm curious. What *did* inspire you to become a doctor?"

She gave him a short, tidy answer that had the advantage of being accurate as well as sounding middle class. "I had a mentor who encouraged me."

"Friend of your parents?" Ethan inquired.

"She was my physician." Jenni didn't care to go into detail.

Her relationship with Susan Leto had been prickly at first. She'd seen the questions in the woman's eyes when she'd stitched a gash on Jenni's arm. The injury had occurred after she'd fallen from a boy's motorcycle the summer before senior year. Jenni had gone on the defensive, before realizing Dr. Leto suspected that she might be an abuse victim.

Even after determining that she wasn't, the doctor had taken the time to ask why she was living with an aunt and what Jenni's future plans were. Jenni had resented the interrogation at first, but, after a bit of coaxing, she'd admitted to receiving high test scores, although she saw no use for them.

Dr. Leto had asked Jenni's permission to talk to school authorities on her behalf. Soon she'd found herself in the honors and AP classes she'd never dared take. Rather than risk disappointing her mentor, she'd studied hard and had applied to several universities.

With the doctor's help, Jenni had received a full scholarship to UCLA, and later had won acceptance to medical school. When Susan retired to Tucson, Jenni experienced some of her old sense of abandonment, but her friend had remained available by phone and had sent her a plane ticket to join the family for Christmas that year.

However, further discussion of her mentor would only make Ethan wonder why Jenni had needed outside help. And her parents were none of his business.

They reached the park, a lovely green square with wrought-iron benches and lush overhanging trees that appeared dark and mysterious in the moonlight. "I love this place."

He escorted her along a cement path. "The Jackson family dedicated it and left money for its maintenance. They used to own my mother's house."

"What happened to them?"

"The last descendant had no children." She heard the sound of a TV from one of the homes. "We bought the place shortly after they died, when I was a kid. I'm glad my parents rented it out rather than selling when we moved to Nashville."

"I can't imagine having roots that deep," Jenni blurted. "Did your parents move around a lot?"

"Something like that."

"You're pretty evasive about your family." In the dimness, his eyes looked even darker than usual.

She'd long ago learned how to dodge when anyone questioned her too closely about the past. "I like to act enigmatic. It makes me seem less ordinary."

"Far be it from me to spoil your fun." Ethan indicated a bench. "Shall we get down to business?" Without waiting for an answer, he removed his jacket and laid it on the wrought iron.

"Wow. That was gallant," Jenni said, impressed in spite of herself.

"I'm the one who dragged you out here. I'd hate to get stuck with your dry-cleaning bill," he joked.

Not wanting to appear ungracious, she sank down. At once, an indefinable essence of him rose from the fabric, filling Jenni with half-realized longings.

Ethan eased into place beside her. Although he carried not an ounce of excess weight, his frame filled the space completely. Perhaps she was growing accustomed to his presence, because the light contact of his thigh against hers felt inviting rather than intrusive.

As she waited for him to speak, Jenni heard the faint strains of a country tune. She couldn't tell whether it came from a home or from someone walking with a radio. Ethan stiffened.

"What's wrong?" she inquired.

"That song," he said. "My wife used to sing it."

Annette had mentioned her daughter-in-law's voice. "She must have sung it beautifully."

"Too beautifully for words."

A powerful yearning to belong in a scenario like that, with a husband who adored her the way Ethan had obviously adored his wife, gripped Jenni. At the same time, his persistent attachment made him safe to be around because she knew that despite the hum of attraction between them, nothing could come of it.

To her, being in a family meant turmoil and conflict. Even though she sometimes ached with loneliness at the thought of gathering around a Christmas tree, she considered that a fantasy for other people.

She'd always kept her boyfriends at arm's length. She supposed she'd subconsciously chosen men who weren't promising marriage material. Knowing that Ethan fell into the same category made her feel wistful and, at the same time, safe.

"So. About the outreach project," he began. "I got the impression you might be changing your mind."

"I think this young woman—Helen—may be in danger if she doesn't get prenatal care," she replied. "I need an excuse to visit that won't make her feel like a charity case."

"What exactly do you want from me?" Ethan asked.

"I'd like you to come with me to Helen's home and persuade her we're part of an outreach project, even though we aren't," she admitted. "Rosie thinks she might accept help if she believes I'm being paid."

"You expect me to lie?"

"You might save a life—or two."

Ethan leaned back and stretched his legs. Rumpled and moonlit, he seemed to invite a woman's caress. But not hers, of course.

"I have a list of children Olivia Rockwell identified as possibly neglected," he said. "Their situations aren't serious enough to warrant an official investigation, but they deserve to be followed up. In some cases, the parents might simply need guidance. Others could probably use a psychological evaluation, and there might be one or two that require intervention."

"Are you negotiating with me?" Jenni inquired.

"You bet."

"You mean that if I refuse to participate in your project, you'd leave a pregnant woman without medical care?"

"You mean you'd leave a whole list of children at risk?" Ethan countered. Despite his obvious enjoyment at trying to one-up her, she could see he took the matter seriously.

"You really view this as crime prevention?"

"Kids grow up fast," he told her. "There's a brief window when a child who turns violent might have been saved if he'd made meaningful connections."

Like me, she thought, reluctantly acknowledging his point. Still, she was neither a social worker nor a psychologist. She'd gone into medicine in part because it was Dr. Leto's field, but also because a doctor operated in a clearly defined manner.

Although medicine was neither perfect nor infallible, it provided straightforward, scientific procedures to follow. The one time she'd made the mistake of trying to rescue a patient from a messy, destructive marriage, where had it landed her? In Downhome, Tennessee, as a matter of fact.

Ethan had gone on talking, she discovered. "Gun safety is another issue that crosses the line between crime prevention and public health. Parents don't realize how often kids die from accidental shootings."

"I've given up on saving the world," she said. "I only want to help this one woman, and I mean strictly in terms of providing medical care—no meddling."

Ethan crossed his arms. "But you need my cooperation. That puts us at an impasse."

Jenni tried another tack. "You make an articulate case for your project. You should present it to the city council."

"Believe me, I've tried. Funds are scarce. I need to show that the town will be getting enough bang for its bucks. What harm can it do to spare me a little of your time?"

A lot of harm, she thought as the starlight glinted in his dark eyes. She'd be spending time alone with a man she found dangerously attractive. By comparison, the fellows she'd dated in L.A. had been little more than boys.

Yet she couldn't abandon Helen, even though they'd never met. The woman's pride touched a nerve in her, and besides, the baby needed her.

She could handle this, Jenni told herself firmly. She'd limit her time with Ethan and project a strictly professional demeanor. No misunderstandings, no giving anyone a chance to cast her in the role of blond seductress. Her involvement with the chief would be strictly business.

"Ten kids," she decided. "I'll trade you visits to ten homes for one visit to Helen's."

His shoulders shook, and she realized he was laughing, although no sound came out.

"You are a piece of work, Doc."

"Ten for one. It's a heck of a good deal." Having sold magazines door-to-door during high school, she could tell when she'd won. "There's a condition, however."

"Uh-oh."

"My patients are entitled to privacy. You can't mention Helen to the council," Jenni told him. "Just the kids."

"I'd like to point out the scope of what we could accomplish by citing her situation. I wouldn't use her name," he countered.

"You think the folks in Downhome won't identify her?" she retorted. "I've never seen such a hotbed of gossip."

"Well…"

"No arguments, Chief."

He flashed her a smile. "Done. We'll go this Sunday."

"Fine. We'll start with Helen." They could work out the rest of the schedule later, she reflected. Maybe in a few weeks, after she'd found a place to live....

"And five kids," Ethan added. "The following weekend, we'll call on the remaining five."

"I'm not sure I'm ready for this." An alarming thought occurred to her. "I don't have to write up a report, do I?"

"It goes with the territory. Sorry, but I'll need your help. Otherwise, the deal is off."

Jenni groaned. "All right." She'd never negotiated this hard for anything in her life. "I know a couple of used-car salesmen who could take lessons from you."

"How do you happen to know a couple of used-car salesmen?" he asked.

Jenni wasn't sure if he was serious or just teasing; however, she hadn't made it up. "I bought my last car from one." She'd driven the dented sedan for four years, then donated it to charity before leaving L.A. rather than risk driving it cross-country. "That was after the other salesman made the mistake of addressing me as Blondie. I told him to stick his fender where the sun never shines."

Ethan laughed. "Remind me never to call you that."

"Don't worry. I will," she said sweetly.

He glanced at his watch. "I hate to rush off, but my son's due home from a party any minute."

"No problem." To forestall any insistence on accompanying her, Jenni added, "I can make it to Karen's by myself." Rising, she lifted his jacket from the bench and was about to shake off the dust, when Ethan's hand clamped around her wrist.

"Whoa," he said. "There's stuff in the pockets."

"Sorry." Despite her instinct to move away, Jenni paused as she registered the warmth of his fingers on her arm. Against the cooling night, his heat formed a cocoon.

Suddenly, she didn't want to think of him as the police chief or as the man who'd once judged her harshly. She wanted to bury her face against Ethan's chest and let him hold her. From his ragged breathing, she suspected he was thinking along the same lines.

Strictly business—that was how she'd sworn to keep this relationship. Was she too weak to keep the resolution she'd made five minutes ago?

Jenni pulled away, leaving Ethan to shrug into the jacket. "It was nice dealing with you, Chief. Say hi to your mother and son for me."

Ethan hurried to catch up, then matched her steps as she strode across the park. "I'm walking you home."

"You shouldn't keep your little boy waiting."

"Move fast, then."

Jenni didn't need urging, when the last thing she wanted was to linger in the scented night with Mr. Dark and Dangerous. Even in her pumps, she made double-time back to the Lowells' residence.

She was pleased to note that the visitors' cars had departed, so at least she wouldn't have to face a roomful of curious women. It also meant she and Ethan must have been gone longer than she'd realized.

At the porch, he said, "We can start right after church. One o'clock, okay? And please don't tell Helen we're coming. If she isn't in, we'll return later."

"You think she'd avoid us?" Jenni didn't really need to ask. In Helen's position, she'd probably have fled from authority figures, too.

"Let's not take that chance. By the way, thanks." He regarded her. "This outreach program means a lot to me. It's time Downhome did more for its poor."

"Glad I can help. Even if you did have to twist my arm."

Only after he disappeared did it dawn on Jenni that she'd

planned to spend Sunday cruising the town, looking for rentals. Well, she'd have to do that tomorrow afternoon, after her clinic hours in the morning.

Ethan Forrest had a disconcerting way of rearranging her life. She didn't plan to let him get away with it often.

JENNI'S EYES STUNG from the pungent odor of livestock as she emerged from the dilapidated duplex. She'd followed signs down Jackson Avenue promising a rental unit, only to find herself in a run-down part of town.

Because she'd phoned ahead, she'd felt obligated to knock on the door and ask to view the vacancy. The place had turned out to be even worse than she had feared. Cockroaches scurried across the floor and old wallpaper failed to hide several holes in the wall. Jenni would prefer to pitch a tent on The Green rather than live there, although she'd offered a more polite excuse to the landlord.

Barry had given her an advance peek at next Tuesday's ads, to no avail. There didn't seem to be a decent place to live in town short of renting an entire house, unfurnished, and she wasn't going to buy furniture while she still faced three months' probation.

Jenni winced at the smell emanating from across the inaptly named Garden Street. On the far side of the road, goats shambled across a rutted enclosure next to a board structure that, judging by the denizens pecking at the dirt, must be a chicken coop.

So much for zoning and urban planning.

In L.A., Jenni supposed, she'd been more fortunate than she'd realized. Although none of her relatives had overwhelmed her with love and support, at least they'd taken her into middle-class homes in well-tended neighborhoods.

Her heart went out to a group of children scrambling through weeds, pretending their sticks were laser wands.

Still, despite the dirt, most of them appeared healthy. If they had loving families, they were luckier in a way than she'd been.

As she was about to climb into her car, Jenni noticed what looked like a yard sale farther down the block, in front of a small apartment building. Visiting thrift stores and garage sales had become a hobby in her college days. Sometimes she came across an intriguing old book or item of vintage clothing that actually fit into her budget. The fascinating part was that you never knew where you might unearth a treasure. Possibly even in a place like this.

She headed toward the site. Her loose stride and trim pantsuit drew the scrutiny of an old woman in a wrinkled housedress, who rocked on a porch swing as she supervised a tricycle-riding tot.

"Hello," Jenni said. "What a cute little girl."

"Afternoon," came the elliptical response.

Jenni wondered how she appeared to the elderly lady. Judging by her stare, like a visitor from another planet.

When she reached the yard, Jenni discovered that what she'd seen was a display of paintings set up on homemade easels. Not simply originals, but works of breathtaking intensity and talent, even if they were a bit rough.

A couple of images showed this same neighborhood in piercing detail, the shabbiness heightened and the sense of despair palpable. From other canvases glared gaunt, angry faces. Why was this disturbing yet gifted artist exhibiting his work in a run-down front yard?

Catching a movement, she sighted a lean, dark-haired young man lounging alongside the building, smoking a cigarette. He wore a torn T-shirt and jeans with the knees patched.

Jenni read the signature on one of the paintings. "Are you Arturo Mendez?" she asked, recognizing the name from the discussion she'd heard last night at Karen's house.

He shrugged. From his slight nod, she gathered that meant yes.

So this, apparently, was Helen's boyfriend and a possible suspect in the break-ins. Yet Jenni didn't feel frightened, only intrigued. While Arturo's technique was still too crude for him to exhibit at the kind of galleries she'd visited with Susan Leto, his vision transcended the ordinary.

"I don't see any prices," she said. "Are they for sale?"

"Sure. Whatever." He was obviously a man of few words.

"They're really good." Although Arturo tried to hide his reaction, Jenni saw his eyes spark with interest. "They wouldn't be easy images to live with, though."

"I'm not a decorator," he muttered.

"Really?" she shot back. "You mean you don't do pastel flower arrangements?"

An edgy smile revealed white teeth. "You're not from around here."

"I'm from L.A." Despite the temptation to tell him that his work was meant for bigger places than a dusty yard in Downhome, Jenni remembered Gwen saying the artist had refused an invitation to exhibit on The Green. As a kid, she'd despised do-gooders, and she had no intention of trying to meddle, even though seeing his abilities wasted bothered her. "How much for this one?"

She'd stopped in front of the portrait of a young woman whose uncombed brown hair and dangling cigarette failed to diminish her natural beauty. What drew Jenni was the expression—a rueful mixture of irritability and affection. Usually, she avoided burdening herself with artwork because of her frequent moves, but the subject's raw honesty struck a chord.

"Not for sale," he replied.

The subject must be Helen, Jenni thought, and knew better than to argue. Remembering his earlier response when asked if the works were for sale, she said, "I guess this falls under the category of 'whatever' rather than 'sure,' right?"

"What?"

"Never mind. Well, thanks for letting me look."

"Anytime." The mask of indifference fell back into place.

Jenni sensed his gaze following her to the car, but not in a threatening way. She decided to suggest to Barry that Arturo might make an interesting story.

It was nearly five o'clock, she saw with a jolt when she checked the car's clock. What on earth was she going to do about a place to live? Jenni wondered as she drove. She couldn't expect the Lowells to let her stay in their guest room indefinitely, and besides, she was eager to find a place to set up her sewing machine.

Within minutes, she reached the lovely Jackson Park. What a contrast to Garden Street! The houses might have emerged from a storybook, especially the blue-trimmed gray Victorian with its gabled roof.

In the front, a woman knelt on a pad, planting pansies from plastic nursery containers. Catching Annette's eye, Jenni waved. Ethan's mother signaled frantically with her spade.

After pulling over, Jenni rolled down the window. "What is it?"

"Perfect timing." Annette brushed dirt from her jeans as she rose. With a scarf tied over her gray-laced brown hair, she looked remarkably neat, considering her activity. "Nick's taking a nap. Why don't you pop in and check out the apartment?"

Jenni blurted the first thing that came to mind. "Is Ethan around?" Flustered, she added, "I don't think he'd welcome my visit."

"He usually works on Saturdays. He's not back yet." Annette collected the empty containers and her other gardening gear. "This won't take a moment. And don't worry about Ethan."

Jenni knew she ought to decline. She had no business inspecting a place that was, in its own way, as unacceptable as the one across the street from the chicken coop. Well, maybe not quite.

But she felt exhausted and discouraged, and Annette seemed so hopeful. "Thanks," she said, and exited the car. What harm could it do to look?

Chapter Seven

It was 3:20 p.m.—twenty minutes past the appointment—on Saturday when Ethan arrived at Archie and Olivia Rockwell's rambling stone house on a large lot south of the high school. The property, with its outcroppings and meandering creek, made a wonderful setting for the Rockwells' occasional barbecues, which Nick always enjoyed.

Today, however, Ethan had come on official business. The search committee needed to find two more doctors, and he knew from previewing the résumés that narrowing down the choice wouldn't be easy.

When he volunteered for the panel, he'd hoped that one candidate would stand out for each position, making their decision easy. That hadn't happened during the hiring process for the job Jenni had eventually landed and it wasn't happening for the other positions, either.

Olivia greeted him at the door, dressed in an African-print caftan that emphasized her height and dark coloring. A native of Memphis, she'd once admitted to Ethan that she hadn't expected to stay in Downhome when she'd first arrived to take a teaching assignment. Then she'd met Archie and fallen in love.

"I didn't figure a black person had much chance of succeeding in a backwater place like this," she'd said frankly. "Archie kind of amazed me."

Her husband had started as a pharmacist leasing space in the dry goods emporium and had eventually acquired ownership of it. Later, he'd added the farm supply store across the street to his possessions. Since Olivia was named principal of two schools, the couple had presided over the town's society and helped bridge any lingering uneasiness among residents of different races.

"Good to see you. We're in the den," she told Ethan. "Come on back."

Although large, the Rockwell house had low ceilings and odd-size rooms, a testimony to its piecemeal growth from a modest ranch house to a residence encompassing well over three thousand square feet. In the den, an add-on that lay two steps below the hallway, Karen greeted him cheerfully.

"Sorry I'm late," Ethan said. "I had to clean up after work."

"No problem." As usual, she'd tucked her reddish brown hair behind her ears. "We started without you."

The women had spread the résumés atop an oversize coffee table. Ethan helped himself to a praline before taking an armchair at one side.

He'd spent most of the day with his men, undergoing physical fitness training and shooting at a range outside the city limits. He placed the same demands on himself as on everyone else, because he believed the head of such a small operation ought to be able to step into any gap.

As he opened his notebook, Karen took an assessing peek at him. Ethan knew at once that Jenni must have told her about their conversation last night. Both Karen and Olivia supported the idea of an outreach program, so he didn't mind.

He wondered if she and Olivia had been speculating about him and Jenni on a personal basis. Well, if so, they'd get over it.

"We realize you were hoping to have a pediatrician on

board next." Karen gestured toward one of the dossiers. "But we've got a ticklish situation here. It's just not going to work."

"You're talking about Chris McRay, I assume?"

"For heaven's sake, he might be a murderer!" Karen burst out. "Even if he is Mae Anne's grandson, he has no business treating this town's children."

"He hasn't been charged with anything. He isn't even under investigation. This is your brother's personal issue," Olivia reminded her. "You know he wants to move closer to his grandmother now that she can't travel anymore. It would mean a lot to her."

"He does have ties to Downhome," Ethan added. "He'd probably stay for at least a few years."

"He isn't part of the community," Karen protested. "And you can imagine what a fuss my brother will raise. Why not leave well enough alone?"

"Which of the other two applicants would you choose?" Olivia asked. "The doctor from Wichita had a drug problem. He was lucky to keep his medical license."

"He smoked pot. He didn't prescribe himself narcotics." Karen lacked her usual forcefulness, however. A pot-smoking pediatrician was out of the question.

"Our other applicant is seventy-two," Ethan pointed out. "I wouldn't necessarily rule someone out because of age, but the information indicates he's showing signs of forgetfulness."

"We're really batting a thousand, aren't we?" Olivia said dryly.

Much as Ethan wanted to get a pediatrician on board, perhaps a delay wasn't a bad idea. "Let's run an ad on a different Internet site," he suggested. "Maybe we'll hear from more people."

"Good idea." Karen sounded relieved. "Don't you think so, Olivia?"

The chairman's mouth twisted skeptically. Her two children didn't have any serious problems that Ethan knew of, but as school principal she had to be concerned for her students. "We shouldn't put it off for too long."

"A few more months," Karen said. "In the meantime, maybe we can bring in an obstetrician. There's an applicant with six-year-old twin girls who sounds very well qualified. I'll bet he'd like to relocate by the time school starts."

"I agree he's a strong candidate. However, I got the feeling he was just putting out feelers," Ethan countered. The man had impeccable credentials, along with a stated desire to move to a small town. However, he had no particular reason to choose Tennessee. "He'll probably end up staying in Texas."

"That doesn't mean we can't try." Olivia passed around the plate of pralines.

Although it was approaching dinnertime, Ethan took another one. Olivia made the best pralines in town.

"I'm all for it," Karen said.

"Okay." Ethan saw no harm in going along. "Let's take a closer look at William Rankin, MD."

So, for now, they'd dodged the issue of what to do about Dr. Chris McRay. But it wouldn't stay out of sight forever.

BY FIVE-THIRTY, THEY'D AGREED to invite Dr. Rankin and one other obstetrician for a visit. The pralines had barely taken the edge off the appetite Ethan had worked up from his earlier exercise, and as he drove home, he could hardly wait for his mother's traditional Saturday night dinner.

He was grateful that he'd chosen to relocate near her. Not only had she provided a mother figure for Nick, but returning to Downhome had inspired Ethan to apply for the job of police chief rather than remaining as an underling in a larger department.

He wanted to do his best for this town. If only he knew which course would turn out best—but how could anyone predict the future? Although Ethan's instincts urged him to support Chris McRay, the guy was bound to stir a painful controversy. And Ethan had been wrong before.

Despite the possibility that Jenni might quickly tire of the place, he had to admit the council had made the right decision in hiring her. She cared about her patients and she'd gone to bat fiercely for a pregnant stranger. Last night, he'd found himself admiring the new doctor. Not to mention being strongly attracted to a woman for the first time since losing Martha.

Ethan's hands tightened on the steering wheel as he remembered his desire to kiss her. When he'd unthinkingly caught Jenni's wrist, he'd realized how much he missed the connection that came from real intimacy.

For all that, she was exactly what he and his son didn't need. Transitory and fiercely independent. Even secretive in some ways. Not warm and giving like Martha, although, he had to admit, his wife had put her career first during the early years of their marriage. But he'd been a different person then, and besides, he'd always known that, fundamentally, Martha had wanted the same things he did.

His thoughts returned to Jenni. Secretive—perhaps that was putting the matter too strongly, but she was certainly full of contradictions.

She wore designer clothes, yet, according to her, she'd bought a used car in L.A. Her sunny, surfer-girl bounciness didn't tally with the comments about her parents' frequent absences, either. And although she'd fought for the chance to help Helen, she'd tried to avoid performing a larger community service.

Her behavior defied any pattern that Ethan recognized. He wasn't sure what to make of her.

Pulling into his driveway, he took a second look at the car in front of his mother's house. The sedan had Davidson County plates with a frame bearing the name of a Nashville leasing agency.

Ethan's breath caught in his throat. It had to be Jenni's. If his mother had called the doctor, something must be wrong.

Heart thudding, he bolted from his car. He cleared the flower bed in a leap and raced to his mother's side door— unlocked, as usual, despite his warnings.

"Mom? Nick?" he called as he burst into the kitchen.

Three startled faces turned toward him. Simultaneously, he noticed that they all looked quite healthy, and he registered the enticing aroma of frying chicken.

Annette, in a bright yellow apron, stood mashing potatoes at the counter. By the wooden table, Jenni held Nick in her lap, helping him sound out words from a picture book.

Ethan didn't know whether to laugh or scold. It wasn't their fault he'd jumped to the wrong conclusion, but he felt annoyed nonetheless.

"I saw the doctor's car," he explained. "I thought Nick might be hurt."

"I'm sorry." Jenni closed the book.

"We didn't mean to frighten you." Annette smiled indulgently. "Hope you don't mind, son. I invited Dr. Vine for dinner."

"No problem." He felt too relieved to argue. Instead, he swept his eager little boy into an overhead lift. "How's my man?"

Nick giggled. "I can read *c-a-t*. Meow!"

"Meow yourself."

"Can I have a kitten, Daddy?"

Ethan pretended to glower at Jenni. "Is this your influence?"

She set the book on the table. "I always wanted a cat myself. So I guess I have to plead guilty."

Ethan pulled Nick close. "How about a dog? A nice big one that can protect you and your grandmother."

Annette scraped the potatoes into a serving dish. "I don't want another dog. The last one broke my favorite vase and ruined the carpet."

"That's because you spoiled him," Ethan responded, citing a point he'd raised many times. "I offered to take him for training." The dog had eventually found a more suitable home with a farmer.

"I'm too much of a softie. Still, I might be in the market for a cat," his mother said. "Not a kitten, though. I'd prefer an older animal. They're less rambunctious and very gentle with children. We used to have one when you and Brianna were small."

"It's up to you." Ethan would have provided his son with a pet sooner, but he lacked the time for one. If Annette chose to get a cat, however, that might work fine.

He helped set the dining room table and serve the food. It smelled so great he was tempted to sample the fried chicken in advance, but that would set a poor example for his son.

They were halfway through dinner, with Nick filling them in on last night's birthday party, when Ethan collected his wits enough to wonder what Jenni was doing here in the first place. After his son finished speaking, he posed the question.

Annette didn't beat around the bush. "I saw her driving past and I waved her down to look at the apartment. She'd been all over town and found nothing. I think she should live here."

He hadn't realized his mother was so eager to rent the place. She leased it only sporadically, mostly to the adult children of friends. Ethan hoped finances weren't a problem. He'd tried repeatedly to give her a stipend. However, she always insisted his father's pension was more than adequate.

"Jenni checked my blood sugar. It only hurt a little." That

was Nick's method of weighing in on the discussion. "And she said she could sew a shirt for my teddy bear."

Ethan didn't know how to react to his son's unexpected advocacy. "A shirt for your bear?"

"She's quite a seamstress." Annette gestured at the tailored suit Jenni wore. "My fingers are getting too stiff for fine work. She offered to make him one as soon as she finds a place to set up her machine."

Blue-gray eyes met Ethan's. "I haven't been lobbying them," Jenni said. "Frankly, I'm not sure moving in here is a good idea, although it's a charming place."

She stopped. He ought to be pleased, Ethan thought. Instead, he experienced both curiosity and an inexplicable sense of disappointment. "Why wouldn't it be a good idea?"

"I'd rather not go into it."

This was maddening. However, Ethan chose not to interrogate her. "Anyone object if we have dessert now?" When no one did, he cleared the table.

"Why can't Jenni live here?" Nick demanded, surrendering his dish.

"It's more fun if I just visit sometimes," she said.

"No, it isn't. I want to watch you make the teddy bear shirt."

"Didn't somebody mention getting a cat?" Ethan hoped the topic would distract his son. "Where do you suppose we can find one?"

Soon they were involved in a discussion over whether to visit the animal shelter in Mill Valley, respond to one of the occasional "Free Kittens to Good Homes" signs around town or set out food for a stray Annette had noticed in the neighborhood.

Jenni, who'd devoted herself to the apple pie during most of the interchange, spoke at last. "I vote for the stray."

"Why's that?" Ethan asked.

"I have a fondness for strays."

"They do make good pets, I've heard," his mother commented. "Some cats crave affection and when you rescue them from a life of loneliness, apparently they become devoted."

Ethan had never heard that about cats. He preferred dogs. They respected order, displayed loyalty and performed useful services. Still, the pet was for his son, not him. "You might as well give it a try. The cat certainly needs a home."

"I'm going to name him Boots," Nick announced.

"Why?" Jenni asked. "Are his paws like little boots?"

"I just like the name."

"I agree," she remarked earnestly. "It reminds me of *Puss 'n Boots.*"

"Me, too," the boy said.

Ethan's chest gave a squeeze at the picture the two of them made, Nick's freckled face tilting upward while Jenni's neck curved toward him. They reminded him of a sculpture of a mother and child.

Annette broke the mood. "Ethan, would you please show Jenni the furniture I've stored for the apartment? I couldn't get that rusty lock to work."

The doctor opened her mouth as if to protest, then closed it in silence. She obviously saw his mother as a force to be reckoned with.

Ethan, however, was less easily cowed. "Are you sure this is a good idea?"

Ignoring him, his mother turned to her grandson. "Nick, let's go watch that funny video of the time your Dad tried to put up the patio cover and it fell on his head. Ethan, you and Jenni are welcome to join us if you like."

He recognized when he'd been outflanked. "I think I'll pass."

Jenni struggled to suppress a grin. "Gee, I'm not sure…"

Catching his eye, she said, "Oh, okay. I'd love to look at the furniture."

"Good, because you'll be needing it," Annette replied tartly. "And don't worry about cleaning up in here. Nick and I can handle that."

Ethan decided to get this over with before his mother hauled out his baby photos, too. Taking the set of apartment keys from a hook, he held the side door for Jenni and they emerged into the fading light of a summer's eve.

Together, they crossed a lawn scented with roses and honeysuckle. His mother had a gift for placing clumps of flowers and decorative grasses so they appeared to have sprung up naturally, and she had replaced the former owners' formal patio with rambling bricks. It was a place for wandering and daydreaming, Ethan mused, unlike his own strictly utilitarian yard.

Alongside the house, the driveway led to the garage, above which rose a cottagelike apartment with a balcony and a peaked roof. At the back of the garage, at ground level, lay a storage space sealed with a padlock.

Beyond that, amid an expanse of decorative rocks, nestled the vegetable garden with which his mother had replaced a fishpond that might have endangered Nick. At the back, tall flowering bushes and a few trees screened off the neighbor's house.

Jenni gazed around appreciatively. "It's so beautiful it scares me."

Ethan stopped by the storage door. "Why?"

For a moment, she seemed on the verge of explaining, and then she drew back. "I don't know. That was a silly thing to say. Let's inspect the furniture and get it over with. I'm sure you're eager to go home and relax after a long day."

"Putting me off?" he challenged.

"You enjoy being contrary, don't you," Jenni retorted. "If

I were eager for your company, you'd get rid of me as fast as you could."

"I told you—I enjoy sparring. Besides, you said earlier that moving in here wasn't a good idea. However, you didn't tell me why. Well, no one else is listening, so fire away."

She wavered. Why so self-protective? Ethan wondered.

"For one thing, people might gossip," Jenni replied. "We're going to be spending time together on the outreach project, and now we'd be living next door. Rumors may not harm your reputation, but I'm an outsider."

"If there are rumors, they'll be good-natured ones." Ethan had never found the townspeople to be malicious. "After a while, they'll come to see that it's strictly platonic."

Jenni didn't debate the point. "Number two, I doubt this place is private enough for my taste."

The comment saddened him. He'd had the impression she liked his son. "You think Nick would drop in too often?"

"I'm not worried about that. He's a sweetheart, and so is your mom. I just don't want to become part of a family. I'm used to living alone."

"A hermit?" For a young, single woman to be so intimacy-averse seemed unusual.

Again, she gave a truncated answer. "More or less."

Ethan decided he'd questioned her enough. He inserted the key into the lock. The thing required several hard twists to open.

Inside, he switched on the overhead bulb. An assortment of chairs, a bureau and some shrouded objects that he guessed were a sofa, box springs and a mattress packed the shallow space. "The last tenant had his own furniture, so we put this away." He eyed a thick cobweb. "This could use a good cleaning."

"If I were going to rent, it would be fine," Jenni assured him.

"You must be accustomed to better."

"What makes you say that?" she asked.

"Well, you're a doctor." That seemed an inadequate answer. "And you dress like a million bucks." Ethan remembered his mother's comment, which he hadn't had a chance to absorb until now. "You make your own clothes, right?"

"Right," Jenni said.

Absent parents. Used car. No furniture. "I guess I figured you wrong. I thought you were rich."

To her credit, she didn't rub it in. "Lots of people do."

"Why don't you set them straight?"

"Why should I?" came the response. "As you said, I'm a doctor. Now that I've paid off my med school loans, I *will* be able to afford better stuff."

"Including expensive clothes?" he couldn't resist probing.

"I like sewing. I don't plan to stop."

The more Ethan learned about Jenni, the more curious he became. He'd never had the urge to pry into anyone's life before, and he had no right to do so now.

Nevertheless, his mother had raised a good point. "You're not likely to find a place as nice as this elsewhere in Downhome, and you're good for Nick. It would be a shame to say no because you and I got off on the wrong foot."

"Both wrong feet, in my opinion," she retorted.

"I apologize." Based on what he'd been told, Ethan believed he'd done the right thing by passing the medical director's comments along to the city council. Still, he regretted having upset Jenni. She'd obviously had to struggle to get where she was, and he hadn't made things easier.

"Also, I can't help wondering if having me next door isn't just a way to keep an eye on me," she said.

"What?" Then he remembered telling Olivia something along those lines. "Karen repeated that?"

"Never mind where I heard it."

She was right. What mattered was his formerly opposi-tional attitude. "I apologize for that remark, too," Ethan said. "Now I don't see any reason you shouldn't rent here. You have a very humbled police chief willing to help move you in, unless that would intrude too much on your privacy."

Jenni shifted from one foot to the other. "You shouldn't do this."

"Do what?"

"Act so sweet. It goes against the grain."

"I have many facets," he told her. "Like a diamond in the rough."

"I don't want diamonds," Jenni replied. "Rough or other-wise."

"Why not?" he asked.

"Because they tie you down."

She'd already said she didn't want to be part of a family, Ethan recalled. And diamonds—well, there was a lot of sym-bolism wrapped up in those stones. They hinted at engage-ment rings and commitments.

He would have expected a professional woman in her early thirties to want what most people wanted—a home, kids, a spouse. The same things he'd wanted when he'd met Martha, although he didn't expect ever to find them again. But Jenni had a right to be different. She certainly had noth-ing to worry about from him.

"I can't promise not to be charming," Ethan joked. "How-ever I'll do my best to stay out from underfoot. Take the place. At least it's not a dump."

A smile lit up her face. She became nearly irresistible when she let down her guard.

"'At least it's not a dump.' There's a sales pitch the adver-tising gurus never thought of," she said. "As an admirer of originality, I feel it should be rewarded."

"Is that your way of saying yes?"

"Yes, but I'll hold you to your promises."

He didn't remember what promises he'd made, other than to help her move in and to try not to act like a pest. That must be what she meant.

"Absolutely," Ethan confirmed. "You can count on me."

Chapter Eight

That evening, Karen greeted the news of Jenni's decision with approval. "It's a terrific place," she said. "And you'll only be a few blocks away. I'd like to have a friend nearby, especially now that Leah's planning to move."

Barry, who'd acted grumpy since his meeting with Ethan the previous night, made no comment. However, when Jenni described her earlier experiences while apartment hunting and mentioned Arturo Mendez as a possible subject for a story, he shook his head.

"I tried to interview him once," he said. "He's a pain in the neck. Acted like he was a movie star and I was some kind of paparazzi. When we finally made an appointment, he stood me up. The guy has too many issues for his own good."

"Maybe we all do," Karen muttered, but she didn't elaborate. Jenni guessed she was referring to Barry's attempt to substantiate his innocence.

The next morning, Jenni awoke wondering if she'd made a mistake in agreeing to rent the place. Ethan had vowed to not intrude on her privacy, but how could he help invading her thoughts? When Annette showed Jenni around the flat, she'd observed that the bedroom window overlooked his yard and patio.

She imagined him wandering outside with his coffee in the

morning, perhaps remembering how he and his wife used to sit there and make plans for the future. It bothered Jenni to visualize Ethan with another woman, although she had no right—and no desire—to claim him for herself.

He'd shared his whole heart with Martha. She'd been beautiful and talented, and it seemed terribly unfair that she'd died so young. Everything Jenni heard and everything she saw in Nick's dear little face confirmed her impression of Martha being an ideal wife and companion. All the things she herself could never be.

Well, if there was one thing Jenni knew, it was how to give people space. She'd make sure Ethan enjoyed his memories undisturbed.

After breakfast, she prepared for their outing. She swung by the clinic and picked up brochures on prenatal care, child development and vaccinations. She also collected lollipops and coloring books.

Ethan arrived at one o'clock sharp. He'd left the jacket and tie at home today, perhaps to avoid intimidating people. Even in a sports shirt and slacks, however, he radiated authority.

Jenni had paired white slacks with a blue cotton sweater and a short-sleeved white jacket. "That shade of blue matches your eyes" was the first thing Ethan said. Noting her skeptical expression, he added, "Not that I care about things like that."

His attempt at a bluff amused Jenni. "You're a natural flirt, but I'll overlook it. Now, let's move on."

"I got Helen's address from Rosie," he mentioned as they descended the steps. "Apparently, she lives with her boyfriend."

She heard a note of caution in his tone. "Is that a problem—as far as we're concerned, I mean?"

"It could be. But frankly, I doubt the guy will raise a ruckus with me standing by."

Jenni had no illusions about the possibility that a father-to-be might be more concerned with his pride than with his girlfriend's well-being. Still, Arturo hadn't struck her as a violent man. "I intend to keep this strictly factual. I'm not here to pass judgment on anybody's lifestyle or personal history. These are medical issues."

"I agree," Ethan said.

They drove down Jackson Street toward Garden Street. "I was here yesterday, looking at a rental."

"Cockroaches? Barnyard odors?"

"You got it."

"Hope you don't mind going there again," he said.

"Of course not. This isn't a pleasure outing." She'd become impatient when some of her fellow med students reacted squeamishly to unpleasant sights and smells. Granted, it took a special kind of guts to handle the worst cases, but for the most part Jenni sublimated her personal sensitivities at work.

"You're a tough cookie," Ethan remarked.

"It's my job."

He made a left and she saw the chickens and goats again. Their shabby surroundings hadn't improved, and neither had their smell.

Jenni noticed that the children at play wore better clothes than she'd seen on Saturday, probably indicating they'd just returned from church. Attendance was apparently more commonplace in Downhome than in L.A.

The car stopped in front of the small apartment building. The paintings had disappeared, making the place seen even more depressing.

"We're not going to mention that we heard about her from Rosie, right?" Jenni said.

Ethan nodded. "As far as the clients are concerned, we're part of a pilot outreach project, paying random visits."

"To random pregnant women."

"With random potential health problems." He gave her a conspiratorial smile.

"Got it." Grabbing her clipboard and some brochures, Jenni scooted from the car before Ethan could come around. Men in this town had an unexpected habit of opening doors for women. After the every-man-for-himself attitude in L.A., Jenni doubted she'd ever get used to Southern courtesies.

Inside the square building, the smell of frying bacon and the blare of a TV emanated from first-floor apartments. Ethan proceeded up a steep staircase to unit 2B.

After knocking, he moved back and gestured Jenni to do the same. She hoped he didn't expect bullets to come flying out, but had to admit stepping away was a sensible precaution.

When the door opened, Arturo Mendez stood there in a T-shirt that, if anything, displayed even more rips than the one he'd worn the previous day. He frowned as his gaze traveled between her and the police chief. "Is this about the painting or what?"

"I'm sorry?" Ethan said.

"I asked about one of his paintings yesterday," Jenni explained. To Arturo, she said, "We're doing outreach. I'm a doctor, and one of your neighbors mentioned that a pregnant woman lives at this address." She hoped he wouldn't demand to know which neighbor.

"Since when do doctors pay house calls with the police chief?"

"It's a pilot program," Ethan interjected smoothly. "I'm assisting Dr. Vine."

"I don't have to let you in." Jenni could see Arturo's anger in the hunch of his shoulders. "Helen's fine."

Before he could slam the door, she said, "May I talk to her?" Impulsively, she added, "She's the woman in the painting, isn't she? I'm concerned that smoking could endanger her health."

"I don't believe that crap." Defiantly, he produced a pack of cigarettes from his jeans pocket and lit one. "Anyway, it's none of your business."

Ethan tensed. As a police officer, he obviously didn't like being in a situation he couldn't control. But these people weren't criminals and they had a right to their suspicions, Jenni thought.

As she was trying to figure out how to defuse the situation, the beautiful brown-haired woman from the portrait appeared behind her boyfriend. "Who is it, Artie?"

"A lady doctor. And Chief Forrest. Poking their noses into our business," the painter said.

As he spoke, he turned, leaving a slight opening. Making an instant decision, Jenni ducked into the room. Startled, Arturo swung around, which had the effect of blocking the doorway so Ethan couldn't enter.

"Jenni," the chief said warningly.

"Hi. I heard you're expecting a baby. That's fantastic!" Jenni addressed the young woman.

"Thank you. We're excited." Although Helen wore no makeup, she looked spectacular. Her skin glowed and her face had begun to fill out, although her figure showed only the slightest curve beneath her embroidered smock.

She and Arturo had put a lot of care into their home. The walls had been papered, the furniture shone, and the dramatic paintings were displayed with care, some on their easels and some on the wall. The smell of turpentine masked any odors from outside.

An unusual shade of green splashed one unfinished canvas. From the roughed-in shapes of surrounding houses, Jenni realized Arturo had begun a scene at Jackson Park.

"I'm Dr. Vine. Call me Jenni." She shook hands with the

young woman, who appeared uncertain how to deal with this uninvited guest. "May I ask, have you seen a physician?"

"She doesn't need one."

Arturo appeared to be deliberately objecting to every suggestion. Jenni doubted either of them was over twenty, so they hadn't had much time to outgrow adolescent attitudes.

"I haven't seen anyone," Helen answered softly.

"Don't talk to them!" her boyfriend growled.

While he was distracted, Ethan eased into the room. Arturo countered by shifting his position to prevent access to an inner hallway.

"You smoke, right?" Jenni continued talking to Helen, who nodded. "That's a risk factor for high blood pressure. In a prenatal exam, that's one of the first things I test for. High blood pressure can damage the mother's kidneys and contribute to premature delivery. It can endanger her baby's life."

The young woman glanced nervously at Arturo. "I'm fine."

"As part of our pilot program, we're offering free prenatal examinations at the clinic," Jenni explained. "You know where it is, on Home Boulevard across from The Green? You don't even need an appointment. I'll work you in anytime." She handed the young woman one of the business cards Barry had printed for her that week, along with a brochure about the first trimester. "Things can go wrong without warning during pregnancy, but many problems can be prevented. It's really important that you come in."

Arturo folded his arms. "Does Mr. Police Chief hang around your office?"

"Of course not," she said. "He's just accompanying me today."

"This isn't charity, is it?" Helen asked.

"Not at all," Jenni improvised. "We find that proper preventive care reduces the likelihood of an emergency later on.

We actually save money this way." She wasn't sure that remark made a lot of sense. However, if it encouraged Helen to visit the clinic, she didn't care.

"Nice paintings," Ethan observed. "Is your studio back there?" He indicated the hallway.

"Just the bedroom," Arturo replied.

"One bedroom?" Ethan asked.

Jenni had an urge to shake him. What was the matter with the man? They hadn't come here to snoop.

"Maybe I'll see you Monday," she told Helen. "The clinic hours are on the card."

The young woman clutched it with perfectly shaped red fingernails. "I'll try."

Jenni didn't like the way the two men were sizing each other up like a pair of roosters. "We'll be on our way, then. We have other calls to make."

Since Ethan didn't stir, she caught his arm.

"Right," he said as if recalled to their mission. "Congratulations on the baby, ma'am."

To Jenni's relief, he went along quietly.

They didn't speak until they reached the sidewalk. "What was that all about?" Jenni didn't bring up the portrait thefts. She didn't intend to spread other people's suspicions about Arturo without proof.

"Nothing."

She hated to get into an argument, but Ethan had come close to ruining the entire visit. "I took you at your word when I agreed to cooperate on this outreach program. In there, I got the distinct sense you have a secret agenda. Do you?"

"Of course not." Ethan's face settled into the stonewall lines she'd come to know over the years from confronting principals, social workers and other authority figures.

Jenni refused to let him dodge the issue. "Either you come clean or I walk home."

"We made a deal. You owe me five visits to kids' homes today and five more next week," he said doggedly.

"If you didn't disclose your real reason for pursuing this project, the deal's null and void." Jenni planted herself on the sidewalk, feet apart and arms folded. She hoped Arturo and Helen weren't watching, although she had a feeling they might be.

Ethan must have been thinking the same thing. "We can talk in the car."

"Fine."

They drove a few blocks and stopped where the road yielded to woodland. When the engine cut off, Jenni heard birds twittering and the repetitive chirp of an insect.

"I didn't invent the outreach program for some nefarious purpose." Ethan draped one arm across the steering wheel. "I've been trying to get it started for a long time. Still, I'll admit, I take a particular interest in Arturo Mendez."

"Why?" she demanded.

"Recently, Downhome has suffered an unusual series of break-ins. The only things stolen were family portraits," he said. "I can't divulge the details of the investigation, but Arturo's name has been mentioned."

"I know."

"You do?"

"Word gets around fast. But having been slandered myself, I'm not quick to pass judgment."

"Fair enough," Ethan responded. "However, there are two bedrooms in that unit—I can tell from the windows outside—and he said there was only one. If I knew for sure that those pictures aren't stashed in the spare room, it would go a long way toward clearing Arturo."

"And if they were there, you'd arrest him," she retorted.

"Obviously," Ethan replied.

Jenni had no sympathy for crooks. Still, there was a larger

issue at stake. "Regardless of his guilt or innocence, your attitude might dissuade Helen from seeking the help she needs. You should have told me what you were up to before we went in. You betrayed my trust."

"You're exaggerating."

She opened her door. Ethan put a hand on her arm.

"Wait." He released a long breath. "Let me think about this."

"What's to think about?" But she closed the door. At least he'd dropped the smug expression.

"Okay," Ethan said as if he'd reached a decision.

"Okay what?"

"This has been my project for so long, and mine alone, that I tend to assume I own it. It didn't seem like a big deal to use our visit to check out a theory about a crime. I didn't consider the fact that I now have a partner."

His willingness to reconsider impressed Jenni. Still, she wasn't ready to excuse his actions. She waited, her arms folded.

"I can see why you believe I used you, but that wasn't my intention," he continued. "However, I concede that it was wrong. All the same, the kid's obnoxious."

"That's what I call a kiss-your-sister apology," Jenni told him.

"What does that mean?"

"Not much passion in it," she clarified.

Ethan winced. "I truly and deeply apologize for giving offense."

"And for possibly endangering Helen."

"I certainly didn't mean to do that."

It was Jenni's turn to make peace. "Apology accepted. But I don't think Arturo's obnoxious. He's just hostile."

"Which makes him a pain to be around," the chief responded.

"But not necessarily a criminal."

"If you discovered that he was, would you tell me?" he asked.

That was a tough one. "It depends on the circumstances," she answered truthfully. "I'm not going to deliberately protect a robber. However, our priorities are different, Chief."

"I can live with that." He handed her a stack of papers. "These are the kids Olivia suggested we contact. You want to pick five, or shall we simply start at one location and work through them geographically?"

"Let me see." She stared at the top paper but couldn't concentrate. Her brain was replaying their interchange.

She'd never met a man like Ethan. Initially, he'd come across as arrogant and judgmental, yet she'd learned that he listened and communicated well. After hearing his point of view just now, she'd seen his actions in a somewhat different light. And he wasn't afraid to admit when he made a mistake.

The guy had possibilities. Dangerous possibilities.

The fact that he stirred a physical response in her hadn't bothered Jenni because she'd figured it would wear off fast. But he wasn't bigheaded, just confident. And she found confidence appealing.

At this moment, she felt more keenly aware of Ethan's nearness than ever before. She noticed the grip of his hand on the wheel, the digital watch encircling his furred wrist and the way humidity made the sports shirt stick to his broad chest.

She wanted to touch him.

The urge was so strong she had to resist the temptation to smooth her palm over his arm. Or to pluck off a leaf clinging to his dark hair. She didn't dare, because any little feminine gesture would mark a new stage between them, one that she chose not to enter.

Jenni stared at the paper in her lap. A name jumped out: *Angeletta Amos*. "Pretty name," she said.

"Which one?"

"Angeletta." She read the note. According to Olivia, the first grader was small for her age and painfully shy. That didn't necessarily indicate anything wrong, but Jenni agreed it merited looking into. The causes could range from heredity to neglect.

"We'll stop there first." Ethan hadn't glanced her way since he'd resumed driving. Yet his mouth curved softly and his torso angled slightly toward her.

He feels it, too. The possibility that the chief was attracted to her sent a delicious shiver through Jenni. It also sounded an alarm. They needed to put the lid back on Pandora's box before that devilish thing called hope sprang out.

Fortunately, they arrived shortly at the small house listed for Angeletta's grandmother. While the paint had weathered to a dull gray and weeds overwhelmed the grass, she didn't see any rubbish strewn about. The windows were cracked but had been polished to a sparkle.

"Vinegar water and crumpled newspapers," Jenni said without thinking.

"What?" Ethan asked.

"That's how you get glass to shine that way," she told him. "You should try it on your windshield." She'd saved a fortune in cleansers over the past few years by relying on vinegar.

"You're a little scary," he joked. "I'll bet you're a whiz with a tool kit, too."

She might as well admit it. "I attended a class in how to tune my car. Very useful in L.A."

"Let's see if you can tune Angeletta. The kid sounds like something's missing in her life."

The girl's grandmother turned out to be disabled. Although

only six, Angeletta fixed meals and did laundry for her Nana, two cousins and a younger brother. Her parents didn't appear to be part of the scene.

"You should feel proud of yourself," Jenni told the child after posing some gentle questions. "You could be a nurse or a doctor someday if you wanted to."

"Me?" The little girl beamed. "Really?"

"You're smart and you're responsible." Jenni glanced at the grandmother, who sat with two canes close at hand. "But you know one of the first things a doctor has to learn?"

"What?" Angeletta asked.

"To care for her own health." Jenni produced a pamphlet on nutrition. "I'll leave this with your Nana. From what you've told me, you need to eat more fresh fruits and vegetables. Also protein—that's eggs, cheese, meat and chicken."

"I thought boys need that, not girls," she said.

"You need it, too." After making sure that lack of money wasn't the problem, Jenni arranged for the grandmother to bring all the children in for a health screening.

In each of the next four houses, they encountered small problems with potentially significant implications. One mother was feeding a baby store-bought milk from a bottle, unaware that infants required either breast milk or special formula, and she fed her older children primarily fast food. At another house, a boy's father explained that he'd missed school because he'd outgrown his clothes and shoes and they couldn't afford new ones. Ethan promised to outfit the boy with the help of a local service club.

The families took pride in their self-sufficiency, Jenni observed. Persuading most of them to accept charity was hard, and several seemed wary of officials. Working together, however, she and Ethan managed to allay people's discomfort and secure their cooperation.

"We form a good team," he said as they retreated down the walkway from the last house of the day.

Emotionally wrung out from their work, Jenni could only nod.

"Planning to move in tonight?" He held the car door for her.

She groaned. "I was thinking about it, but I haven't finished packing. And I want to give the place a scrubbing first, too."

"My mom planned to clean it this afternoon." He raised a hand to ward off her protests. "She made me swear not to tell you so you couldn't object. And I made her promise to wear gloves if she tackled the storage area. Some of those spiderwebs were big enough to snare an elephant."

"I didn't mean for her to do that."

He slid into the driver's seat, then fastened his belt. "She's thrilled that you're coming. Not me, though."

As she buckled herself in, Jenni hoped he was kidding. "You're the one who told me to accept. Change your mind?"

"Sure thing." Ethan started the motor. "I realized how much I'm going to miss frolicking nude in the backyard."

"Please don't stop on my account!"

They both chuckled.

When he dropped her off in front of the Lowells' house, Ethan added, "I'll help you haul the furniture upstairs tonight if you're not too exhausted. Can I pick you up at seven?"

Jenni didn't have the strength to fight Ethan at every turn. Besides, she didn't want to. Instead, she said, "I'll drive over myself. But I would appreciate the muscle power."

"Anytime."

She went inside to grab a bite and pack her bags, trying hard not to imagine Ethan frolicking in his backyard, nude or otherwise.

Chapter Nine

After dinner, Ethan gave Nick a bath and read to him from *Winnie-the-Pooh*. It was one of the books Martha had bought while pregnant, part of a collection she'd anticipated sharing with her son.

If she were here… Over the years, Ethan must have begun a million thoughts with that phrase.

At first, it had wrenched his heart, but at the same time it had provided the comforting illusion that he still had Martha's companionship. When he'd bought this single-story house next to his mother's Victorian, he'd pretended his late wife was choosing the home with him. He could almost hear her voice exclaiming over the airy layout or pointing out a cracked fixture in one of the bathrooms.

These days, though, he thought of her less often. Perhaps that was because he filled so many hours with work, Ethan mused. He supposed he ought to cut back for Nick's sake, but the boy seemed to be flourishing. And for Ethan, accomplishing something meaningful in the community meant setting an example.

Today's visits had confirmed Ethan's belief that the town needed an outreach program. Although none of the problems had been life-threatening, they'd reminded him how lucky he'd been to have top-notch medical care when Nick had developed diabetes.

"You have a choice," he told his son as they set the book aside. "Grandma invited you to watch a video with her tonight. Or you can come up to Dr. Vine's apartment and help us unload furniture."

"Can I carry stuff?" Sitting on the glider on Ethan's screened porch, the little boy looked impossibly tiny.

"I'm afraid it's too heavy. But you could help us decide where to put it."

Nick's nose wrinkled. "Boring!"

Ethan didn't see it as boring at all. "I thought you wanted Jenni to move in."

"I do. So she can play with me!" his son said. "What's the video?"

"She mentioned Veggie Tales."

"Funny!" Nick said. "I pick Grandma's."

"Whatever you want. Now, gimme five." They exchanged their secret handshake, which was so secret that neither of them ever remembered it, so they improvised. Then Ethan hoisted the pajama-clad boy onto his shoulders.

On their way next door, he spotted a black-and-white cat slipping around the corner of Annette's house. "Is that the kitty Grandma wants to adopt?" Ethan asked.

"Yeah. It's Boots," his son replied.

"Why do you suppose he's running away from us?"

"He's scared of you." Nick apparently didn't consider it possible that a cat could be scared of him. "You're big."

"And I have a deep booming voice." Ethan mounted the steps to the side door. As usual, he found it unlocked. "Do I scare you?"

Nick giggled. "Of course not. You're my daddy."

Annette welcomed them with a large bowl of popcorn. Although Ethan had fixed a respectable dinner of spaghetti and salad, his son dug in as if he were starving.

While taking a handful for himself, Ethan remembered

his concern. "Mom, you need to start locking your side door."

"Maybe I'll stack the family photographs in the side yard and the thief can help himself," she teased. "I've got more than I know what to do with, anyway."

He grimaced at her light tone. "He acts harmless enough, but if he were cornered—" noticing Nick's rapt attention, he tempered his warning to avoid frightening the boy "—he might get scared."

"Point taken," Annette said. "Now, you'd better go help that young lady."

Ethan kissed them both before leaving. When he emerged, he glanced toward the front, but Jenni hadn't arrived. In the dusky light, a middle-aged couple strolled hand-in-hand along the sidewalk. From a nearby house, he caught a tanta-lizing whiff of pot roast.

Ethan wondered if Jenni cooked. He had a feeling that, if she did, she wasn't about to cook for him.

What made her so prickly? As he circled to unlock the stor-age area, he noted how completely his thinking about her had changed. Usually, he sized people up speedily and accurately. Far from being a surfer girl, however, she'd turned out to be a dedicated physician.

Could he be wrong about Arturo Mendez, as well? For the sake of the man's pregnant girlfriend, Ethan hoped so.

Upstairs in the unit, he unloaded a couple of stools in front of the dining bar that separated the kitchen from the front room. Annette had repainted after the last tenant left, and this afternoon she'd removed several months' worth of dust. Jenni ought to enjoy the place.

"Anybody home?"

Ethan opened the door to find Jenni toting two large suit-cases. "You should have called me to carry those up."

"I'm not helpless." Jenni's manner of dressing for physical labor was startlingly sexy, he noted as she set the cases in a corner. A black T-shirt and jeans clung to her slender build.

His mother and son were just a short hop across the yard, he reminded himself. Besides, he doubted either he or Jenni wanted a casual entanglement, and they certainly weren't suited for anything deeper.

"Let's get started," he said. "I'm not sure we can manage the sofa, but everything else is fairly light."

"Sofa too heavy for you?" she challenged, hands on hips.

She looked so cute and feisty that Ethan had an urge to rumple her hair, except that if he did, she'd most likely poke him in the eye. "I think I can manage." Abandoning his usual good manners, he strode ahead of her out the door. If she wanted to prove how strong she was, he wouldn't insult her with gallantries.

The lady didn't shirk, he had to admit a few hours later as they finished their moving job. She'd scarcely reacted when she scraped herself on a door frame or banged her hip on the stair railing. Somewhere along the line, she must have adopted toughness as a self-protective mechanism.

Jenni hadn't dithered around rearranging the furniture, either. Instead, she'd assessed each room thoughtfully as if drawing a mental chart, then directed the furnishings to exact locations. With pinpoint accuracy, she'd made space for a sewing center in her bedroom and set up a small office in one corner of the parlor.

"You've got this down to a science," he observed as he washed his hands in the kitchen. Despite Annette's assault on the storage space, he and Jenni both bore traces of grime.

She wiped her hands on her jeans. "I've discovered it saves frustration if I get things right the first time." Standing in the center of the living room, she rotated slowly, taking in her surroundings. Apparently, what she saw met with her approval, because she concluded, "I just have to unpack a few overnight things, then I can collapse."

Ethan opened the refrigerator and removed the wine and two glasses he'd placed there earlier. "Allow me to assist in relaxing you. Hope you like white zinfandel."

A pause warned that he'd miscalculated. "You don't happen to have any soda pop, do you?" Jenni asked at last.

"At my house, sure."

"Never mind." She regarded him across the dining bar. "Water will be fine."

"It's a California label I thought might appeal to you," Ethan said. "Sorry, I'd have picked something else if I'd known."

"I don't drink," Jenni told him.

Lots of people didn't drink for any number of reasons, but Ethan put two and two together. Her avoidance of alcohol, coupled with the other things she'd said, indicated a pattern. "Alcoholism in the family?" he hazarded.

From the way her eyes widened, he could tell he'd scored a hit. It made him a little ashamed, but since they would be thrown into each other's company a lot, he preferred not to keep tripping over skeletons.

Jenni sat down on one of the stools, and propped her elbows on the counter. "Let's get this over with," she said.

He filled her glass with tap water. "Shoot."

"Dad ran off when I was five." She scarcely seemed to notice when he set the tumbler in front of her. "Mom abused drugs. She'd go through rehab, get clean and find work as a waitress. We'd have smooth sailing for a few months, sometimes even a couple of years, but sooner or later something would set her off. A lost job, a broken relationship or her own demons."

"What happened then?" Ethan asked.

"Social services rattled my family tree and located a few

sound branches." Jenni spoke with world-weary composure, as if she'd told this story more than a few times, which undoubtedly she had. "One aunt took me in for a long stretch during my teen years. I lived with some cousins on and off. My paternal grandmother even made a guest appearance on the list."

"Was your dad a total washout?" Having seen his share of deadbeats, Ethan harbored no illusions about the innate nobility of fathers. Even so, it was hard to envision a levelheaded person like Jenni emerging from a totally dysfunctional background.

"Well, he was better than my two stepfathers," she said. "They both knocked Mom around when they got drunk. Dad never hurt anybody."

"Your stepfathers beat you?" Ethan asked angrily. Despite all that he'd seen in his years as a police officer, he'd never developed a thick skin when it came to child abuse.

"Never more than once." Jenni took a sip of water. "I paid back at least as good as I got, and I'm a pro at dialing 911. Cops weren't always the most sympathetic people in the world, especially when they arrived to find I'd decked the jerk with a skillet, but I learned how to make my case."

"Good for you." No wonder her attitude bordered on the pugnacious, Ethan thought. "What kind of person was your dad?"

"He resembled his mother. Grandma Alice had an almost mythical ability to avoid unpleasantness. She never read my report cards, never returned a phone call from the school and never noticed what time I came home. Getting to know her helped me understand that when Mom's addictions became overwhelming, Dad simply bailed out. He was a master at avoidance."

"What happened to him?" Ethan leaned against the kitchen

counter. If Jenni had lived with her paternal grandmother, he reflected, she couldn't have lost track of the man completely.

"He moved to Florida—as far from California as he could get. Never married again, but once in a while he did remember to send me a Christmas card. Even a few gifts, although way too late for my birthday, as if he couldn't quite remember when it was."

"What kind of gifts?" Curiosity prompted him to ask.

"Weird stuff, like doll clothes for a kind of doll I didn't own, or one of those snowball paperweights with flamingos in it that was so ugly you almost had to like it," Jenni said. "When Dad's heart gave out, three days passed before anybody checked his apartment. With what I know now, I'd guess he had a borderline personality disorder that worsened over the years."

"Is your mom still alive?" If so, a reconciliation might be possible.

"She died when I was nineteen," Jenni replied. "Ran into a freeway barrier while driving under the influence."

What a grim story, Ethan reflected. "Any theories about how you turned out so healthy?"

"Who says I'm healthy?" she asked wryly.

"You're an incredible person," he told her frankly. "Resilient, effective, outspoken and productive. That's not flattery, either."

"I can tell." She ran her finger around the rim of the water glass. "You're not the flattering type. As to whether I have a theory, I don't know where I got my survival instinct. Well, no, that's not entirely true."

He waited while she considered, pent-up energy evident in her face. Jenni must have been born a dynamo, although that quality might as easily have landed her in jail as in med school.

"Mom used to leave me with a baby-sitter when I was little. Terry and I stayed close until I was seven, when I went to live with my cousins the first time," Jenni explained. "She taught me to live by the Golden Rule and to demand that other people treat me the same way. Wow. I haven't thought about Terry in a long while."

Ethan didn't want to trouble her with too many questions but one sprang to mind. "How'd you manage to become a doctor?"

"I had a mentor, as I mentioned before. Her name's Dr. Susan Leto and she lives in Tucson."

A few significant individuals had had a tremendous effect on her life, he thought. On the other hand, she deserved most of the credit.

"The reason I don't drink," Jenni added, "is that I tried it a few times and it made me feel too good. I don't want to risk losing control."

"Wise decision." He raised his glass in a toast, suspecting she would appreciate the irony. "I hope you don't retreat from everything that makes you feel good, though."

"Is that a pass?" she shot back.

Ethan nearly choked on his wine. "Good Lord, no! I'd better watch my innuendos around you or I'm likely to get clobbered with a frying pan."

She smiled, banishing all signs of tension. "I should have known better. You seem to have this incredibly trustworthy quality."

"How romantic." He decided against refilling his glass. He didn't want to give the impression that he drank much, since he didn't. "I've always longed for a beautiful woman to murmur sweet nothings about my trustworthy qualities."

"Your wife was lucky," Jenni said. "I mean…" She stopped, obviously realizing that a person who died young could hardly be called lucky. "That came out wrong."

"I'll take it as a compliment." Usually, when people talked

about Martha, he felt as if they were infringing on his memories. This time, Ethan didn't mind.

It struck him that, like Jenni, Martha had been a restless soul. From the night they'd met, she had made it clear that she refused to let anything, even love, interfere with pursuing success as a country singer.

Dreams changed sometimes, but this one had never entirely faded. Five years later, although her pregnancy wasn't planned, she'd welcomed their child. However, she'd intended to continue touring and singing at clubs. Ethan doubted she'd have agreed to move to Downhome.

In the years since then, he hadn't given that side of her personality much thought. Without intending to, he'd come to idealize Martha as the perfect companion and mother. The fact that she'd been a person with her own needs didn't mean they'd have become unhappy, of course, only that their marriage would inevitably have undergone its share of adjustments.

None of that had anything to do with Jenni, he supposed. Still, her presence reminded him that Martha in the flesh had been much more interesting and unpredictable than her counterpart in his memory.

Jenni broke the silence. "Ethan? I'm sorry. I guess I touched on a sore subject."

"You're entitled. I certainly poked into your business," he replied. "That's enough introspection for one night, though."

"I figured it was better to lay all my cards on the table." Coming around the bar, she collected his empty tumbler.

"I'll take care of those. I've got a dishwasher."

"I don't mind." She stopped inches away. The air simmered as they regarded each other.

Ethan stepped closer. Sensing her warmth and vulnerability, he couldn't tear his gaze from her slightly parted lips.

Jenni fumbled the glasses, barely catching them in time. "Oh, heck, I'm not sure what I'm doing."

"Set them down," Ethan suggested.

She complied. Even in the flat kitchen lighting, her eyes shone with a longing that mirrored his own.

He ran his palms along Jenni's arms. At her shoulders, he massaged gently, lifting the wisps of blond hair away from her neck. She eased closer, lids half closed, face tilted.

Lowering his head, Ethan savored the scent of shampoo that clung to her. His lips grazed her earlobe and found the pulse point below.

Jenni rubbed her cheek against his hair. She touched him tentatively—first his muscular forearms, then his chest. Stroking the heel of her hand over his roughened jaw, she kissed him.

Despite Ethan's resolve to take it slowly, the sensation of her mouth against his inflamed him. He pulled her tight, his body catching fire as he deepened the kiss. His hands played down her back and brought her hard against him.

Jenni wrapped her arms around him while her tongue tested the edges of his lips. Ethan couldn't breathe with wanting her. If he hadn't suddenly become aware that his mother and son might decide to check on them at any moment, he didn't think he could have stopped.

Carefully, he disentangled himself. "I didn't mean to rush things. I don't know what came over me."

"Sex," Jenni answered breathlessly.

Laughter rumbled through him. "You got that right. I haven't felt anything like that since—" He stopped, realizing he'd been about to mention his late wife at a completely inappropriate moment.

"You think too much, Chief," Jenni murmured.

He gazed at her longingly. "I'm afraid so."

She straightened her T-shirt. The movement threw her breasts into relief, which had a painful effect on Ethan's groin.

"I am not going to get one wink of sleep tonight," he muttered.

"You should have ravished me while my brain was taking a hike. It would have been fun."

"I want more than sex," he warned.

"I was afraid you might. You're that kind of guy, the kind who sticks around." Jenni turned away to rinse the glasses. "I'm more the shallow, what's-in-it-for-me type. Sorry if that fits your stereotype of a blond heartbreaker."

"You don't fit anybody's stereotype." In five years, Ethan hadn't met a woman he wanted to date, let alone sleep with. Maybe she saw only a surface attraction. However, he sensed deeper possibilities. "Maybe you ought to take a chance."

"I'm not cut out for the whole home and family thing," Jenni replied calmly.

Yes, she was, he thought, but they'd reached an impasse. Although Ethan was tempted to pursue a relationship and prove Jenni wrong, he might still lose her in the end. In such a small town, a breakup could create a nasty mess. He also had his son's well-being to consider.

She reached out, then reluctantly curled her fingers to avoid touching him. "I'm going to miss doing more of this. I've been thinking about it for a while."

"Me, too." Now that he'd taken the first step, Ethan could no longer deny the wildfire raging inside him. He needed a real woman to wake up with instead of a memory, but it obviously wasn't going to be Jenni.

At least, not anytime soon. He enclosed her hand in his two large ones. "We ought to set boundaries."

"That may be hard if you really frolic nude in the backyard."

He reached around to land a light smack on her bottom. "You're shameless."

She pulled away. "It's temporary, believe me. I'll be Miss Priss again in no time."

"Is everything temporary with you?"

"No. I plan to stay around Downhome for a while," Jenni replied. "Just to prove your initial assessment wrong."

Ethan regarded her with regret. "Are you still holding my remarks against me?"

"Not exactly," she admitted. "But tell me one thing."

"Okay." They stood only a few feet apart. Ethan struggled to remember that it might as well be a million miles.

"You felt it was your duty to tell the council what you'd learned about me," she said. "What about that other guy, my competition? Did you find anything negative about him?"

"He's a recovering alcoholic. And yes, I passed that information along."

"Was that why they hired me?" she asked.

"You got hired because people were impressed by how much you cared about your patients," Ethan said. "And because the women liked you better. Period."

Behind the joking manner, he saw that she was pleased. "Thank you for telling me that. And for carrying my furniture."

"Is this the part where we shake on it and vow to be friends?" he asked skeptically.

"You're more than a friend." Jenni spoke seriously. "I'm probably an idiot not to take a chance with you. But it wouldn't work."

"Thanks for being honest." He collected the glasses and started out. In the living room, he paused to add, "If you need anything...."

"I'll throw balled-up messages on to your patio."

"I was about to tell you to call my mother. She's the landlord, not me." With a wink, Ethan skedaddled.

Full darkness had descended, spangled with stars that shone brightly away from the glare of a city. Martha had written a song called "Country Lights" that used to resonate in

Ethan's mind whenever he went out at night. Yet for the first time in years, he found he couldn't summon the sound of her voice.

He still felt Jenni's heat imprinted on his body. Even if nothing further developed between them, she'd helped him to acknowledge that he was ready to move on with his life. The scary part was that it seemed tangled up with a woman who might break his heart without even trying.

Pulling his jumbled thoughts together, he headed for his mother's house to collect Nick.

Chapter Ten

By Wednesday, two of the outreach children had come for exams, but Jenni had nearly given up on hearing from Helen. When she checked the appointments on her computer after lunch, the manicurist still hadn't scheduled one and there was no sign of her in the waiting room.

However, Leah Morris had arrived for a checkup. Jenni was flattered that the teacher had chosen to consult her instead of seeing a more established doctor in Mill Valley.

A striking woman with black hair and blue eyes, Leah had only a few minor illnesses and injuries in her medical history. Her mother had died of cancer eight years earlier, but her father was alive and had remarried, the patient explained.

When they'd finished the physical exam, Jenni returned after Leah had dressed. She often learned important information about a patient's overall health by asking questions and listening.

With her cover-girl looks and sweet, open expression, Leah struck Jenni as a woman who should have no trouble finding suitors. Yet when asked what she used for birth control, she said, "Are you kidding? I haven't needed any for ages."

Jenni made a note for her records. "You mentioned you might be moving. Would you like me to prescribe something in case you want it before you find a new doctor?"

"No, thanks." Despite declining the offer, the teacher didn't appear ill at ease. "I'm only going for a couple of visits this summer. I don't expect to meet anyone yet."

"Don't wait until the heat of the moment," Jenni warned.

"I guess I'm naive, but I can't imagine anything happening that fast." Leah rotated her stool restlessly. "In big cities, is it really common for women to jump into bed with men they've barely met? Around here…well, around here, you can't do that because you know practically everybody."

"Anonymity has its temptations," Jenni agreed. "Yes, it happens."

"And when they do that—go to bed with someone they've just met—is it really cold and heartless, and they never see each other again?" Leah asked. "As a doctor, you should know."

"To tell the truth, I consider that kind of behavior extremely risky." Despite her preference for short-term relationships, Jenni avoided one-night stands, with good reason. "I've heard of woman being drugged or worse. Once in a while, I suppose people connect that way. However, I'd recommend checking out a man thoroughly before getting involved."

"Well, of course!" Leah smiled tremulously. "That kind of behavior sounds exciting in the abstract. Still, I wouldn't want to try it."

"Good attitude," Jenni said. "In a new place, you'd be vulnerable, especially if you're trying to find Mr. Right."

"I'm not sure I want to find Mr. Right." After retrieving a brush from her purse, Leah worked it through her shiny, straight hair. "The longer I'm single, the more I like doing things my way. It's taken a while to gain the confidence to leave Downhome, but now I can't wait to spread my wings."

"If you think of any questions or you change your mind about birth control, please give me a call," Jenni said.

"Absolutely." Leah shook hands firmly. "You survived the

jungle out there, right? How bad can Austin and Seattle be compared with L.A.?"

"There's good and bad everywhere."

The teacher radiated an innocence that, despite her intelligence, might make her susceptible to the wrong kind of man. As Jenni watched Leah go, she wished she could have shared some of her street smarts, but at least she'd given a warning.

At the reception desk, Patsy Fellows looked up from the computer. "Another one of your outreach kids is coming in tomorrow," she said. "You and the chief must have made a big impression."

Especially on each other. Their close encounter had stirred Jenni in a way she found almost shocking. She'd have made love with him right then and there if common sense, and his scruples, hadn't intruded.

She wished she didn't keep wondering what the man was doing and whether he'd decided to give up on her entirely. She wanted him off her radar screen. Apparently, he'd reached the same conclusion. Although she caught occasional glimpses of Ethan at home, he hadn't dropped by, and, in an attempt to establish her privacy, she'd deliberately avoided much contact with Annette and Nick.

"We're going to visit families again on Sunday," she told Patsy.

"How can you spend all that time with him and act so indifferent?" the receptionist asked. "He's way too old for me, but he's such a hunk!"

"Not my type, I guess," Jenni lied.

"I saw how he looked at you the other day. I suspect you're *his* type," the teenager confided.

"I hope you're not discussing this with anyone outside the office," Jenni cautioned.

"Absolutely not! I mean, my dad works with him. I'd die if he found out I think the chief is sexy!"

"Good girl," Jenni said.

Then she saw him.

Ethan strolled across the waiting room as if he belonged there, pausing to exchange greetings with a woman who'd come to see the nurse practitioner. In a dark suit with his trademark loosened tie, the chief radiated male vibes that made Patsy sit up straighter and Yvonne, who'd just emerged from the lab, give him a trace of a smile.

Ethan hefted a portable cooler. "Pepe got a shipment of real spumoni at the diner. That's a rare event and I happened to be having lunch there, so I decided to share the wealth."

Jenni had bought take-out tortellini from the Italian restaurant one evening and been surprised by its quality, although she couldn't say much for the cheesy murals and fake grape clusters that passed for decor. "What's real spumoni? Isn't it just ice cream?"

"For a woman of the world, your education is sorely lacking." From a sack, the chief produced half a dozen paper plates, plastic flatware and a knife. "This is a treat that should never—I repeat never—be scooped, only sliced, as everybody in Downhome knows. Well, almost everybody."

"I knew that," Yvonne said.

Estelle, who'd obviously overheard the conversation, poked her head out of the business office. "Me, too."

"So why haven't you bought me any?" demanded her daughter. "I've only heard about it. I figured Pepe's spumoni was some kind of legend."

"It is—a legend that now becomes reality." After setting the cooler on the counter, Ethan lifted out a cake box. He opened it to reveal a molded loaf, which, he explained, consisted of two layers of ice cream—one chocolate, the other pistachio—with a filling of rum-flavored whipped cream mixed with nuts and candied fruit.

Jenni's stomach issued a growl at the enticing scents. Fortunately, her fellow staff members' oohs and aahs covered the sound.

"Do I get some, too?" asked the patient.

"You bet." Wielding the knife with surgical precision, Ethan dished up the spumoni. "I don't want to hear any comments about being on a diet, either. Finicky eaters will be handcuffed."

Everyone gathered around the reception desk. Although Ethan hadn't paid any special attention to Jenni, his sideways glance indicated his awareness.

He'd staged this event for her benefit, she thought, amused. He could be a very hard man to resist if he set his mind to it.

As he'd indicated, the spumoni far surpassed the knock-off Italian desserts she'd eaten previously. Closing her eyes, Jenni let the exquisite flavors percolate. When she looked up, Ethan lifted his plate in a kind of salute. First wine, then spumoni. This time, he'd found a vice she couldn't refuse.

A murmur of appreciation arose from the others. "If I weren't already taken, I'd marry you for this," Estelle confessed.

Patsy giggled. Yvonne sighed.

"By the way," Ethan said, "I wondered if I could ask you something privately, Dr. Vine."

"Of course. As soon as I finish." The second and third bites tasted almost as transcendent as the first, she discovered.

By this time, Ethan had used the side passageway to bypass the desk. He made himself at home wherever he went. Well, almost everywhere, Jenni amended. He hadn't exactly fit in at Arturo's home.

At last she discarded her empty plate. "That was sensational. This way, Chief." A bevy of female heads swiveled to watch as he followed her past the business and records offices into the rear hallway. "You enjoyed that," she teased when they were alone.

"Enjoyed what?"

"Creating a stir," she said. "Not that you didn't earn it, but you're a bit of a rogue."

"If I wanted to act like a rogue, I wouldn't do it in front of witnesses," he murmured in a tone that sent a quiver down Jenni's spine. She forced herself to walk faster.

Her office lay in one corner, its window facing Tulip Tree Avenue, the nursing home and the community center. After closing the door behind him, Ethan gestured at the walls, which were nearly bare except for her medical degrees and a few reference books on a shelf. "This place is practically naked."

Jenni knew he'd used suggestive language on purpose, so she ignored it. "Most of my medical books are on CD-ROM."

"Do you keep your plants and knickknacks on CD-ROM, too? No criticism intended." He made a pacifying gesture. "My point is, the monthly crafts fair and farmers market takes place Saturday on The Green. Nick and I were hoping you'd join us. It's an opportunity to shop for unique items."

"That's why you brought the spumoni? As an excuse to ask me out?"

"I didn't want to come empty-handed," Ethan said with mock solemnity.

She couldn't believe he'd made such a production out of a simple invitation. It flattered her and, reluctantly, made her aware of how special Ethan was. So special he scared her.

Nonsense. Maybe her heart rate speeded a little at being alone with him, and the lingering sweetness of the spumoni on her tongue made her think of kisses, but....

He'd already beaten her to the punch. His mouth brushed hers, and then he moved to the window. "Great view."

"What?" Jenni shook off her momentary daze. "Chief, you ought to write yourself a ticket for hit and run."

He ducked his head in acknowledgment. "I didn't expect to do that."

Not to beg him to do it again took a great deal of fortitude. "Also, you didn't need to come by the clinic. We live next door."

"That would mean intruding," he protested.

"As opposed to cornering me in my office and kissing me?" She glanced past him, hoping no one had seen through the blinds.

"Like I said, I didn't intend to do that."

"I'm not going to argue your intent. I'm not the DA and you haven't committed a crime. Well, stealing kisses might qualify, but given your record of community service, I'll let you off with a warning."

"Does that apply if I do it again?"

Before she could react, Ethan cut across the intervening space, cupped her face with one hand and lowered his mouth to hers. This time, his tongue traced the inner edge of her lips.

Longing pulsed through Jenni as she instinctively caught hold of him. She relished both his audacity and his unmistakable arousal.

As Ethan's mouth traced the line of her throat, his thick hair pressed against her jaw. He smelled wonderful. Jenni wanted more of this, much more, but she had to come down to earth.

It was the middle of the afternoon and they stood in front of an open window. Had they both lost their minds? "We'd better stop."

"Are you sure?"

She struggled to regain control of herself. "Is anyone watching?"

Reluctantly, he drew away and glanced outside. "Mercifully, no. Your blinds are angled upward." He took a deep breath. "It's a good thing we'll have a chaperone on Saturday, since we seem to have trouble controlling ourselves. Can Nick and I pick you up here at noon?"

"Better make it one. We got a lot of walk-ins last Saturday so I presume it'll happen again." Although technically the clinic closed at noon that day, Jenni disliked turning away patients. "By the way, a couple of our outreach kids came in and another one's scheduled tomorrow."

"That's terrific," he responded. "Heard anything from Helen Rios?"

"Not a word." Jenni straightened her clothes, although they weren't really creased. "Remember, you agreed not to mention her in your report."

"Of course not," Ethan said. "I was concerned about her pregnancy, not my project."

"Sorry. It's not that I don't trust you." She moved behind the maple desk. "It can be tricky sorting out your various roles, Ethan."

"Police chief, search committee member, landlady's son and general pain in the neck," he summarized. "That is a handful."

"Not to mention purveyor of indulgences." Jenni checked her watch. She had a patient scheduled. "I'm afraid duty calls."

"Mine, too." He regarded her. "I don't know where this is going. We have enough chemistry to set off our own Fourth of July fireworks."

"Is that a big event around here?" Jenni knew her attempt to change the subject must be transparent, but she refused to respond to his comment. It was too incendiary, in more ways than one.

"We hold a community picnic on The Green," Ethan replied. "The high school marching band plays, the drill team drills, the cheerleaders cheer and a good time is had by all. You should plan to attend."

"I'll definitely be on hand to patch up anybody who gets too friendly with a sparkler," Jenni said.

"Can you recommend a treatment for grown-ups who get burned playing with fire?" Ethan asked.

"Afraid not."

"Then I guess I'm out of luck."

After they said goodbye, she let him exit unescorted. If the nurses saw her pink cheeks, Jenni suspected, they'd spend the rest of the week speculating about what had occurred in her office.

For the next few hours, she saw a few more patients and spent the breaks familiarizing herself with the office record-keeping and billing systems. Although technically the city required everyone to pay except in emergencies, the rules appeared flexible enough for her to write off a few individuals such as the outreach children. As for the tests that needed to be sent out, Ethan had mentioned that one of the service clubs might cover the expense.

At four-thirty, Patsy came into the records room. "We've got a walk-in. It's Helen Rios from the Snip 'N' Curl."

Jenni hurried to her feet. "I'll see her."

"You sure?" the receptionist asked. "You won't be finished by closing time."

"You can leave at five." Jenni didn't expect other employees to stay late just because she chose to. "I can handle Yvonne's duties myself."

"She isn't alone. Her boyfriend's with her." Patsy frowned.

Jenni caught the note of uneasiness in the young woman's tone. "Is something wrong?"

"I went to high school with Arturo." She paused.

Jenni kept her voice low so no one else would hear. "What do you think of him, Patsy?"

The receptionist appeared pleased to be consulted. "He's not mean or anything, but he can be real rebellious. Freshman year he kind of liked me until he found out my dad worked for the police department."

"How did he react?"

Patsy made a face. "The next time I ran into him, he acted like he didn't recognize me. It's just as well, I guess. If I were in Helen's spot right now, my father would have a fit!"

Pregnant, unmarried and living with an unemployed artist. Jenni wouldn't want to be in that situation or have it happen to her daughter, either.

In any case, she couldn't turn them away despite the late hour. She knew instinctively that if she did, Helen would never come back. "We'd better get moving," she said.

Patsy nodded. "I'll ask Yvonne to make up a chart."

"She'll have to confirm the pregnancy, also." Jenni requested several other tests as well, emphasizing blood pressure. Although taking it was a standard part of exams, it had special significance in this case.

"Okay. I'll tell her."

By the time Jenni entered the examining room, Yvonne had completed her tasks and departed. Helen's blood pressure turned out to be slightly elevated.

Arturo leaned against one wall, arms folded over his ripped T-shirt. Helen sat on the paper-covered examining table with a wrapper pulled around her.

"Hi." Jenni shook hands with them both. "I'm glad you came in. This is an important step toward guarding your baby's health."

She proceeded to examine the patient in a friendly but impersonal manner, explaining her actions as she went. Helen relaxed enough to ask about her due date—it was in November—and whether it was dangerous for an expectant mother to work at a beauty shop.

"Make sure there's good ventilation and that your nail polishes don't contain toxic substances," Jenni advised. "Also, don't spend too much time standing or you could develop swollen feet and ankles."

Both of them nodded. Arturo appeared younger than he had previously and was clearly concerned about his girl-friend.

Jenni gave Helen some brochures on pregnancy along with samples of maternal vitamins and a prescription for more. "There's one other thing we need to discuss. Why don't you get dressed and we can talk in my office."

"If you've got something to say, Doctor, say it now." Arturo resumed his defensive manner.

"Artie!" Helen protested.

"I know what she's going to say!"

Jenni doubted that. "Please enlighten me."

"You're going to tell us to get married," he snapped. "That I'm some kind of jerk because I haven't waltzed her down the aisle. Well, I don't believe in those things. If people love each other, that's enough."

Helen glanced from one to the other uncertainly. Jenni had a suspicion she didn't share her boyfriend's liberated views.

"That wasn't what I want to discuss. I'm her physician, not your spiritual leader." Registering the skepticism on Arturo's face and the anxiety on Helen's, she plunged ahead. "Miss Rios, your blood pressure is on the high side. That would concern me in any patient, but particularly during pregnancy."

The young woman's eyebrows puckered. "Why?"

"As I mentioned before, it increases the risk of problems." Jenni handed Helen a pamphlet she'd held in reserve until they could discuss the topic. "High blood pressure can be a factor in premature delivery. In the most serious cases it's implicated in a condition called preeclampsia, which may be life-threatening."

"For her or the baby?" Arturo demanded.

"Both." Not wanting to worry them excessively, she added, "You should be all right as long as you're monitored. My preference would be to refer you to an obstetrician, but we don't have one in town right now. I can continue to treat you or make a referral to someone in Mill Valley, whichever you prefer."

"We can't afford a specialist," Helen said. "And we've only got one car, anyway. I'd rather see you."

Arturo shrugged, apparently assenting.

"That's fine, with the understanding that if a crisis should develop later in the pregnancy, we'll have to hospitalize you." Jenni decided not to mention at this point that serious complications might have to be treated at a major medical center such as Vanderbilt. These two had enough to deal with at the moment. "In the meantime, I'll need to examine you regularly. As for the blood pressure, I can teach you how to check it at home, and if it continues to rise, I may have to put you on medication."

Helen seemed relieved. "That doesn't sound so bad."

"Hopefully, it won't be. Also, it's essential that you quit smoking. I can't tell you how harmful it is to your baby."

"Does that include secondhand smoke?" the young woman asked. Arturo scowled.

"It would be better if you weren't exposed to it." Jenni left the subject at that. "I'll learn more when I get your test results. We'll be watching for protein in the urine, although I don't expect to see it at such an early stage. You should cut down on salt intake, also, and be sure to exercise moderately. No alcohol, either."

"I knew that." Helen smiled tentatively.

Arturo balanced on the balls of his feet like a boxer. Jenni supposed the analogy might be accurate, because he was preparing to do battle, although with an invisible foe: Helen's condition.

"I'm sure you can both handle this," she said reassuringly.

"Yeah?" Arturo's fidgeting grew more agitated. "I don't know. This sounds like a lot. I mean, I'm not good at taking care of people."

"Honey, we can do it," his girlfriend responded.

He gestured helplessly. "I can't give up smoking. It calms me. And what if you get sick? You better move in with your mom till the baby comes."

Helen's eyes filled with tears. "I don't want to. She's got Dad to look after." To Jenni, she explained, "He had a stroke." More forcefully, she added, "I'm not leaving the apartment. You'll have to throw me out."

Arturo shook his head. "Have it your way. I'd just upset you like I always do and make things worse." After taking a set of keys from his pocket, he handed them to his stunned girlfriend. "I'll leave the car outside for you. I'm going to borrow my cousin's old clunker and pick up my stuff."

Ignoring Helen's plea to wait, he hurried out.

Frantically, the young woman collected her pink uniform from the Snip 'N' Curl. Although Jenni normally left while a patient dressed, she didn't think Helen should be alone right now.

"I can't believe he's breaking up with me!" On went the underwear, followed by the uniform. "It's his baby, too!"

"He may not mean it as a breakup—more of a time-out," Jenni said. "He may feel guilty because he got you pregnant and now he sees it as a threat to your health."

"You think so?" Helen buttoned her blouse wrong the first time and had to start over.

"This is more about his insecurities than about you." During her undergraduate years, Jenni had taken psychology courses to better understand her own background. "He's just beginning to deal with the reality of what it means to be a father."

"I thought he'd stick by me," the young woman said miserably. "I thought he loved me."

"He probably does," Jenni replied. "He needs time to sort out his doubts about his self-worth. In the meanwhile, my concern is your well-being."

"I'll be fine." Helen slipped on her shoes. "He makes me so mad. Still, I want him back. Do you think he'll come around, Dr. Vine?"

"I hope so." She'd sensed his anger focusing on himself rather than his girlfriend, but the man had a lot of issues to deal with.

Jenni made sure her patient had all the necessary supplies. Patsy, who'd stayed late on her own initiative, walked Helen to the parking lot.

As Jenni locked up, it struck her that without Dr. Leto, she might have ended up in a similar situation. No, perhaps not. Jenni might have gotten pregnant by accident, but she would never have centered her life on a guy.

At least when you were alone, no one could let you down. She'd learned that lesson a long time ago.

Chapter Eleven

On Saturday morning, Ethan met with his captain and lieutenant about the still-unsolved portrait thefts. The good news was that there hadn't been any more incidents since the burglary at Pepe's apartment two weeks earlier.

The bad news was that they were as far as ever from catching the perpetrator.

"One of the officers scoped out the flea market in Mill Valley," Ben reported. "No one's tried to sell family portraits, which isn't surprising. Who'd buy them?"

"What about the frames? Someone might want those." From across the street at The Green, Ethan heard the once-a-month clamor of cars parking and shoppers chattering. He tuned them out.

"There's a booth that carries frames and art supplies," replied Ben. "The owner said no one's brought in anything resembling the stolen property." One of the missing frames, decorated with gilded cupids, ought to be highly recognizable.

"Any mention of Arturo Mendez?" Ethan had requested that the investigator make a discreet inquiry.

"Yes and no," Ben said. "The dealer sells Mendez supplies but hasn't taken anything in trade. Of course, if he's fencing stolen goods, he's not likely to admit it."

Ethan turned to the lieutenant. "What did you learn, Mark?"

"I chatted up Helen, like you asked," the young man explained. "She says Arturo keeps one bedroom off-limits and goes ballistic if she peeks inside. He won't even let her clean it. According to her, that's his studio."

"You didn't say why you were asking, right?"

"I acted like I was shooting the breeze while waiting for Mom," he said.

Ethan tapped his pen against the desk blotter. "I got inside his apartment during our outreach visit but I couldn't see into the bedrooms. My instincts tell me the guy's hiding something. I realize Helen wouldn't voluntarily spy on him. Still, keep after her. She might notice something without realizing it."

"That's not likely," Ben said. "He's moved out."

"Oh?" Ethan hadn't heard about that.

"My daughter says the two of them visited the clinic Wednesday afternoon. Arturo stalked out of there, apparently because his wife—excuse me, girlfriend—might need his help with her pregnancy. I guess it's asking too much for him to think about anybody except himself." Ben's voice dripped sarcasm. "Patsy says Helen told her afterward that he was leaving. My daughter doesn't normally discuss anything that happens inside the clinic, but Helen told her she didn't care who knew it. She was really torn up."

"Too bad." Ethan hadn't talked with Jenni since then. Even if he had, he doubted she'd have mentioned the subject, out of respect for patient confidentiality. "Well, let's not narrow the scope of our investigation too quickly. Arturo may not be our guy after all."

They'd had several other petty thefts reported, he noted, including a digital camera stolen from a house on Bennington Lane and a CD player missing from Willow Avenue.

There could be a second thief at work, or the same person might have changed his MO.

"Considering that Mendez doesn't have a steady job, I wouldn't put it past him to traffic in small electronics," Ben said.

"Let's assume we've got two different perps." Ethan didn't want this turning into a witch-hunt. "Whoever took those family photos was most likely motivated by hostility rather than profit. You could sell a camera or a CD player easily enough, but a picture of Pepe and his kids? Not my idea of a hot item on the Internet."

They all chuckled. Ethan glanced at his watch. "Well, guys, speaking of family values, I've got a date with my kid."

"And I've got plenty to keep me busy." Mark was working the weekend shift.

"I'm off," Ben said. "Estelle asked me to fix our house fan. I told her I have a sermon to prepare for tomorrow, but she says I can think just as well while I'm working."

"No doubt you'll find the experience inspiring." During his marriage, Ethan had never minded doing repairs around the house. It wasn't quite on a par with hunting down a mammoth or killing a marauding cave bear. Still, he liked taking care of a woman that way.

Now all he needed was the right woman. In fact, he was beginning to suspect he might know one.

ETHAN HAD BEEN RIGHT, Jenni mused as she surveyed her office after collecting her purse. The place *was* naked.

As a rule, she opted for bare walls and simple decor because she preferred not to own anything that wouldn't fit into a suitcase. Possessions weighed her down. Or at least, they had until now.

Jenni's gaze wandered out the window. A van drove by, windows rolled down, two kids and a dog visible in the back seat. A happy family, going to the fair.

Something twisted in her chest. There was a part of her that had never stopped being a little girl, had never stopped believing that Mom was finished with drugs and that Dad would show up on her birthday.

However, another, even stronger part hated that vulnerability. It was determined not to let anyone or anything hold her down.

She didn't want to be the old Jenni anymore, but she didn't know how to be anyone else. One step at a time, she supposed. She didn't need to make major changes, just a few little ones.

Oh, for heaven's sake, why make such a big deal about buying a few pretty things? It's not as if you can't afford the shipping costs.

It was nearly one and Ethan might arrive anytime. Suddenly, Jenni couldn't wait to lock up. The crafts fair ought to have something suitable for her office or her living room. Maybe both.

Worst-case scenario: she'd use the stuff for a few years before leaving it behind. What was wrong with that?

ETHAN RARELY BROUGHT NICK to the fair. Annette had given up long ago because trying to keep candy out of the hands of a five-year-old was so painful. Although he seemed to understand when they talked about the risks of high blood-sugar levels, that didn't stop him from craving the multicolored pinwheel lollipops and giant cones of cotton candy that other kids took for granted.

Jenni, however, had planned for that eventuality. "I bought some sugar-free ice cream at the grocery yesterday," she told the boy as they made their way between booths of hand-woven baskets and corncob dolls. "Which do you like best, chocolate or vanilla?"

"Both," he said.

"That's good, because I bought both kinds. I'd hate to waste either one. We can have some when we get back to my place."

"Let's go now!" Ethan had never seen his son this impatient on an outing, especially since they'd only been wandering through The Green for a quarter of an hour.

"The ice cream's in the freezer. It won't melt if we shop a little while longer," Jenni conceded.

"I want to see Boots," Nick explained. "He lets me pick him up. Did I tell you?"

Although his son had mentioned it at least a dozen times before, Ethan assumed a fascinated expression. "Did he squirm?"

"Only at the end." The boy's dark eyes contrasted with his reddish brown hair, giving him a serious air. "I think he forgot to be scared."

"Sounds like you two are getting along." Jenni examined a large painting of a woodland. It captured the flowing lines and the spirit of wildness. "This would look good in my office, don't you think?"

Ethan remembered one of the few things his mother had taught him about interior design. "Shouldn't you pick a theme first? So everything fits?"

"I don't want everything to fit." Jenni eyed the price tag. "I like artwork to stand out so people can tell I bought it because I love it." To the artist, who'd been watching them from a discreet distance, she said, "Will you take a check?"

"Sure, Doc." Her fame had obviously preceded her. "I can drop the painting off at the clinic on Monday."

"That would be terrific!"

They concluded the transaction quickly. But by then, Nick had begun fidgeting big-time.

"Maybe we should go see if that ice cream's still there." Jenni bestowed one of her sunny smiles on Ethan. He couldn't remember why he'd ever considered her fluffy. Radiant, yes. Outspoken, opinionated, funny and sexy, but never fluffy.

"I thought you wanted to check out the cheese selection," he said. She'd mentioned it earlier.

"Thanks for reminding me. Do you like cheese, Nick?" Jenni asked Nick.

He wrinkled his nose. "It stinks."

"It does," she agreed. "Some of it, anyway."

"Cheddar is okay," the boy conceded.

"You want to try a scientific experiment?" Jenni asked.

Nick eyed her dubiously. "Okay."

"Come on." She grabbed his hand and tugged him toward the food booths.

Ethan, striding alongside, met her gaze above the boy's head. "What do you have in mind?"

"Children's relationship with food ought to be healthy," she told him. "Dietary restrictions turn everything into a chore. Trying new things makes eating an adventure."

"Sounds good to me."

Jenni seemed to be having a nice time—and Ethan certainly was—as they passed among the booths selecting pretzels, a sugar-free chocolate bar, a small jar of green olives and a wedge of Camembert. The little boy considered each purchase gravely, listening with interest as his companion explained that foods could be salty, sweet, bitter and either sour or tart.

She led the way to a bench. "How clean are your hands?"

"I washed them before we came." He studied his palms. "They look clean."

Ethan was about to suggest they go across the street to use the rest room at the police station, when Jenni said, "He hasn't been handling anything dirty, so I think we're okay. Too sterile an environment interferes with building up immunities."

"If you say so, Doc." Ever since the diagnosis two years ago, Ethan had bent over backward to protect his son. He wasn't keen on loosening his standards, but with the boy starting first grade in the fall, they couldn't wrap him in cellophane forever.

"What we're trying to figure out is which part of your tongue tastes which type of flavor." After taking a pocketknife from her purse, Jenni cut three small pieces of Camembert. "This should be tart or sour. Roll it around and see where the flavor is strongest."

Ethan tried to give the cheese his full attention, but several people stopped by to say hello. After swallowing, he explained that Jenni and Nick were conducting a taste test.

"What a good idea!" one woman enthused. "I'd like to try that with my kids."

Despite making a scrunchy face at the taste, Nick dutifully sampled the cheese. "The side of my tongue doesn't like it."

"Very good," Jenni told him. "The sides are most sensitive to sourness. Too strong, huh?"

The boy nodded vigorously.

"You know what?" she said. "We're born with zillions of taste buds on our tongues and around the mouth. Some of them disappear as we age, so when we're grown, we can eat food that tasted too strong when we were young."

"So I might like it when I'm older?"

"That's right."

More people gathered. By the time Jenni worked her way through the pretzels and the chocolate bar, a small crowd was listening avidly to her mini-lecture.

She opened the jar of olives and, after plucking out three, passed the rest around. "Anybody recognize this flavor?"

"Bitter!" several chimed along with Nick, who must have arrived at the answer by process of elimination.

"Tell me whether it's stronger on the front or the back of your tongue," she instructed the boy.

Everyone sampled the olives. "Back!" Nick cried, and nearly choked.

"Oops." Jenni regarded him with concern but no panic. Sure enough, he coughed up the olive readily and then chewed it manfully before swallowing.

Ethan's heart, which had nearly stopped beating, steadied slowly. Having undergone first-aid training as a police officer, he realized a pitted olive wasn't large or solid enough to block a five-year-old's airway, but to him, Nick seemed incredibly fragile. He ought to stop overprotecting the boy, he thought.

Nick grimaced. "I won't like olives even when I'm big!"

"Maybe not," Jenni replied. "Hey, did you know that your tongue is a muscle? You use it for talking, tasting and what else?"

"Sticking out at people you don't like!" responded another child, to general laughter.

"Licking suckers!" Nick announced.

"Bravo to both of you!" She dusted pretzel salt off her lap. "Now, I think we've taken up this bench long enough, don't you?"

"Thanks for the lesson," said the young mother, who'd returned with salty and sour foods for her youngsters. "You ought to do this as a regular thing."

Olivia, who'd stopped by with her nine-year-old daughter, seconded the suggestion. "I'd like for you to speak to the elementary students—tie it in to some of our lessons. If it's all right, I'll give you a call and we can work out a schedule for this fall."

"I'd love to." Despite Jenni's sparkling response, she seemed flustered by the attention. Or, perhaps, by the general approval.

Ethan hoped she'd get used to it. Because although she didn't realize it yet, she fit into this town in ways she clearly had never anticipated. And neither had he.

THEY ATE THEIR CONES in the backyard. Annette hadn't yet returned from an interior design job, so they had the place to themselves.

Jenni was still marveling at the positive response her taste test had aroused. It surprised her because she had so little personal experience with kids. She hadn't expected to have anything new to show to parents.

Also, as a perpetual outsider, she'd usually encountered disapproval whenever she drew attention. Even in medical school, when she earned a professor's praise, she heard grumbling from fellow students about blond bimbos. At the L.A. hospital, her concern about patients had drawn more than one caution from superiors about maintaining a professional distance, even before the false claim.

In Downhome, people acted as if they admired her. Although their respect felt wonderful, Jenni didn't entirely trust it. One misstep could make her an outcast.

She could tell she'd impressed Ethan. And despite her resolve not to get involved, she valued his esteem above anyone else's.

"Boots has to be around here somewhere." Nick started looking for the cat as soon as he finished eating. "He's glad to have a home."

"He may not be so glad after Wednesday." Ethan, who'd set up a lawn chair for Jenni, sat on the steps that led to her apartment, watching his son prowl about calling the cat.

"What happens Wednesday?" Jenni asked.

"Boots has a date with the vet in Mill Valley," Ethan said. "His doom is set."

"They're neutering him?" She was glad to hear it, given

the number of unwanted kittens turned in to animal shelters each year. "That's a kind thing to do. It's healthier for him and… Oh, heck, why am I giving you a lecture?"

"As a man, I can't help sympathizing with the victim here."

"As a woman, I empathize with the female cats," she retorted. "Pregnancy can be tough."

"Don't you want kids?" he inquired unexpectedly.

"Well, that came out of the blue!" Her gaze went to Nick, but he'd wandered out of earshot. "I certainly wouldn't like to be in Helen's situation."

"Most pregnant women aren't involved with flakes," Ethan said. "Besides, you're dodging the question."

She didn't know how to answer. "I never pictured myself as the maternal type."

"You're good with children."

"Around Nick, who wouldn't be? He's so cute." Jenni didn't think she deserved credit for something that came easily. "I'm sure it's a lot harder dealing with him as a parent."

"What makes you say that?" Although Ethan spoke lazily, she sensed a serious undercurrent.

"You have to be patient even when you're tired and irritable. Plus, there's an automatic power struggle as kids exert their independence." She'd not only studied those issues but witnessed them in her examining rooms.

"Learning to rise above the fray is part of maturing." He finished his cone and looked around as if a refill might be hiding somewhere nearby, but of course it wasn't. "You learn to deal with it."

"Sure, if you have good examples to draw on from your parents," Jenni responded. "Kids from dysfunctional families have nothing to fall back on except fight or flight. It's unfair to subject a kid to that."

"If you're talking about yourself, you might have better instincts than you think."

"Thanks, but one day in the park isn't much to judge by." With half her attention, she'd been watching for a small furry creature, and now she spotted it before Nick did. "There's Boots! By the rosebush."

"Here, kitty!" The boy pelted toward him.

The cat braced for flight. "Whoa," Ethan told his son. "You'll scare him."

Nick stopped. After a moment, Boots ventured forward, sniffing.

"It'll take him a while to get over being scared," Ethan observed. "Still, he seems like a loving cat. Ever have a pet?"

"Me?" Jenni watched as the boy squatted and gave Boots a hug. She feared the animal might scratch him in an escape attempt, but it held still for a moment before slithering out of his grasp. Even then, it remained close by. "No."

"Seems like there are a lot of things you haven't experienced," Ethan murmured. "And here I thought you were a woman of the world."

Although she knew he was joking, his seductive tone reminded Jenni of other things she hadn't experienced, either. Like making love to a man who wanted more from her than she felt safe giving. A man she already dreamed about too often.

The hum of a motor alerted her to Annette's return. "Have a good time at the fair?" the older woman called when she'd emerged from her sedan in the driveway. Despite the gray woven through her chin-length brown hair, her energy made Ethan's mother seem too young to be a grandma.

"We sure did." Jenni got to her feet. "How about some ice cream? It's low cal."

"Just let me unload first."

"More dessert for me, too?" Ethan asked hopefully, like an overgrown kid.

"Sure. Another round for everyone."

Annette beamed at Nick. "Looks like Boots has figured out where he belongs."

When the boy gave the cat another hug, it held still slightly longer than before. Already getting acclimatized, Jenni thought.

"Won't he be scared when we take him to the vet?" Nick asked. "Can we stay with him?"

Annette sighed. "Honey, we have to drop him off Tuesday night. They'll do the operation Wednesday morning and we can bring him home that afternoon."

"We can't leave him!" he protested. "Can't I sleep there?"

"At the vet's?" Ethan said. "I doubt they have cages for little boys."

Tears welled in the child's eyes. "Then we won't nutter Boots."

"Neuter," Annette corrected. "Oh, dear, I'm afraid we have to."

Nick's distress touched Jenni. All children had fears of separation, and although he was too young when his mother died to remember, he must feel the loss at some level. Since he'd begun identifying with Boots, she feared that, in emotional terms, the cat might recover from the procedure before the boy did.

"Is there a motel close to the vet's?" Jenni asked. "He might feel better if you stayed nearby."

"What a good idea! That way, we could pop over to the vet's last thing at night and be there when Boots wakes up," Annette said. "You wouldn't mind if we stayed in Mill Valley on Tuesday night, would you, dear?"

"Please, Daddy!" Nick added.

As Ethan took in the pleading faces before him, Jenni sensed his reluctance. However, he ducked his head in assent.

"I'd like to join you, but I have a presentation to make to the city council that night."

"You'd sleep over in a motel to comfort a cat?" she asked, startled.

"To comfort my son," he corrected gently. To Annette and Nick, he said, "Don't forget your jammies and toothbrushes."

"Yay!" Nick dropped the cat and came running.

Lifting the boy on to his shoulders, his father paraded him around the yard, with both of them whooping and hollering. Boots took refuge around the corner of the house.

"Thank you," Annette told Jenni.

"I didn't do anything."

"You did more than you know. I'm going in now, but I'll be back for that ice cream."

"I'll get it ready!" As Jenni climbed the stairs, the sight of father and son circling the garden made her heart squeeze with unfamiliar sweetness.

She wasn't really a part of this scene, she reminded herself. If only Ethan weren't so incredibly desirable. If only she weren't perilously close to the point of no return.

Jenni vowed to put the brakes on, no matter what it took.

Chapter Twelve

"I hope you plan to make good use of your time while we're gone," Annette said Tuesday evening as she and Ethan washed the dishes. Nick was sitting in the den, trying to reassure Boots, who'd been meowing piteously in his cat carrier ever since they captured him.

It was a little after six and they'd have to leave soon, since the veterinary clinic closed at seven-thirty. The city council meeting started earlier, but of course it wasn't twenty miles away.

"I doubt I'll have any free time." Ethan polished a dish with the towel and set it in the cabinet. At home, he left plates dripping in the drainer. However, his mother couldn't abide spots. "If you've got a list of chores, I'll try to get to them on the weekend."

"I'm not talking about chores." She stole a glance toward the den, no doubt to be sure Nick wasn't within listening range. "I'm referring to Jenni."

"You? Matchmaking?" Ethan asked with pretended dismay.

"You need to seize the moment," Annette responded tartly. "It's hard to romance a woman with a little boy underfoot. Here's your chance."

"It's also hard to romance a woman while persuading five curmudgeons to fund a project," Ethan grumbled.

"The council members aren't curmudgeons!"

"Granted, except for Beau," he conceded, "but they're careful with the taxpayers' money. I have to persuade them that outreach is cost-effective."

"If you win, the two of you should celebrate." Using a stiff brush, she scrubbed her meat-loaf pan. "If you lose, then console each other. For heaven's sake, Ethan, I haven't seen you come alive like this since Martha died. Don't let that woman get away."

Too bad things weren't so simple. Ethan had hoped he and Jenni might draw closer on Sunday when they'd visited seven more children, but she'd kept the focus on work. Grateful that she hadn't objected to his adding two extras to the list, he'd respected her limits.

He'd tried to lighten things up Monday night, offering to fix dinner while they prepared the preliminary report. Instead, she'd insisted on working at the police station, where she'd arrived with take-out food from Café Montreal.

Since the desk officer kept popping in on various pretexts, mostly in an attempt to flirt with Jenni, progress had been slow. Ethan had had no choice but to concentrate on business until they got the job done. Afterward, Jenni had fled, declining his invitation to help read Nick a story.

He recognized a full-out retreat when he saw one. The woman had constructed a mile-high wall around herself. He wished he had a machine to fly into her past so he could have a few sharp words with the jerks who'd done this to her.

Tonight, in addition to his presentation on the outreach project, the doctor search committee was scheduled to make a report, which meant Ethan would be in the council's line of sight all evening. Jenni had promised to drop by, but she'd claimed that, as a new city employee, she wouldn't feel comfortable speaking.

Realizing that his mother awaited his reaction to her comments, he said simply, "Jenni's complicated."

"And Martha wasn't?"

"What does that mean?" he asked.

"You prefer complicated women, so why let that stop you?" she noted. "Easygoing gals bore you. My biggest fear when you moved back to Downhome was that you wouldn't meet anyone independent enough."

"Are you kidding?" He dried the meat-loaf pan as he talked. "If you think Downhome females are pushovers, you must have missed something."

Annette laughed. "I'm referring to the young, single ones. Not Gwen and Mae Anne and Olivia."

"I wouldn't describe Karen or Leah as clinging vines. Besides, I didn't mean that I object to Jenni's complications." He replaced the pan in a drawer. "What I meant was that she's hard to get close to. I have my doubts whether she wants a relationship."

"She likes you. How could she help it?"

He gave his mother a hug. Although she barely reached his chest, she managed to hug him back. "Thanks for the vote of confidence."

"Just remember," she told him, "you won't have many evenings by yourselves. Don't get so tied up in your obligations that you forget how to have fun."

He had to admit, a late-night supper might be just the thing to lower Jenni's defenses. "Mind if I rummage through your fridge? I doubt milk and peanut butter will inspire much conversation."

"Help yourself." Annette removed her apron and hung it on a peg. "There's cheese in the drawer and the whole-wheat loaf is a few days old, so it needs to be used."

"That gives me an idea." Ethan helped himself. "Do you have any special plans for Mill Valley other than cat sitting?"

"The motel gets premium cable channels," she informed him. "There's a Harry Potter movie on tonight, and I'm taking that package of bran muffins on the counter."

"Well, there goes my other snack idea," he joked.

When they adjourned to the den, a distracted Nick gave Ethan a peck on the cheek, then raced back to the cat carrier, where he spoke soothingly to Boots. The boy was growing up with a kind heart, Ethan noted, pleased.

His good mood dissipated a few minutes later as he climbed into his car. With the city council, you never could tell what kind of response you might get.

He hoped his planned celebration wasn't going to be replaced by a wake.

JENNI SLIPPED INTO THE COUNCIL CHAMBER as the meeting started. She walked in beside an older couple and, to avoid attracting attention, took a place behind them in one of the dark, pewlike rows.

Ethan sat near the front, between Olivia and Karen. She was glad he didn't turn around.

Still, from the back, she enjoyed studying his broad shoulders and dark hair. To Jenni, he seemed to tower over the dozens of people in the audience.

The chamber resembled an old-fashioned courtroom, with a curving platform at the front. The five council members sat behind a solid bench, with Mae Anne's face barely visible.

Although Jenni had arrived in town only a few weeks ago, she recognized all the faces. She knew Gwen, Rosie and Mae Anne from Karen's party, and Olivia had introduced her husband, Archie, during Jenni's initial visit. Beau had said hello to her at his grocery store.

She listened with interest as the city manager, a fortyish fellow named Alton Tucker, described a developer's preliminary proposal to build a shopping center on the outskirts of

town. The types of businesses he hoped to attract included a
supermarket, a coffee specialty shop, a restaurant and movie
theaters.

As might be expected, Beau and Gwen bristled at the possibility of competition. Mae Anne brought them up short.

"When my husband, Abe, was mayor, some upstart proposed building a café right next to The Green, with outdoor
seating," she reminded Gwen. "Oh, wait, I believe that was
you. And no offense intended, Beau, but I've heard folks
grumble about the limited selection at the grocery and the
long wait for service at peak hours."

"What am I supposed to do? Let some big chain steal my
customers?" he shot back.

"What should you do?" Mae Anne repeated. "Adapt! Stock
gourmet items. Beef up your staffing. Besides, in that location, people will always stop by because of the convenience."

"If we reject this development, they'll buy farmland across
the city line and Mill Valley will get the taxes," Archie added.

Since the subject had been raised as an information item
only, with no action required, the council left it at that. More
stores would bring more jobs and probably a new housing
tract, Jenni mused. It could be a blessing if it meant that, at
some point, Downhome might grow large enough to build its
own hospital.

Next, Olivia described the search committee's quest for an
obstetrician. Jenni would have come to hear this item even if
she weren't involved in the outreach project. She hoped
they'd soon have an OB on board to take over several high-
risk pregnancies she was treating, including Helen's.

"There are three candidates we've asked to visit during August," the principal said.

"Why three?" Beau demanded. "Two was enough last time."

"We're hedging our bets. We suspect at least one might
drop out of the running," she answered.

The prospects included a man from Texas, who had two children but no wife—"No, we didn't ask why not," Olivia said when Beau inquired—as well as an older woman weary of the harsh winters in her native Minnesota and a young doctor finishing his residency in Boston.

"Anyone have skeletons in the closet?" Archie queried. "We'd like to be warned in advance this time."

Perhaps he hadn't noticed her in the back, Jenni thought with a touch of embarrassment. She wished now that she'd made her presence more obvious.

"Not that I know of, but from my experience, the best doctors aren't necessarily the ones that please everyone from the get-go," Olivia told her husband. It was a safe bet she hadn't missed a single detail of who came and went in the audience.

"Your committee is doing a terrific job. You should be commended," Gwen remarked, and the other members agreed. "We look forward to meeting the candidates."

"So do I." Olivia sat down.

Archie glanced at his agenda. "We're ready for the police chief to report on the outreach program."

"I was surprised to see that on the agenda," Beau said. "I don't recall us approving a pilot project."

"You didn't." Ethan approached the microphone set up for guest speakers. "However, at no cost to the city, Dr. Vine and I decided to test the waters."

Rosie spoke up. "Good for you. If people didn't show a little initiative, nothing would ever get done around here!"

Archie politely cut off further comment. "Chief, why don't you make your report?"

"Ladies and gentlemen, I hand-delivered copies of the report to you this afternoon, but with your permission I'll review the key points." Ethan raised his notes.

Jenni listened tensely as he sketched the visits they'd paid to a dozen children and the ways in which they'd been able to help. "Although we identified only one case of possible abuse"—the child's bruising had seemed excessive, given the explanation that he'd fallen off the bed—"we identified a number of nutritional and other health deficits that could interfere with learning. I'd say at least nine of the twelve youngsters were helped in some way, thanks to Dr. Vine."

"What are you going to do about the abuse case, Chief?" Archie asked.

"We've arranged for the child to undergo a full medical exam to check for suspicious old injuries," Ethan replied. "We'll also keep an eye on the situation, although we don't want to overreact. Taking a child out of a home wrongfully can be an abuse in its own way."

He concluded by describing his hope for a larger program that could expand as funds became available. Jenni was impressed by his vision.

Beau, however, thought otherwise. "It sounds like a lot of bureaucracy to me. Too much nosing around in people's private business."

"We all want to help kids," Gwen conceded, "but aren't you mixing social services with crime prevention, Chief?"

When Ethan paused to collect his thoughts, several of the board members glanced at Jenni. Realizing that her contribution might influence the outcome, she stood and caught Archie's eye.

The mayor cleared his throat. "I believe Dr. Vine has something to contribute."

As she approached, the welcome on the chief's face made Jenni blush. She hoped the council members attributed her pink cheeks to shyness.

"Children who suffer undiagnosed nutritional and health problems tend to fall behind in school," she explained. "That puts them at risk for dropping out and abusing drugs. In L.A.,

I'd have said they were susceptible to joining gangs. However, I don't know if that's a problem here."

"Chief?" The mayor looked his way.

"We don't have gangs per se, but last year Mill Valley encountered some gang wanna-bes," Ethan said. "A group of kids adopted the kinds of clothing and initiation rites they'd seen on TV. They were caught vandalizing cars."

"You mean this project really is crime prevention?" Beau sounded surprised. "Not just back-door socialism?"

Chuckles rose from the audience. To Jenni, it seemed people were sympathetic to the chief.

"I assure you, Mr. Johnson, I'm a police officer, not a socialist," Ethan replied.

"Thank you," Archie told him. "You two may take your seats, but please stay handy in case we have any more questions."

"Thank *you.*" Ethan gestured Jenni toward the row where he'd been sitting.

Since she couldn't return to the rear without making a production of it, she slid in beside him.

Her spontaneous participation had come too quickly for her to get nervous. However, now that it was over, she began to shiver. Based on prior experience, public speaking made Jenni fear her statements would be challenged or belittled. Even though, intellectually, she knew her status had changed, her nerves remained frazzled.

As the council members discussed the project, Ethan rested his arm against Jenni's. His touch reminded her that, for once, she wasn't alone.

At last Mae Anne made a motion for the city manager to investigate sources of funding for an expanded outreach program. When the matter was opened for public discussion, Olivia spoke in favor.

The motion passed four to one, with Beau dissenting.

Jenni's apprehension lifted. No one had jeered at her. In fact, as the meeting ended, a small knot of well-wishers surrounded her and the chief.

"You did great!" Karen told her. "I was proud."

Barry, who'd been taking notes for the newspaper, gave her a friendly wave across the room. His gaze flicked coolly over Ethan.

Too bad not every issue could be settled so swiftly, Jenni thought. She knew Ethan would help if he could.

Still, her spirits refused to be dampened. Tonight felt like a triumph.

By the time they left the chamber, it was past nine o'clock, but she didn't feel remotely tired. "Is there any place to party around here?" she asked Ethan.

"On a Tuesday? We roll up the sidewalks in half an hour."

From the front steps, she saw a couple of street lamps glimmering in The Green. At Pepe's Italian Diner, only a safety light shone through the glass front. "You're not kidding."

"However," he said, "I know of a lovely small establishment, very private. The music they play is…jazz?"

She believed he meant his house. "Light jazz, preferably."

"Of course," he replied at once. "And while I can't vouch for the chef's Cordon Bleu credentials, he makes a valiant effort to please. Would you care for a midnight supper a few hours early, mademoiselle?"

Ethan was the perfect person to share her buoyant mood with. Jenni couldn't resist.

"Maybe for a little while," she said.

Chapter Thirteen

Ethan poured them each a glass of root beer while the cheese was melting in the fondue pot and the bread cubes toasting in the oven. What he really needed was a second chafing dish full of chocolate and some strawberries to top it off, but even a police chief couldn't command food to appear at will.

There'd been a moment in front of the council when he'd feared the project might fail. Not that he couldn't have explained its value in preventing crime, but Jenni had made a more eloquent case. Moreover, her recent experience in an urban setting had carried extra weight.

They'd made a good team.

"Something smells fabulous." Jenni wandered in from the living room, where a Monica Mancini CD was playing. "Oh my gosh. Fondue!"

"Like it?" He enjoyed seeing her here in the kitchen. The remodeled room had been one of the main attractions of the house, aside from its location. However, it had always lacked something. Now he knew what that was.

"It's one of my favorite dishes, but I hardly ever run across it." She accepted the glass appreciatively. "That's premium root beer, unless I miss my guess."

"A good host serves only the best." He raised his goblet. "To future triumphs."

"To triumphs."

Ethan hooked his arm around Jenni's so they could drink with elbows entwined. Despite a slight awkwardness, they managed it without spilling.

As they broke the connection, he caught a whiff of Jenni's delicate fragrance. She'd removed her suit jacket, and the pale blue blouse clung to gentle curves.

"Warm," he murmured.

"What?" She looked up, startled.

"You're radiant tonight," Ethan said boldly.

For the space of a heartbeat, Jenni didn't move. Then she made a gesture that encompassed the kitchen. "I love these cabinets. And the countertop. Your wife did a great job here."

He knew she was trying to put a distance between them by summoning the ghost of Martha. But it had lost its power.

"She never lived here. She never even lived in Down-home."

"No?" Jenni stopped roving. "I pictured you all nested here."

Discussing one's late wife hardly qualified as a romantic gesture, yet Ethan discovered that he wanted to. And he decided Jenni had a right to hear the story.

"Let's eat while we talk." He carried the fondue pot and burner into the front room and settled them on a mat on the coffee table. By the time he returned, Jenni had opened the oven and taken out the cookie sheet with a pair of pot holders. "Thanks for pitching in."

"Survival tactics," she joked.

They transferred the bread cubes into a basket and carried it, along with a pair of fondue forks, to the table. Sitting side by side on the couch, they twirled the cubes in the cheese and ate. The flavor melted in Ethan's mouth.

"My wife was a country singer," he said when he came up for air. "We met in Nashville when some fellow officers and I stopped by the music bar where she was performing."

"Was she from Nashville?" Jenni asked.

He shook his head. "She grew up in Georgia. Her parents still live there. I try to stay in contact with them, but they haven't made much of an attempt to play a role in Nick's life."

"That's too bad."

He rarely thought about Martha's folks. They were likable people although hard to pin down. "Anyway, we had an off-and-on romance for a while. She was always going on the road, performing or auditioning. Took me a while to convince her to get married."

When he paused, a stillness descended around them. The flame beneath the pot and a lamp in one corner left gentle shadows.

"I pictured her as more of a homebody," Jenni admitted. "Was she eager to have kids?"

"I think we both assumed that would come, and it did," he replied. "We'd dated five years and been married for three when she called from the road to say she was pregnant. She didn't expect it to make any difference to her touring, but then she started feeling sick."

Jenni nodded. "That's not unusual."

"In her case, though, the symptoms struck me as excessive. She lost all her energy and complained of feeling bloated and uncomfortable. By the second trimester, her doctor got concerned when she didn't get better. That was when Martha told him her mother was a breast cancer survivor and her aunt had died of ovarian cancer in her thirties."

Jenni hugged herself. "That's not a medical history I like to see."

"An ultrasound showed a suspicious growth on one ovary, but Martha refused treatment because of the pregnancy," he explained. "She fell in love with the baby as soon as she felt him move inside her. The thing that scared her most was the possibility of losing him."

"What happened?" Jenni had stopped eating, he noticed.

"The doctor delivered Nick by caesarian section and then performed a hysterectomy. Nick came out fine and Martha handled the surgery all right. Unfortunately, the growth turned out to be cancer."

He halted as a rush of tears blurred his vision. Although Ethan had recovered in many ways, the memory still tore at his heart.

"That's unusual," Jenni said. "Normally, pregnancy helps protect against ovarian cancer. I'm sorry, Ethan."

Both her sympathy and her clinical understanding eased the tightness in his chest. "She died three months later. Three months. I couldn't believe it happened that fast."

"We've made a lot of progress against cancer, but some cases are unusually aggressive," Jenni observed.

"I kept thinking that if she hadn't met me, if she hadn't become pregnant, the cancer might have been treated early enough to save her," Ethan admitted. "I love Nick so much I couldn't imagine what my life would be like without him, but maybe I'm being selfish."

"Ethan," Jenni said gravely, "if she hadn't been pregnant, they probably wouldn't have diagnosed ovarian cancer as soon as they did. The symptoms can be vague and it isn't the first thing you look for in such a young woman."

To keep his hands busy, he twirled more bread into the cheese. "I underwent grief counseling—that's standard for police officers who've suffered a trauma—still, I guess it takes time."

"Lots of time," Jenni agreed.

The way she accepted the tragedy without emotionalism steadied Ethan. And a scarcely recognized burden of guilt, the sense that perhaps his wife might have been saved, lifted from him at her words.

Discovering that he had an appetite, he popped the heavily loaded cube into his mouth. The gooey stuff nearly choked him, but he relished it all the same.

Jenni stared at the tiny blue flame beneath the burner. "One of the hardest parts of being a doctor is facing the fact that I can't save everybody."

"At least you save some of them." Without thinking, he fingered a wayward strand of her fine blond hair. It floated against his fingers like spider silk. "Three years later, when Nick fell ill, I thought I might lose him, too. Thanks to medical science, he's fine."

"Yes, he is." After moving the fondue pot aside, Jenni propped her feet on the coffee table. "Your wife sounds interesting, but not the kind of woman I'd expect you to go for."

"In what way?" Reluctantly, he quit toying with her hair.

"She sounds offbeat," Jenni summarized. "Like someone who charted her own course."

"Does that mean you think I'm conventional?" Ethan challenged. "It's not exactly the picture I have of myself."

She gave him a slow smile. Tonight, she seemed less guarded than usual. "You *are* part of the establishment."

"That doesn't mean I have to be stodgy." He reflected before continuing. "I'm an innovator and a liaison between different parts of the community. As for my taste in ladies, I prefer a woman who stands out from the crowd."

"I should guess you'd scare off most independent women," Jenni said. "You're so…overwhelming."

Ethan didn't know whether to be flattered or deflated. "You mean, like a steamroller?"

"No, I mean…confident, take-charge, the kind of guy who dates the prom queen in high school because she suits his image." She curled her legs beneath her.

"I didn't have a steady girlfriend in high school. Come to mention it, I'll bet my prom date was shocked when I asked her. She was the class intellectual. Went to Harvard, I believe."

"Somebody from Downhome went to Harvard?"

"I graduated from high school in Nashville." Ethan was still trying to absorb Jenni's description of him. He liked the word *take-charge,* although he wasn't thrilled with her idea that he picked his dates for their social prominence. "As for being confident, maybe I come across as cocky, but I don't care. I've always gone after what I wanted and I intend to keep doing it."

Right now, what he wanted was Jenni. She'd tossed off her suit jacket and discarded her shoes. Her soft blouse had come partly untucked from the skirt, which hiked up to reveal long, stocking-clad legs. He swayed forward to see how she would react.

"Are you making the moves on me, Chief?" Holding her position, Jenni sent him a provocative look.

"Certainly not. I never take advantage," he demurred, only half meaning it.

"Advantage of what? Or whom?" The pupils of her eyes had dilated in the reduced light.

By way of an answer, Ethan brushed his finger across Jenni's temple. When he traced a path to her ear and circled it gently, her lashes lowered.

He angled closer, fighting his instincts. The longer he held back, the less likely he'd frighten her. At the same time, every inch of his skin tingled.

"Are you going to kiss me or what?" Jenni demanded.

Ethan restrained himself, barely. "We make such a good team, Doctor. I wouldn't want to put you in an awkward position and spoil everything."

"You're doing this on purpose," she said.

"Doing what?" he asked innocently.

"Driving me crazy."

"I'd say it was the other way around."

She caught his face between palms that felt smooth against

his rough cheeks. They stared deeply into each other's eyes, locked in a mock battle for control.

Jenni broke first. With a startling abruptness, she swung about and settled onto Ethan's lap. Grasping the knot of his tie, she said, "I always figured a guy like you should be on a leash."

He ran his hands along her legs, easing the skirt up to her hips. When he stroked her inner thighs, he heard her breath quicken. "Still think you've got me under your thumb, Doc?"

"I've got you exactly where I want you." Jenni stole a quick kiss. "You owed me that from your hit and run in my office."

"I always pay my debts. Preferably with interest." Ethan pulled her closer and claimed her mouth. As he stroked her hips, molten gold flowed through him.

The buttons on her blouse glided easily and her blouse fell away. When he touched her breasts, Jenni gave a little cry that was almost a sob. She drew away only long enough to open his shirt.

Her tongue outlined a path down his chest. Ethan gripped her waist, but she wiggled free to remove his belt and free his taut member.

When her mouth grazed him, he could hardly bear the tension. "Let's not waste this."

"Who said we were going to?" Jenni demanded, and, pushing him down on the couch, straddled him. She stretched above, only a thin layer of cloth between them.

It occurred to the tiny sliver of his brain still functioning rationally that he hadn't intended a seduction tonight and that this might not be the wisest course of action. But he couldn't stop now.

Arching upward, Ethan caught her nipples between his lips. Hearing her gasp, he lowered her panties. A yearning to join seized him with such power that he struggled to delay even a moment longer.

"We ought to…I have some protection…" he managed to say.

"I'm on the pill," she replied. "Don't worry, Chief. I know what I'm doing."

As she slid onto his length, raw hunger roared through Ethan. Its intensity demolished the last shred of self-control.

Above him, Jenni played her hair across his chest. Ethan touched her everywhere, wondering at the freedom of it and at how much he relished every breath she took.

He wanted many things and he wanted them now: to thrust so hard they would both be sore for days. To merge into Jenni until she could think of nothing except him. To enchant her the way she'd enchanted him.

But he couldn't capture her, he could only hold on for the ride as her stroking intensified. Power flooded him, spilling between their bodies until they seemed to glow with an unearthly radiance. He lost awareness of everything except their union as a firestorm swept them.

A series of explosions rocked Ethan's body, and Jenni answered in kind. The inferno threatened to carry them into the sky, but at last it muted and she came to rest against him, lovely and ephemeral as a spark of light.

As he held her gently, Ethan knew better than to stake a verbal claim or act possessive. He had to proceed with caution.

Yet, as he'd said, he always went after what he wanted. And he didn't let it go easily once he took it.

AT SOME LEVEL, Jenni had always separated her essential self from her sexual responses. She had managed to keep her boyfriends happy and satisfy her physical needs without risking too much emotionally.

Tonight, she'd forgotten how to do that.

It had started out safely enough. When she realized how

much she wanted the chief, she'd taken charge of their love-making. She'd sensed him surrendering to his desire, and she'd relished his excitement.

Passion had caught her unprepared. She'd been expecting a spring rain and instead a hurricane had whirled her off her feet.

Instead of trapping her, making love to Ethan had freed her to soar to new heights. Now, lying in his arms on the couch, she allowed herself to toy with possibilities.

If he could love a free spirit like Martha, why couldn't he love an outsider like Jenni? And why couldn't she, who'd doubted her ability to establish a real home, finally settle in a place where she felt more accepted than she'd ever dreamed possible?

Hope terrified her, because she knew the devastation that could follow when it died. But she'd never been afraid to run a risk if the payoff merited it. And this one did.

"Bedroom?" Ethan murmured.

For an instant, Jenni considered objecting. She ought to go home...but maybe she *was* home.

They had tonight. Tomorrow Annette and Nick would return and they'd need to be careful, at least until...unless...

She wasn't foolish enough to expect permanence—not yet. Transferring from the couch to a bed was as ambitious as Jenni dared become in her current frame of mind.

"Sure," she said.

AWAKENING IN AN UNFAMILIAR SLANT of morning light, she lay still. She'd learned to take her bearings, emotionally as well as physically, before stirring.

She felt elated but uncertain, as if she'd crawled too far along the branch of a tree that might not support her weight. Beside her, Ethan dozed, his handsome face sweetened by a rare trace of contentment.

How dangerous and fragile happiness was. Yet for some people, it lasted. Could they be that lucky?

Reluctantly, she checked the bedside clock. A few minutes past seven. The clinic opened at nine, but she ought to arrive early to be ready for the first patient.

Jenni sat up. Instantly, Ethan's hand clamped onto her wrist. "Going somewhere?"

Bending, she kissed his stubbly cheek. His arms closed around her, pulling her down.

When she resisted, however, he relented. "I need to go change," she said. "What time do you start work?"

"Eight," he grumbled. "What a ridiculous hour. I ought to cut myself more slack."

"You're the top cop. You have to set an example."

"Ah, but what kind of example?" Dark, appreciative eyes gazed up at her. "Did anyone ever tell you you're gorgeous when you're naked?"

So was he, with powerful muscles evident even in relaxation. "I vote for a rematch. But not today."

"I'll have to arrange for Nick to sleep away again soon," he murmured. "How many stray cats do you think we can neuter before my mother gets suspicious?"

Jenni laughed. "Dozens, I hope. The Humane Society should love you." She got to her feet, debating whether to shower here or at her apartment.

"We have frozen waffles," Ethan offered.

"I'd better get going." She whisked into the bathroom for a quick cleanup, then collected her clothes from the living room. Ethan came out in his bathrobe, but after a brief kiss, Jenni waved him back. "I don't want anyone to see you when I go outside."

"Like they wouldn't think it odd that you're coming home fully dressed at seven-thirty in the morning?"

"House call," she improvised. "Doctors work weird hours."

"Whatever."

He didn't seem concerned about gossip. Jenni took that as a good sign. A man as prominently placed as Ethan wouldn't want to be associated publicly with a woman unless he really cared about her.

The notion gave her an unfamiliar goose-bumpy sensation.

She exited through the side door, wishing a fence didn't separate the two properties. However, she saw no one on the street, and Annette's house sat shuttered and silent.

Jenni hurried along the driveway. A slight breeze stirred, although the humidity warmed the air even at this early hour. The rear yard burst with June blossoms, bright blues and whites and reds.

Her body tingled with the memory of last night. She knew she should to put it out of her mind and prepare for the day ahead; yet she yearned to savor it a little longer.

Next to the garage, Jenni mounted the steps. A sudden movement above on the landing startled her and she halted, her heart hammering.

A man moved into view, his expression hooded. With a jolt, she recognized Arturo Mendez.

She considered shouting for Ethan, but then told herself, for heaven's sake, the young man hadn't done anything wrong. Besides, if she hoped to help him reconcile with Helen, she had to earn his trust.

"Hi," Jenni said as casually as she could manage.

If Arturo noticed anything odd about her returning home in business clothes at such an hour, he didn't comment. "Can we talk?"

"Certainly."

"It's private. Or aren't I good enough to invite inside?"

"I'd be delighted to ask you in," she replied. "The problem is, you're blocking my way."

"Oh. Sorry." He moved to a corner of the landing.

"Care for coffee?" she asked as she unlocked the door.

"Sure."

It occurred to Jenni as she admitted Arturo that Ethan probably wouldn't approve of her being alone with such a troubled young man, especially one under suspicion. But she had to follow her instincts.

Just because she'd made love with Ethan didn't mean he had the right to rule her life.

Chapter Fourteen

"I have to get away from here." Arturo paced through the sparsely furnished living room. "I can't expect Helen to understand. She actually likes this town. I was hoping you might know somebody in L.A."

Jenni poured two cups of the coffee from the pot she'd brewed while she and her visitor exchanged wary pleasantries. Although normally she took cream, she decided to drink it black to avoid interrupting the flow of conversation.

"What exactly do you want to do?" she asked. "Despite your talent, you need training."

"That's what I mean." The young man gestured vaguely. "There's, like, the Art Center in Pasadena. I thought maybe you could get me in."

Jenni found his naiveté frustrating. Of course she'd like to assist, but why on earth did this young man believe a doctor had connections with art schools, let alone that she could gain him admission to a highly competitive institution?

She chose her words carefully. "I don't know much about it. Still, that doesn't mean I can't help you. I'd be happy to do some research."

Sinking on to the arm of the sofa, Arturo blew out a puff of air. "I guess I'm really dumb, huh? I figured an important doctor like you could fix it up for me."

Jenni decided to level with him. "I wish I were as important as you assume. Arturo, I just finished paying off my med school debts. Since I came to Downhome, it's the first time people have looked up to me."

"You're kidding!" In his surprise, he seemed very much the nineteen-year-old kid he was.

She hadn't intended to make a play for sympathy. "I'll need some information. Are you interested in a four-year degree, assuming you can win a scholarship?"

"A degree? You mean, like, college?" Hopelessness showed on his face. "Man, I barely graduated from high school. I don't have those kinds of grades or anything. And I was hoping—I thought maybe I could learn fast, so in a year I could support Helen."

Jenni understood enough about artists to be aware that very, very few earned a living in the studio. Some might land jobs in graphic design, but that required lengthy preparation.

"Let's be blunt," she said. "As I told you, I'll do research. What I'd like to know, Arturo, is whether you're going to act like a prima donna if I find something that involves hard work and delayed gratification." In case he hadn't heard the term before, she added, "That means having to wait for what you want."

He stared at the wall so long, she began to doubt he would answer.

Finally, he said, "You don't have any artwork in here."

"I tried to buy a painting, but the artist wouldn't sell it to me," she reminded him.

"Oh, yeah." A dimple flashed, then disappeared. "I don't want to be a nobody for the rest of my life. I don't have some big ego, either. If I can see a goal, yeah, I'd be willing to work hard. And I want to make a life with Helen and the baby. Is that possible?"

Jenni never made promises she couldn't keep. "I'll do my

best to find out. I agree about one thing. At this stage of your career, you deserve a more stimulating environment than Downhome."

She supposed she didn't owe Arturo anything, but he'd trusted her enough to ask for help. Besides, she owed something to Susan Leto. When Jenni had asked how she could repay her mentor's many favors, the answer had been, "Give a hand to someone who needs it."

That person was standing right in front of her, his shoulders a little slumped but his head high. "Most folks around here don't have a very high opinion of me," Arturo confessed. "And maybe they're right. I've done things I'm not proud of. But I'm ready to start over."

"This may take a few days." Jenni hoped it wouldn't be longer. "Where can I reach you?"

"I'll have to contact you. The place I'm staying...it's this abandoned farmhouse out on Long Trail Way. It's posted No Trespassing." He blinked a couple of times. "Whoa. I don't want anyone to know I'm there."

"I promise not to tell," Jenni answered. "Do you have a phone?"

He shook his head. "Like I said, I'll get in touch with you."

"Obviously, you're good at that."

"Huh?"

"Well, you found this place," she pointed out.

"Everybody knows you're renting from Chief Forrest's mother," Arturo answered.

"Everybody" meant the people at the salon where Helen worked, Jenni supposed. "Promise me one thing."

He glanced at her warily. "What's that?"

"No matter what happens between you and Helen, you won't abandon your child. Even if you can only visit now and then, promise that you'll do what you can."

Arturo didn't hesitate. "Yeah, of course. I'd do it anyway. But we're going to be a real family."

"Good," Jenni said.

After a quick thanks, he went out. It was after eight o'clock and she'd have to hurry to prepare for the clinic, Jenni noted. At least by now Ethan should have left, which meant he wouldn't see Arturo departing.

Maybe, she reflected, she ought to mention the visit to him. However, she didn't wish to give Ethan the impression that he'd acquired the right to run her life.

It occurred to Jenni abruptly that she'd done the one thing she'd vowed never to do again. She'd involved herself with a patient's private life.

With luck, the situation would soon be resolved. On that tentative note of reassurance, she headed for the shower.

ETHAN COULDN'T RESIST dropping by the clinic at noon, bringing croissant sandwiches from the Café Montreal. Although Jenni could spare only a few minutes to eat with him, her appreciative smile made the effort more than worthwhile.

He took care not to whistle as he strolled diagonally back across the intersection of Home Boulevard and Tulip Tree Avenue toward the police station. He didn't want to draw the attention of anyone walking on The Green or looking out of City Hall. If they noticed his trajectory from the clinic and the lilt in his stride, they might draw conclusions.

On the other hand, gossip seemed unavoidable. When he bought the sandwiches, Gwen had smiled knowingly, and, at last night's council meeting, he'd caught a few meaningful glances when he mentioned working with Dr. Vine on the outreach project. For once, the folks might even have their facts straight.

The two of them were definitely involved. Ethan didn't kid himself that one night cemented a relationship, but what a launch.

He'd barely entered the lobby when his cell phone rang. "Forrest," he answered.

"Ethan! Oh, thank heaven!" His mother's voice trembled. "Nick and I just got home, and…" She swallowed audibly.

Ethan went cold. "Is he all right?"

"He's fine. I'm sorry, I didn't mean to scare you," Annette said. "There was a man here."

"In your house?"

"Yes. I—I only caught a glimpse of him. He ran out the front when we came in the side door."

In the background, a little voice asked, "Is that Daddy?" and he heard his mother say, "I'm talking to him now."

"I'll be right there." Ethan strode through the station. "Did you see who it was?"

"All I made out was a silhouette."

"Did he take anything?"

"Not that I can tell." Annette inhaled deeply. "It frightened me. Maybe I got carried away."

"Your reaction is normal." As Ethan approached the watch commander's office, he considered how to make sure his mother played it safe without further alarming her. "Why don't the two of you go outside and lock yourselves in the car till I get there?"

"Too late," she said. "Nick's getting Boots settled in the laundry room. I feel so stupid. I ran back inside last night to grab my purse and I must have forgotten to lock up."

"Don't worry about it. I'm on my way and we'll dispatch a patrol officer as well."

After clicking off, Ethan sketched the situation for the watch commander, and half ran to his car. He'd begun to hope the thief might have tired of his game or left town. Instead, he'd struck close to home.

Perhaps the intruder didn't know whose house he'd violated. But Ethan took it very, very personally.

* * *

"I WAS HOPING you could recommend a type of shoe insert that wouldn't show." Sitting on the paper-covered examining table, Olivia wiggled her aching feet.

The principal had arrived promptly for her two p.m. appointment, impeccably dressed in a suit despite the summer weather. An exam and a few questions had left Jenni with no doubt about the source of her discomfort.

"Olivia, you don't need a shoe insert," she replied.

"I don't?" her patient asked hopefully.

Stooping, Jenni collected one of Olivia's stylishly strappy pumps. She recognized the designer logo on the insole, not because she ever wore foot gear like this but because she'd heard the name bandied about on TV. "Very attractive."

"I always try to look my best. My mother taught me that we're judged by our appearance," Olivia said. "It's especially true when you're African-American and have to cope with stereotypes. Power dressing makes small-minded people think twice, which is quite an improvement, since most of them don't even think once."

Jenni reached for her prescription pad. On it, she wrote the name of an Internet search engine, along with the words shoe and stylish and orthopedic. Before handing it over, she said, "You know, sometimes it's hard to take our medicine."

"No, no, no." The principal pretended to panic. "You are not going to tell me what I don't want to hear. Forty-three is not old enough to wear old-lady shoes. I'm going to pretend you wrote down 'Have Archie massage feet daily.'"

"That wouldn't hurt," Jenni agreed. "I want you to search the Web for a design that isn't totally ugly."

Olivia frowned. "Not unless they make orthopedic shoes with at least a three-inch heel."

"I doubt it," Jenni replied.

"I can't give up my favorite shoes!"

"You don't have to." She leaned against the counter, smiling.

"I don't?"

"No, you can have them encased in Lucite and display them on the mantel."

Olivia sighed. "Doc, you are one tough cookie."

"This isn't solely about your feet—no pun intended." Jenni kept a straight face, because she took the subject seriously. "High heels throw your body out of alignment. As the years go by, you'll distort your hips and spine. You could virtually cripple yourself. Olivia, you don't need to prove anything to anybody. At least try a pair of flat shoes with good arch support."

The principal stared gloomily at her feet. "I'll let Archie search. He's a genius with the computer."

"Maybe I should ask for his help, too." Jenni hadn't intended to mention Arturo's request, but who would know better about art schools than the town's leading educator? "Do you know Arturo Mendez?"

"I certainly do." With Jenni's help, Olivia eased down from the table. "You can't believe what a labor it was to keep him in school. If it weren't for some of our dedicated teachers, he'd have dropped out in junior year."

Jenni explained his request. "Despite his attitude, he's still a kid. I doubt he'd do well in New York or L.A. with no money and no contacts. Are you familiar with any art schools in the state?"

"The University of Tennessee has both an undergraduate and a graduate program in art, but that doesn't sound like what he's looking for." The principal retrieved her panty hose.

Jenni averted her gaze tactfully as Olivia put them on. "Any other suggestions?"

"I have a friend in Knoxville who raises funds for the arts.

I'll ask her. She's the kind of person who loves problem-solving."

"Thank you," Jenni said. "I don't mean to be impatient, but I think Arturo's in a hurry."

"I'll get right on it." Stepping into her shoes, the principal winced. "These really do hurt."

"In a few years, you could be consulting me about back problems," Jenni warned. "Let's avoid that, okay?"

Olivia sighed. "I suppose it might be time for a change."

As soon as she left, Patsy popped in. "Chief Forrest is here to see you."

For Ethan to return so soon after lunch seemed odd. "He's not injured, is he?"

She shook her head. "He said it's police business."

"Show him into my office. Do I have any appointments?" Jenni asked as she emerged from the examining room.

"Your two-thirty canceled," Patsy replied.

"Wasn't that Helen Rios?" Jenni had noticed her name on the list this morning.

"She said something came up. She sounded upset." Before Jenni could speak, the receptionist added, "I suggested she reschedule, but she put me off."

"I'll give her a call later." Right now, she needed to find out why Ethan was here.

As soon as he entered, she noticed his reserved expression. "What is it?" Jenni inquired from behind her desk, where she'd used a few spare seconds to sign some insurance documents.

He stood with legs braced and hands folded in front—an official-looking stance. He wasn't a stranger anymore, and yet in some ways, he'd become one.

"About two hours ago, someone broke into my mother's house. He fled before she could get a good look at him," he said grimly.

Jenni's chest squeezed. "Was anyone hurt?"

"Fortunately, no." Ethan's tone didn't soften. Obviously, he hadn't come here merely to inform her of the break-in. "One of the neighbors noticed Arturo Mendez poking around the premises this morning. Did you happen to see him?"

She didn't believe the young man who'd applied to her for help had repaid her kindness by committing a crime. Then it occurred to her that Ethan wasn't asking casually. He must have more information than he'd let on, or he simply would have phoned. "Yes. Why?"

"The neighbor saw him exiting your unit about eight a.m.," he admitted. "Jenni, what's going on?"

"Arturo asked me to help him get into art school." She saw no reason to keep it a secret. Besides, she'd already told Olivia.

"How did he find you?"

"He told me everybody knows I rent from your mother," Jenni replied. "But you said the break-in occurred two hours ago. That's four hours later."

"Burglars frequently case a place before they strike."

Ethan had to do his job, but, all the same, she knew how it felt to be suspected of whatever went wrong simply because you were the kid who didn't fit in. "That doesn't prove anything." Another point occurred to her. "Helen canceled her appointment for this afternoon. Do you know anything about that?"

"We're questioning her."

"What does that mean?" Jenni rounded her desk. "She has a complicated pregnancy! She can't handle a lot of stress."

"For Pete's sake, we're not working her over with rubber hoses." Rubbing his chin, Ethan added, "We took her to the station because we don't want her destroying evidence while we get a search warrant."

"For their apartment?" Arturo would be furious, but it did

make sense. "That's probably good, because it would clear him—except that he moved out."

"Where's he staying?"

Jenni refused to feign ignorance. "I promised not to tell."

"You did what?" Anger laced his voice.

"I'm trying to help…"

"He isn't even your patient!" Ethan snapped. "This man showed up at your apartment this morning and you didn't think to mention it at lunch? And now you're protecting him."

"You can't be sure he's committed a crime," she shot back. "He's a confused kid who's trying to put his life in order. Apparently, I'm the only person in town that he trusts—and I'm supposed to betray him based on vague suspicions?"

"Betray?" Ethan stopped to compose himself before continuing. "I'm sorry, Jenni. When my mother called about a break-in, I hit the roof. Now I find out that one of our suspects paid you a visit that could have compromised your safety."

"He didn't act even remotely threatening." Impulsively, Jenni crossed the carpet and caught Ethan's hands. They felt firm and dear. "I see a lot of myself in him. He's at a crossroads and he's trying to make the right choices. He reached out to me."

"And he might be innocent," Ethan concluded. "Honey, I hope so—"

The endearment touched her.

"Still, I have an obligation to the residents of this town. And I shudder to think what might have happened if Mom had cornered the guy."

Jenni wanted to argue that Arturo wasn't violent, but she couldn't say how he might react if trapped. "When are you going to serve the warrant?"

"As soon as we get it. Hopefully, this afternoon." He released her hands. "Even though he's moved out, he might have left evidence."

"You won't find anything." She wished she felt certain of that.

"I'll let you know," he said, and then he was gone.

Why did this have to happen the morning after she and Ethan made love? Jenni wondered. And while she was so new in town, still an unknown quantity to most people. Would they understand why she chose to champion an underdog?

Her gaze fell on the painting the janitor had hung on the wall. For the first time, she'd dared to buy something too large to pack. What if, when her provisional period ran out two months from now, the town sent her on her way?

Surely this made no difference. One small incident wasn't going to ruin everything.

She had another patient scheduled. Resolutely, Jenni pulled her thoughts away from speculation. With luck, the police would soon arrest whoever was really guilty of the break-ins. Arturo would prove himself worthy of her trust.

And the endearment that had slipped from Ethan's mouth gave her hope that they could soon put this incident behind them.

Chapter Fifteen

It was after six by the time Jenni left the clinic on Wednesday. She'd heard buzz all afternoon from patients and staff about the break-in at Annette's. This town didn't need a news station, she reflected; word spread like lightning.

She'd learned from Estelle that the judge had delayed issuing a search warrant at least until tomorrow. This bit of information arrived courtesy of Estelle's husband.

Helen had called to reschedule her appointment for Friday morning and told Jenni she planned to stay with her mother for a while. "I'd give the police permission to search the place, because they won't find anything, but Arturo would never forgive me," she'd said. "I'm glad he went to see you this morning. At least I know he's talking to someone responsible."

"He told you he came to see me?" Based on her impression of Arturo, Jenni had expected him to keep the matter to himself.

"No, they were discussing it at the salon."

She stifled the urge to groan aloud. Someone, perhaps the neighbor who'd seen Arturo, must have shot his mouth off.

She was glad the busybody hadn't figured out she and the chief had slept together. That would *really* set the town back on its heels, she reflected as she drove home.

Despite her hunger, Jenni didn't think she could bear answering the questions people were likely to ask if she stopped at a restaurant or the grocery store. So she tried to convince herself that yogurt and lettuce would allay her pangs.

Wearily, she trudged up the steps, trying to ignore aromatic smoke wafting her way. At the top, taped to the door, a note in bold masculine handwriting said, "Follow your nose to the barbecue." Childish flowers and curlicues filled the page, indicating Nick had contributed to the effort.

She didn't even consider resisting the peace offering. After she let herself inside, Jenni threw open the bedroom window and peered down. In Ethan's yard, she saw Nick splashing in an inflatable pool while his father tended the grill.

When Ethan glanced up, she waved. "Be right down."

He saluted. Then he put a cautionary finger to his lips, a reminder that the neighborhood was full of curious ears.

Jenni shut the curtains and changed into jeans and a blouse. Although she wished she hadn't broadcast her dinner plans, she looked forward to spending time with Ethan.

The fact that he didn't hold their dispute against her lifted her spirits. There was nothing petty about the man.

And the more she thought about Arturo, the more confident she became of his innocence. If the missing portraits had been stashed in the apartment, Helen surely wouldn't have claimed there was nothing to find.

Downstairs, Jenni skirted the fence into Ethan's yard. She found him wearing a bright red apron and a chef's hat, rakishly askew, as he turned chicken pieces on the grill. Around the coals, he'd tucked foil-wrapped items—potatoes and corn, judging by the shapes.

"Impressive," she said, and gave him a hug. When her cheek came to rest on his shoulder, he brushed a kiss across her hair.

He smelled of charcoal smoke and men's cologne. And

something unique that she privately dubbed "eau de police chief."

Self-consciously, she glanced at Nick. Splashing in his pool, he grinned back.

"Jenni! Did you see Boots?"

"Is he allowed out yet?" She recalled hearing Annette mention that they had to keep the cat indoors for a day or so.

"He isn't out." Ethan indicated the house's screened side porch.

A black-and-white kitty face stared at Jenni from atop a glider. When she approached, he issued a plaintive meow before darting away.

Not wanting to alarm the cat, Jenni retreated. "He doesn't look any worse for wear."

"You wouldn't say that if you were a guy." Ethan added another dash of barbecue sauce to the chicken before calling to his son. "Hey, sport, time to dry off. Dinner's almost ready." To Jenni, he added, "I invited my mother to join us but she has a church social."

"She keeps busy. Should I help Nick?"

"That would be great." Ethan wielded the grilling tools. "I'm a little tied up here."

The little boy stood dripping on the concrete as Jenni dried him; he was sturdy and at ease beneath her rubbing. Although Jenni examined children all the time, she didn't touch them any more than necessary, but this felt different.

She pulled Nick close. Without hesitation, he wound his arms around her neck and planted a smooch on her cheek.

"Pretty lady," he said, and gave his father a thumbs-up.

Jenni burst out laughing as Nick trotted into the house.

"What a lady's man!" Mischievously, she added, "He's a chip off the old block."

"He likes you." Ethan transferred the food on to plates. "So does Mom."

"She actually said so?" Jenni asked.

"She practically read me the riot act. Something about knowing a good thing when I see it." He winked.

Speaking of Annette reminded Jenni of the break-in, an uncomfortable thought. "How's she doing?" she asked. "Is she angry about my protecting Arturo?"

Ethan removed the foil-wrapped vegetables from the briquettes. "She doesn't blame you."

"I'd hate to disappoint her." Whether or not Annette had championed her with Ethan, Jenni valued the woman's friendship.

"My mother's been through a lot, but she's strong-minded," he said. "I don't just mean today, either. Once she takes a liking to someone, she doesn't let go easily."

Jenni carried two plates of food to the cloth-draped patio table. "I would never, ever do anything to put your family at risk, Ethan."

His eyes flashed as they met hers. "I know that. And I respect your position. The more I think about it, the more I realize you're behaving the way you believe is right."

"But you're still a cop," she murmured.

"Well, yes." He brought a third plate along with a serving platter. At the table, where he'd set out condiments and flatware, Jenni poured sugar-free drinks for the three of them.

Nick bounded out of the house. "I'm ready!"

"Did you wash your hands?" Ethan asked.

The little boy extended them proudly. "I was in the pool. They cleaned themselves."

"Have you petted the cat since then?" his father asked.

"Oops. Okay, I'll wash them." Nick dashed inside again.

"He's a sweetheart," Jenni said. "And you're a great dad."

"Not with my work schedule. I don't know how I'd manage if I didn't have family to help." He sounded pleased at the compliment, though.

"It has to be a balancing act," she noted. "Some parents with diabetic children become overprotective. You've let him develop appropriate self-sufficiency."

"Spoken like a doctor. I'm glad you understand. At school, he needs to fit in with the other kids. He's likely to stay with most of his classmates all the way through high school, and first impressions count."

"He'll do fine," Jenni assured him. "He'll probably turn out to be a natural leader like his Dad."

Leaning forward, Ethan lifted his palm to her cheek, tracing the outline of her lips with his thumb. Jenni's mouth tingled and a soft glow spread through her.

Even when he withdrew his hand, the sensation lingered. She felt especially close to Ethan, sitting here on his patio amid the homey noises of the cat mewing and the back screen door slamming to announce Nick's return.

He helped his son butter a potato, skewer his corn and cut up the chicken. Jenni thought she had never smelled anything so good.

As they ate, the boy happily described his experiences in Mill Valley. Staying at a motel with grandma had been a big adventure, and he was fascinated by the veterinary clinic.

"Do you suppose you might want to be a vet when you grow up?" she asked.

"I'm too little to know what I want to be," he responded.

Jenni was wondering what he thought about the intruder when he raised the subject himself.

"When we got home, there was a man in our house." Nick nibbled his ear of corn. "I think he wanted food."

"Why?" Jenni said. She could tell Ethan was listening intently.

"Because Grandma bakes the best cookies. But Boots scared him away."

The boy had concocted an explanation that minimized the

frightening nature of what had happened, she thought. "Boots is one fierce cat."

"He was even fiercer before they cut his privates off," Nick added.

Ethan choked on a bite of potato. Jenni, who'd just taken a swallow of her drink, felt it shoot through her nose as she laughed.

"Where on earth—" Ethan didn't finish the question.

"That's what Grandma said," Nick assured them earnestly.

"Your grandma has a colorful way of putting things." Jenni wiped her face with her napkin.

"However, there are some matters we don't discuss while we're eating," Ethan explained. "They might spoil our appetite."

"Not mine," Nick chirped, and stabbed another chunk of chicken.

"Delicious food, by the way," Jenni commented.

"And such original conversation," Ethan deadpanned.

"They don't know what they're missing over at Pepe's and Gwen's," she chimed in.

After dinner, they moved into the living room, where Nick put a CD on the player, his skill making it clear that he did this often. A stillness came over Ethan, and Jenni knew without asking whose voice they were going to hear.

Guitars, fiddles and a steady country rhythm filled the room. The singer's throaty voice soared above them, reaching inside her with its honesty and pain.

Martha sang of lost love as if from a vast store of experience. Watching Nick, Jenni realized how wonderful it was that he could visit this side of a mother he'd never known.

Ethan didn't try to hide his bittersweet longing. He must be remembering his wife's face the way he'd seen her when they met or perhaps when she'd sung for him privately, Jenni thought. A voice like that was a gift.

When the song finished, Nick turned off the player. "Time for bed," he announced. "Who's going to read me a story?"

"We both are." Ethan sounded a bit hoarse.

Jenni accompanied the two males into a room full of toys, with a patchwork quilt covering the bed and cartoon characters cavorting on the curtains. After Nick hurried through changing into pajamas and brushing his teeth, the two adults took turns reading a new book about a cat, which Ethan had bought as a welcome-home present.

Nick gave them both kisses and curled contentedly beneath the covers. Jenni wished every child in the world could share the same sense of security.

Minutes later, in the living room, Ethan said, "Don't run off. I've got root beer if you want some."

"Just a bit." Much as she wanted to linger, she knew it wasn't wise. "Half the neighborhood is probably sitting in the park with a stopwatch, timing my visit."

"I wouldn't put it past them." Ethan fetched two tumblers from the kitchen. When he returned he said, "I've been thinking about installing a gate between the yards so the whole world can't watch when we go back and forth."

"That's a good idea." She accepted her root beer with thanks. "For Nick's sake, of course."

"Naturally."

Nestling beside Ethan reminded Jenni of what had happened last night. This time they shared a companionable closeness instead of roaring desire, and that seemed special in its own way.

"I enjoyed hearing your wife sing," she said. "Thank you."

He turned his glass in one hand, examining the root beer as if it were wine. "You didn't mind?"

"It was a privilege."

He put the glass down and set hers beside it. When their mouths met, Jenni relished the scratchiness of his cheek and the curve of his shoulder.

I could fall in love with him. She wouldn't say anything, though, because it was too soon, for either of them. In his slow exploration, she felt Ethan's awareness of the fragility of their situation, too.

They held each other for a while longer, and when it was time to leave, Ethan came out on the front porch and watched until she reached the shadows of Annette's backyard.

Hurrying toward her apartment, Jenni registered a silver-black world patched with shades of gray. In such a realm, you had to be careful not to lose your footing, she reflected, and wished she had Ethan's hand to guide her.

But he wasn't far away. She hoped he never would be.

ON THURSDAY MORNING, Ethan and Mark let themselves into Helen's apartment with her key. She'd provided it after the judge issued a warrant.

To be on the safe side, they knocked and called out "Police!" There was, however, no sign of Arturo—not surprising, as Ethan had posted a patrolman in front since the day before to prevent anyone from disturbing the scene.

By big-city standards, he knew this case wouldn't rank high. But in a town like Downhome, the break-ins disturbed people. With his own family having been targeted, he shared that feeling.

Wearing gloves and carrying plastic evidence bags, Ethan and Mark took a quick turn through the rooms to avoid any unpleasant surprises. Their quarry appeared to have moved out, as his girlfriend had stated. There was no shaving gear in the bathroom and no male clothes hung in the closet.

Arturo had left behind a number of paintings. An unfinished scene from Jackson Park rested on an easel in the front room, where Ethan had noticed it during his previous visit. In light of the intrusion at Annette's, the reminder that the artist had been working right in front of her house seemed ominous.

The investigators launched a grid-pattern search, ensuring that they neither missed an area nor repeated themselves. They took pains to replace everything so as not to leave a mess for Helen.

Mark kept a log showing the time and detailing what they saw. However, they didn't find the missing frames or the portraits.

In the second bedroom, Ethan did observe some empty easels. Of course, they might have held Arturo's paintings.

So far, they'd discovered nothing. Maybe they owed Helen and her boyfriend an apology. Ethan hoped for Jenni's sake that this was the end of it, but his gut told him otherwise.

He spotted an envelope propped on a chair. It bore the words "For Helen," but apparently she hadn't noticed it yet.

Picking it up, Ethan untucked the flap and found a wad of hundred-dollar bills. Although it wasn't easy with gloves, he counted them. Six in all.

Elsie and Joe Ledbetter, two of the theft victims, had reported the loss of an envelope containing six hundred-dollar bills, which they'd hidden in the back of their stolen picture frame. They'd considered that a safe place, Joe had explained ruefully.

The police hadn't released the information. They often withheld a strategic detail so that if a suspect blurted it out, he couldn't get off by claiming he'd read it in the newspaper. Such details also helped rule out false confessions.

Arturo probably hadn't known about the money when he took the picture. Later, when he found it, he might have believed the Ledbetters had forgotten about it, since the loss hadn't been cited in the paper.

Still, unless the bills or envelope bore a distinguishing mark, their discovery proved nothing.

Ethan held the envelope toward a window. In the bright

light, he saw an erasure beneath the newer writing. At an angle, he could make out two names: Elsie and Joe.

"We've got him," he said. After examining the envelope, Mark nodded in agreement.

Ethan wished he didn't have to break the bad news to Jenni. But at least she could no longer refuse to cooperate.

Chapter Sixteen

"I made a promise." Jenni took a shuddering breath.

"Don't be ridiculous. The man deceived you." Ethan struggled to hold on to his temper. He'd marched over to her office confident that they could wrap up this matter quickly. "You didn't promise to protect him from facing the consequences of his crimes."

"There has to be another explanation." She braced her hands on the desk. "Maybe he found the envelope in the street."

That she insisted on excusing the man who'd endangered his mother and Nick irked Ethan. "Jenni, you're interfering with an investigation."

"I'm trying to figure out the right thing to do!" she retorted. "Besides, we're not talking about a murder case!"

The fiery expression on her face both moved and infuriated him. The past few nights, he'd drawn closer to Jenni than to anyone since Martha. He didn't want to let a creep like Arturo come between them.

"I've got to bring this man in for questioning," he said. "Tell me honestly, Jenni. Do you still believe he didn't steal the portraits?"

Her shoulders sagged. "I wish I could."

"Wishes don't cut it."

"But I don't believe he broke into Annette's house. Believe me, I'd turn him in if I thought he posed a danger to anyone. He told me he'd done things he's not proud of. All he's asking is for a second chance."

"Everyone wants a second chance." Ethan didn't try to hide his impatience. "Only a minority of criminals—twenty percent, by some estimates—are sociopaths. The rest are capable of remorse. Most of them believe they ought to be forgiven once they say they're sorry. It doesn't work that way. We have laws and penalties for a reason."

Her chin lifted defiantly. Instead of a mature woman, he saw an angry adolescent preparing to stick up for one of her buddies.

Ethan braced himself for an outraged retort. However, it didn't come. Instead, Jenni took a deep breath and transformed back into Dr. Vine. "Yes, we have laws. We also should have mercy."

"Only after the accused has been tried and convicted," Ethan countered. "We don't let people off the hook because they paint pretty pictures or tell a good sob story."

At the last phrase, resentment flickered in her eyes, but she held it in. "I need to think about this."

"I don't see what there is to think about. We found evidence. At the very least, the man needs to explain it."

"I'm hoping he will," Jenni said. "I plan to give him a chance to show what he's made of before I turn him in."

"This isn't up to you," he replied regretfully.

"Oh, yes, it is."

Ethan hated the position she'd put him in. But he couldn't place anyone above his duty, no matter how he felt about her.

"You have twenty-four hours to think it over, which is more than I'd give most people. Then I'm booking you for obstruction of justice."

Her face tightened. She was pulling inside herself, he realized, putting up barricades as she'd no doubt learned to do over the years.

Ethan realized he'd become the enemy. It was the last thing he wanted, but she'd left him no choice.

"I'll let you know what I decide," Jenni answered tightly.

There was nothing more to say. And everything to say—yet if he tried, he might only make things worse.

With a heavy heart, Ethan marched out of the clinic.

JENNI WISHED she could run after him. This was awful. She'd just put her freedom and her career on the line, and she was driving away the best man she'd ever met.

She loved Ethan. Her feelings scared her. Ironically, she'd realized this while he was reading her the riot act. She loved the man even when he stood there threatening to lock her up. She loved his strength and his integrity.

Integrity, however, was the issue right now. *Her* integrity.

Although she hadn't sought out Arturo, his trust placed her under a heavy obligation. She suspected that, now more than ever, he desperately needed to know that someone believed his life had value.

She remembered what it was like to be sixteen, ditching school and running around with a dropout. If she hadn't fallen off his motorcycle and met Susan Leto, she might have been caught in a downward spiral of unplanned pregnancy, drugs or petty crime.

Once Arturo had a criminal record, even if he got off lightly, he'd face extra difficulties in trying to make something of himself. Yet he'd apparently broken the law and, as Ethan had said, the outcome lay out of Jenni's control.

Sooner or later, Arturo would be arrested. But at least if he knew he could trust one authority figure—her—maybe he'd try again when he got out. Maybe he'd at least stand by Helen and their child.

How much, Jenni wondered, would she have to sacrifice to help him? Only a little over two months remained of her probation. Would people hold this against her?

She got her answer an hour later when a patient called to break his appointment. Several more cancellations followed.

Estelle, who'd learned about the situation from her husband, asked what was going on and frowned at Jenni's explanation.

"I don't get it," she said at last.

Olivia called to say her friend in Knoxville had promised to look into a possible position for Arturo. "I'm putting it on hold right now. We have to let the police sort this out."

"I know," Jenni replied. "Thanks."

Olivia didn't offer advice or issue a warning, although as chairman of the search committee and wife of the mayor, she had considerable influence. Jenni appreciated the fact that one person, at least, appeared to be suspending judgment.

Taking her courage in her hands, she crossed Home Boulevard after work to pick up a sandwich at the Café Montreal. As she entered, conversations stopped. Amid an uneasy lull, the young man behind the counter hurried to fill her order. Jenni had barely closed the door behind her when she heard a buzz rising inside.

Everybody knew. No one had spoken rudely, but that might be only a matter of time.

A sense of dread twisted her stomach. Despite her hunger, she barely managed to eat the sandwich.

Through her front window, she saw lights shining at Annette's house. Were she and Ethan eating dinner, perhaps avoiding the awkward subject in Nick's presence? Jenni felt like running over there and apologizing, but she couldn't.

The twenty-four hours ended tomorrow afternoon. What was she going to do?

Her phone rang, startling her. After picking it up, she said hesitantly, "Dr. Vine."

"Jenni? It's Karen. I thought you could use a friend right now." The warm voice dispelled some of her anxiety.

"I sure could." She plopped on to the couch. "I guess everybody thinks I'm either insane or soft on criminals."

"They're confused," Karen said diplomatically.

"Why aren't you?" Jenni asked.

"Because…" The other woman paused. "When I was leaving the nursing home a little while ago, I noticed there was nobody using the swimming pool at the community center. Why don't you throw on a swimsuit and I'll pick you up? I'll bet we could both use some exercise."

The pool lay out of sight of the street, Jenni recalled from when she'd toured the center during her first visit to Downhome. "I guess that would be okay. I mean, yes, sure."

"I'll be over in a second."

Jenni pulled a T-shirt and shorts over her bikini before going out. The last thing she needed was to run into Ethan in a semi-undressed state.

Or maybe that was exactly what she needed. But not under these circumstances.

The awkwardness of living on his mother's property sank in as she made her way quietly along the drive. From inside the kitchen came the clatter of dishes, along with wonderful scents.

She heard Ethan say, "Good for you, Nick. You ate all your stew."

"He cleaned up his lunch, too," came Annette's response. "The boy must be having a growth spurt."

Jenni missed them keenly. Why couldn't she just give in? Maybe Arturo had left the farmhouse by now, anyway. It might not even make a difference.

Still, it made a difference to her. And if he learned she couldn't be trusted, it would make a difference to Arturo.

Karen's smile was welcoming as Jenni slid into the car beside her. "I want to get in a few laps while we still can," she said as she put the car in gear. "Starting tomorrow, the pool will be jammed."

"Why's that?" Jenni asked.

"In case you missed it, it's the Fourth of July weekend."

She hadn't given it much thought. Although the clinic would be closed Monday, Jenni remained on call. "Ethan mentioned something about a picnic at The Green. I don't suppose I'd be very welcome, assuming he hasn't thrown me in the hoosegow by then."

"He wouldn't do that!" Karen gasped.

"Oh, yes, he will if I don't 'fess up," Jenni said. "I don't exactly blame him, either. I suppose I'm acting like an idiot, but I promised Arturo I wouldn't tell anyone his whereabouts. I keep thinking there ought to be something I can do to put things right."

A few blocks farther along, Karen pulled into the nursing home lot, which sat next to the community center. "There's a locked gate on this side, but they gave me a key. Sometimes I work out in the mornings."

A few judiciously planted trees screened the pool, Jenni was pleased to note. Once Karen let them inside, they were able to disrobe in privacy.

Jenni dove into the deep end and completed two laps before slowing. She hadn't realized how much pent-up energy coursed through her.

Karen swam her laps crossways. "You're quite a swimmer," she commented when she came up for air. "Must be those California ocean currents."

"I was on the swim team my first two years in high school," Jenni explained. "That was before I had to get a part-time job."

After their laps they sat on the edge, feet dangling in the water. "I guess part of the reason I called tonight was that I understand what you're going through," Karen said. "I told you about Barry, how he was framed."

Jenni nodded.

"Nobody would give him a break. It was awful during the trial. People stared at us everywhere we went. Because our parents owned the paper, at least we didn't have to deal with unfair coverage, but he got hate mail." In the fading light, shadows hollowed her face.

"Did people take it out on you, too?"

She nodded. "Because I refused to turn against him, some people called us two of a kind. I understand why they sympathized with Mrs. Anglin because she'd lost her husband. Still, that didn't make Barry guilty."

"Does he truly believe he can solve the case after so many years?" Jenni asked.

Karen hugged her knees. "He thinks he's identified the culprit. I'm not sure I agree, but *somebody* has to be guilty."

"Who does he suspect?"

"Chris McRay, who used to be his best friend." Karen spoke the name haltingly. "I had a crush on him for years before that. It was horrible when his testimony clinched the prosecution."

"That's why you sympathize with me," Jenni murmured.

Her friend nodded. "Yes. Don't worry about getting skewered in print, either. Barry will make sure of that."

"But he moved back, despite the way he was treated."

"He stayed away until our mother's accident. Somebody needed to edit the paper, and, with a prison record, he was having a hard time finding work as a journalist anywhere else. Mom and I were glad to see him," Karen said. "And by then, folks weren't angry anymore. Most of them, anyway."

"What happened to the other boy?"

"Chris?" Karen wrinkled her nose. "Believe it or not, he became a pediatrician. He's applied for a job here. What makes it tricky is that he's Mae Anne's grandson and she'd love to have him close by."

So Jenni might end up working with the guy. That is, assuming she passed probation, which at this point was seeming less and less likely. She didn't even want to think about what she'd do or where she'd go if that happened.

Maybe the peace corps had openings for doctors. That would put as much distance between her and Downhome as possible. And between her and Ethan. Jenni's heart ached at the thought.

"Maybe I should resign from the search committee, because I can't be objective about Chris," Karen admitted. "I'm not sure what I'm going to do if he gets hired. There'll be no way to avoid seeing him."

There was more here than met the eye, Jenni thought. "It wouldn't be a problem if you didn't still care about him."

Her friend's jaw dropped. "Wow. You don't pull any punches."

"Sorry," Jenni said.

"It's all right. I'm honestly not sure how I feel about him. But I'd hate to lose you."

Jenni's eyes filled with tears. "I'd hate to lose you, too."

"You have to do what you think is right and let the chips fall where they may," Karen advised.

"If I go to jail, will you bake me a cake with a file in it?" she teased.

"Even better—I'll ask Barry to claim he'd hired you to do some freelance writing. You can say you were a reporter protecting your source. Tennessee has a shield law."

The stoutness of her friend's support amazed Jenni. "I can't tell you how much I appreciate that. However, I'm not going to lie and I wouldn't let your brother perjure himself on my behalf. Thank you, though."

Nearby, a cell phone rang, sending both women searching their bags to find out whose it was. It turned out to be Jenni's.

The sound of Ethan's voice gave her a bittersweet thrill. "This isn't an emergency, but I have a concern about Nick. I don't think it can wait till tomorrow."

"It may take me a few minutes to get there. However, I'd be glad to come," she said.

"You're not home? I'm sorry, I should have looked for your car." His apologetic tone contrasted sharply with his outrage this afternoon. What a complicated relationship they had, Jenni thought.

"It's okay." She decided not to mention that she was at the pool with Karen. Her instinct to guard her privacy had returned. "What's the matter?"

"For the past three days, he's insisted on taking his own blood-sugar readings. The doctor in Nashville has encouraged us to let him manage his own illness, so Mom and I went along with it. We should have double-checked," Ethan said gruffly. "Tonight I decided to run the test myself and it came up low." He gave her a reading that was worrisome but not at a crisis point.

"It should be looked into," Jenni agreed. "How's his temperature?" An infection might account for a drop in blood sugar.

"I didn't take it. I'll do that right now." He sounded as if he were kicking himself for overlooking even a single detail.

"Give me fifteen minutes to get there, okay?"

"Thank you." His voice sounded strained.

Men often resented their sense of helplessness in the face of a loved one's illness, which made them grumpy in hospital situations, Jenni had learned. And she must be the last person before whom Ethan wanted to appear weak. Under the circumstances, he'd reined in his temper admirably.

When she explained that she had to see a patient, Karen

grabbed her towel. "Even if it's not life-or-death, they must be worried or they wouldn't have called you. Let's go."

After drying off, they threw on their clothes and jumped into the car.

The perplexing thing about diabetes was that both very high or very low blood-sugar levels could be dangerous, Jenni reflected on the ride home. Type 1, which Nick had, indicated his pancreas wasn't manufacturing enough insulin to regulate the glucose in his blood. The treatment, available since 1922, consisted of regular injections of insulin—in his case, administered through a pump.

Although unregulated levels of glucose had serious harmful consequences over the long term, including possible blindness and limb amputation, low levels of glucose posed a more immediate danger. When a patient ate too little while receiving steady doses of insulin, his blood sugar might drop low enough to send him into a coma. Untreated, the condition was, on rare occasions, fatal.

Nick hadn't come anywhere near that level. Still, Jenni didn't understand why he'd run into this situation, since he'd apparently been eating regularly. Perhaps his pump had malfunctioned. With no diabetologist in Downhome, she hoped she could figure out the problem.

Karen stopped in front of Annette's house. With a quick thank-you, Jenni sprinted for her apartment, changed and grabbed her emergency medical kit.

When she arrived next door, Ethan answered at once, his forehead creased with anxiety.

"I'm glad you're here."

"Sorry I'm a bit of a mess," Jenni said as she entered. She hadn't even remembered to brush her hair. "Is your mom home?"

"She's having dinner with friends. I don't want to disturb her if I don't have to." As usual, he was prepared to carry the weight of the world on his shoulders, Jenni thought, feeling tenderness for him.

Nick sat curled on the living room couch in his pajamas. Aside from a slight pallor, he didn't look ill.

"His temperature's 98.5," Ethan noted.

Normal. That made an infection unlikely. "Good." Jenni sat beside the small patient, who gazed at her uncertainly. "Hey, sport, what's going on?"

"I'm sorry," Nick said.

"About what?" she asked.

"For not checking his blood sugars when he said he did," Ethan explained. "Otherwise we might have caught this problem sooner."

Nick bit his lip. Jenni's instincts told her he wasn't telling the whole story. Perhaps his worried father hadn't given him a chance.

"Ethan," she said, "I'm going to ask you to step out of the room for a few minutes."

"Nick doesn't mind if I watch his exam—do you, tiger?"

The boy shook his head.

"That's not the point." Jenni struggled to phrase what she had to say as diplomatically as possible. "Sometimes kids feel freer to talk without a parent around."

"Talk?" His expression darkened. "My son has a medical condition. I don't see how talking is going to help."

Jenni regarded him levelly. "Who's the doctor here, Ethan?"

As his jaw worked, she could see how much he wanted to argue. To take command. To fix things. But he couldn't.

Instead of conceding defeat directly, he addressed his son. "I'm going to leave you alone with Dr. Vine for a few minutes, okay?"

"Okay," Nick said.

Ethan spun around and left.

"He's mad, huh?" the little boy asked.

"No, he's worried. Grown-ups sometimes act grouchy when they want to help and they can't," Jenni explained.

Nick clutched a worn teddy bear that probably dated from his infancy. "Am I sick? I mean, worse than usual?"

"Let's find out," Jenni said. "Do you know what a detective does?"

"They catch bad guys," the boy answered.

"They also catch diseases," she told him. "Let's see if we can act like detectives and figure out why your blood sugar dropped. Do you have any ideas?"

From the hall, she heard a rustling that told her Ethan was waiting close by, listening. That suited her fine as long as he didn't interfere.

"I don't know," Nick said.

"A minute ago, why did you say you were sorry?" she probed.

"Because I, um, lied."

"Did you test your blood sugars like you were supposed to?" When he nodded, she asked, "How long have they been low?"

"Since yesterday."

"Why didn't you tell your dad or grandma?"

"'Cause they would have made me stop." He paused.

"Stop what?"

"Feeding Boots," he replied.

A glimmer of light broke through. "You've been giving your food to the cat?"

"Grandma makes him eat that dry stuff," Nick told her. "It tastes terrible. I tried it. Yuck."

"That's because you're not a cat. Now, let me see if I follow this," Jenni said, amused in spite of herself. "You've been sneaking your food to Boots, so you aren't eating enough. Did you know that was why your blood sugars dropped?"

"I figured." He hung his head, the picture of mortification.

Jenni drew him against her. He cuddled close as if it were the most natural thing in the world. "Being kind to animals is a good thing, Nick," she said. "But grown-ups sometimes have facts that children don't."

"Like what?"

She explained about the dangers of low blood sugar, and also how cat-food manufacturers conducted research to make sure they provided both complete nutrition and the flavors that cats preferred. "It's okay to give Boots a treat now and then, but don't overfeed him or he'll get fat and unhealthy. Plus, we have to take extra care with your health, too."

Nick made a small noise of relief. "I've been awful hungry. And I felt bad about lying."

A tap on the door frame announced Ethan's return. At the sight of his son nestling with Jenni, his eyes got misty. "I guess the detectives did their job, huh?"

"Did you hear all that?" she asked.

His head bobbed. "I didn't meant to steamroller his explanation."

"You're his dad. He means more to you than anything on earth," Jenni responded. "You were just trying to help."

Carefully, she slid away from the little boy. "So you're hungry?"

"My stomach's got a big hole in it," he said.

"How about a snack?" Ethan suggested.

"Okay!" Nick jumped up. "I don't have to prick my finger again afterward, do I?"

"I'm afraid so." Jenni rose slowly, wishing she could stay. "It's important to monitor those blood sugars frequently until they level out. I want to make sure we don't need to adjust your dosage."

"Okay." Nick scuffed his bare foot on the carpet. "I'll do what I'm s'posed to, since you say so, Jenni."

"I'm right next door," she told him. "Have your dad call if you need anything."

"Sport, I'll fix you a snack in a minute." Ethan escorted her to the front porch. "I'm more grateful than I can express."

She smiled. "Don't worry. The clinic will send you a bill."

"That's not what I meant." He kept his tone low. "You're so good with him."

"He's a sweetheart."

Ethan got to the point. "I hate what's happening to us. I want you back."

"Me, too." A fierce longing nearly overwhelmed Jenni. All she had to do was give him one tiny piece of information and it would all be over.

What did she really owe Arturo, anyway? He'd evidently broken into homes, and he'd run out on his pregnant girlfriend.

He'd also swallowed his pride and asked her to help put his life on track.

"Tell me," Ethan said.

"I can't." A tear burned a path down one cheek. "I keep hoping he'll turn himself in."

"That would be the honorable thing to do," the chief agreed. "But I wouldn't count on it. I meant what I said today, about taking you in. Don't make me do it."

Jenni tipped up her chin. "We both have to follow our conscience."

His expression was one of both frustration and admiration. For a moment, she imagined he might kiss her, until Nick called, "Can I eat now?"

Ethan seemed to tear himself away. "Think it over, Jenni. Please."

"Believe me, I'll think of nothing else," she assured him, then left, taking her medical bag home in the dark.

It looked as if it would be a long night.

Chapter Seventeen

On Friday, a pall hung over the clinic. Several more appointments were canceled and the patients who arrived to see her, Jenni noticed, were either farmers who probably didn't sit around the Café Montreal, listening to rumors, or people with problems that couldn't wait.

However, she received some forceful support from Yvonne, who drank coffee with Jenni during their mid-morning break. "I can't believe what my uncle's been saying," she grumbled, referring to Beau Johnson. "He claims the men were right all along, as if this had anything to do with that stupid business that happened to you in L.A.!"

Jenni finger-combed her hair, a restless habit she'd been trying to break—successfully, until today. "What I'm doing might cost me my job."

"Then I'm going to speak up," Yvonne said angrily.

Jenni didn't see why the public would listen to a young unwed mother, even the niece of a city council member. "You've taken more than enough heat. There's no reason to put yourself on the line for me."

Yvonne dumped an extra packet of sugar in her coffee. "Oh, yes, there is. I've kept my mouth shut way too long. Uncle Beau thinks the Allens were practically saints. He doesn't know why they really left."

Jenni would have preferred not to dish dirt about her predecessors. On the other hand, this sounded like something she ought to know. "Why did they?"

"Because Luther Allen is Bethany's father!" she burst out. "He could see how hungry I was for affection, so he pretended to care about me. He pretended he'd fallen in love, when all he really wanted was to get in my pants. After he learned I was pregnant, he ordered me to get rid of the baby. Can you believe that!"

"And you never told anyone?" The man's behavior disgusted Jenni on every level.

"No, but his wife found out. How could she help it? We worked together," Yvonne said. "I felt bad for her sake, but not for Dr. Luther's. After Bethany was born, I thought for a while he might accept her—quietly, I mean. I wasn't asking for public acknowledgment, just a little help. But the whole while, they were planning to leave. They announced their retirement and moved out of state with practically no warning."

"That doesn't free the father from his legal and financial obligations," Jenni pointed out.

"I phoned him to try to work something out. He said if I sued for child support, he'd make me look like a complete tramp," Yvonne answered. "I believed him. Public opinion around here wouldn't affect him at a distance, but I'd have to live with it. Besides, I didn't want money from such a hateful person. Mostly, I was so hurt by the way he treated me that I kept it secret."

"You should pursue your legal rights, for Bethany's sake," Jenni said.

"He might sue for custody just to be mean," Yvonne countered. "Anyway, you see why it ticks me off when Uncle Beau says he wants good old-fashioned doctors like the Allens. What I did was wrong and Dr. Dorothy has a right to be angry, but her husband used me."

"I agree. Still, I don't want you going public on my be-half." Although the scandal might deflect some criticism from her, Jenni couldn't let Yvonne make that sacrifice. "Regardless of what happens to me, you and Bethany have to go on living here. Besides, what the Allens did has no bearing on whether I pass probation."

"It should!" Yvonne exclaimed. "You're being unselfish and kind. They ought to respect that."

"I'm also defying the police," Jenni pointed out.

"I don't understand the chief. I thought he really liked you."

"He does." She was a bit surprised to hear herself say this. "But he's too honorable to let that get in his way."

"You call what he's doing *honorable?*"

"Actually, yes."

Patsy poked her head into the lunchroom. "Helen Rios is here."

"Thanks." Jenni stood. "Please don't say anything, Yvonne. Don't let my pigheadedness cause you problems."

"I won't if you don't want me to," the nurse conceded. "At least not now." Clearly, Dr. Luther Allen remained a sore subject. However, he could be dealt with at another time.

Helen's checkup went well. She'd stopped smoking, reduced her salt intake and begun strolling around The Green before and after work.

"Your blood pressure's holding steady," Jenni told her. "You're doing a great job."

"I'm so mad I figured it would skyrocket," the manicurist admitted. "I can't believe Arturo broke into those people's homes! It makes me want to kick him."

"We aren't sure that he did it." The words nearly clogged her throat, because what Ethan had found left little doubt.

"I should have been suspicious," Helen said dejectedly. "Once, Arturo came in with a package he said was a new canvas, only it was framed already. He acted excited, like he'd pulled something off."

"Why would he do something like that?" Jenni asked.

"To get revenge for being picked on in high school." The manicurist shrugged. "He treated every little insult like a big deal."

"You think he held some kind of grudge against the families he robbed?" Jenni asked.

The patient shook her head. "He was generally mad at the whole town. Even if people are a bit standoffish, it's not their fault his stepfather acted like a jerk and his mother didn't stick up for him. Dr. Vine, it's great that you're trying to help, but a lot of us need you. If you get arrested or fired, who'll treat us?"

"We'll make arrangements. And I hope it won't come to that." However, Jenni knew it might.

For the rest of the morning, she found herself watching the time. Ethan had issued his warning at two-fifteen p.m. on Thursday, and she figured he'd arrive around two p.m. to give her one last chance.

A chance she couldn't bring herself to use.

Maybe her motives weren't even all that noble, Jenni mused as she chewed on a vending-machine tuna sandwich at lunch. She had a habit of challenging authority figures. Maybe this was nothing more than a knee-jerk reaction on her part. She hoped not.

The sandwich tasted like cardboard. Grimacing, she tossed it into the trashcan and headed for her office. At the front desk, Patsy signaled to her. "Phone call," she said urgently. "He wouldn't give a name, but I think it's Arturo."

Estelle, who'd been updating a chart, frowned at them. "I didn't realize he was a patient here."

"He's not—unless someone just shot him," Jenni answered tartly, and went to take the call in her office.

* * *

ETHAN HADN'T SEEN MUCH of Barry Lowell in the two weeks since their disagreement about the Anglin murder case. Today, however, the deadline for the weekly *Gazette* and the breaking story of Arturo Mendez had brought the editor-reporter to the station.

"How're you going to play this, Chief?" Barry asked, having invited himself into Ethan's office when Amy wasn't paying attention—not a difficult task. "Are you really going to slap Dr. Vine in the slammer for refusing to do your job for you?"

"I wouldn't put it that way." Ethan kept a rein on his temper. He had no intention of helping the press make a fool of him. "She's withholding key information about a man suspected in a series of felonies."

"Yeah, ripping off a few photographs qualifies as the crime of the century," Barry taunted.

"There's also the matter of the missing six hundred dollars," Ethan noted.

"Right. A guy accidentally making off with an envelope full of money is definitely big-time. It's the equivalent of a Mafia takeover here in Downhome."

Barry obviously relished ragging on him, although, in fairness, Ethan suspected the reporter goaded all his subjects in hopes of getting a good quote. With Beau Johnson, the tactic had worked well on several occasions.

"I have the highest regard for Dr. Vine," Ethan said. "I hope we can avoid a showdown at the OK Corral. By the way, are you and Karen coming to the Fourth of July picnic?"

"I'll be shooting it." Barry meant with a camera, presumably. "You'll have to ask my sister about her schedule."

"I'm sure she'll show up."

Finally, Lowell took himself off to annoy some other unlucky individual. Ethan tilted back his chair as his mind returned to the problem at hand: Jenni.

Last night, she'd been wonderful with Nick, far more sensitive to the boy's subtle clues than Ethan. At every step, she meshed with his family as if fate intended her to belong to them.

He desperately wanted to avoid driving her away. But he had a sworn duty to uphold the law, no matter what that cost him.

Ethan's musings broke off as Ben Fellows dashed into his office. "My wife phoned," he said. "Our suspect just placed a call to Dr. Vine, and she's on her way out of the building."

"I'm on it." Ethan sprang up. If Arturo had arranged to meet Jenni, he didn't intend to leave her unprotected. Also, arresting the man would put an end to their standoff.

"Chief, I'm not sure you should be the one to handle this," Ben cautioned.

Although his judgment might not be completely impartial, Ethan owed it to Jenni to not leave the situation in anyone else's hands. Whatever happened, he would bear responsibility for the outcome. "Thanks for the advice, but I'm going."

"Then let me run backup."

Despite the temptation to refuse, Ethan knew better than to play cowboy. If Arturo turned violent, Jenni's safety and his own might depend on having reinforcements nearby. "Okay, but don't move in until you get the word from me."

"Understood."

They both raced to their cars.

ASIDE FROM A COUPLE of No Trespassing signs, the dilapidated farmhouse looked as if it might have been abandoned shortly after the Civil War, Jenni thought uneasily as she bumped along the rutted drive. Part of the chimney had collapsed, several windows were boarded up and the weeds around the front porch had grown into tall bushes.

Rounding the structure, she halted on a bed of gravel beside a beat-up car. This must be the clunker Arturo had borrowed.

When she killed the motor, the only sounds were the chirp of an insect and the lonely rustle of trees. Coming to such an isolated setting might not be the smartest thing she'd ever done, but on the phone Arturo had made it sound urgent.

He must know she'd arrived, Jenni reflected, yet she saw no sign of anyone stirring in the house. Perhaps Arturo was waiting to make sure she'd arrived alone.

When she got out, the heels of her pumps sank through loose gravel into moist earth, the result of frequent night rains in Tennessee. The smell of old leaves and rotting vegetation hung in the air.

Walking mostly on her toes, she crossed to a back porch so ramshackle she had to ascend on the outside edges of the steps. She knocked loudly, waited, then knocked again.

"Hello?" Jenni called. "Arturo?"

No answer.

"Hey, I left a waiting room full of patients!" She was exaggerating, since the only patients in the office when she departed had come to see Estelle. The claim however, had the desired effect. Inside, a board creaked.

Jenni's pulse quickened. When Arturo appeared in the doorway, she felt relief.

His expression was guarded. "You alone?"

"You still don't trust me?" she countered, irritated. "If I wanted to turn you in, I didn't have to come here personally to do it."

"Sorry, Doc. Old habits die hard." He held the door wide. "I want to show you something."

"Okay." She followed him through a hollowed-out kitchen to a living room gilded by sunlight. The rays had to fight their way through clouded glass on the few windows that remained unboarded.

Jenni blinked at the sight of easels arrayed in a semicircle. Small pictures, large pictures, some framed, some painted on canvas—half a dozen in all. It took her a moment to realize why she seemed to be seeing double.

Pepe's image caught her eye first, in a photograph with his children and then in the adjacent larger painting, which showed the Oteros in an identical pose. The artwork transcended the photo with whimsical lines and fresh colors that enhanced the subjects' personalities.

Gazing from easel to easel, Jenni registered what Arturo had done. He'd created artworks based on each of the three stolen portraits, bringing the subjects vividly to life with an immediacy lacking in the originals.

"These are wonderful," she enthused.

"I've been working on them the past few weeks," he said. "I just finished."

The style differed from the angry realism in his other works, Jenni noticed. Humor and warmth infused these creations.

"Your style is really developing." She turned to him. "These ought to be in a gallery. But, Arturo, why didn't you just ask to borrow the photos if you wanted to use them?"

He ducked his head. "I didn't steal them to make copies."

"Then why?"

"'Cause I was mad," he admitted.

"Mad at who?"

He shook back his shaggy hair with a trace of defiance. "While I was doing odd jobs, I kept seeing walls covered with photos of smug people. You know, the kind whose kids always sneered at me. I guess I wanted to prove I was smarter than them."

"By stealing?" Jenni asked.

"I didn't think they'd care that much," he told her. "It made me feel superior, swiping their conceited faces and making them live in my apartment, but to me, they were just photographs. I mean, I figured they could be replaced."

"Weren't you worried about getting caught?"

"I'm not stupid. I didn't go to homes where I'd worked. I picked places at random wherever I found an open door. I even saved the newspaper clippings out of pride, but I didn't read them. I should have," he added, sounding disgusted with himself.

"What changed your mind?"

"It started when Helen told me about the baby." Arturo stared down at his worn sneakers. "One day, the pictures looked different—I kind of understood how the parents felt about their kids. Then I read the articles I'd saved and I saw the one about that guy who'd died and his parents didn't have another copy of the picture. I wanted to give them back, but I couldn't figure out how."

That didn't let him off the hook. "I don't understand why you broke into Annette's house, then."

"Whose?"

"Mrs. Forrest," she said. "The chief's mother."

"I didn't take anything from her." Arturo's blank expression underscored his protest.

"She saw a guy in her house the day you dropped by my flat," Jenni persisted.

"I don't know about that," he insisted. "It wasn't me. Honestly."

"Haven't you at least heard about it? The chief's furious."

"I haven't talked to anybody since Wednesday. I was busy finishing the paintings." He folded his arms. "I thought maybe you could help me talk to the people and return their pictures, along with the new ones. As an apology."

So he didn't realize his apartment had been searched or that she'd risked jail rather than break her promise. No wonder he hadn't turned himself in, Jenni thought, her spirits lifting at this evidence that Arturo was genuinely trying to redeem himself.

"I'd like that," she said. "The problem is, the cops found the money—"

"They sure did."

Both of them pivoted as Ethan stepped in from a side room. How he'd managed to approach the house undetected, let alone sneak inside, Jenni had no idea.

Arturo glared from her to the chief. "You tricked me."

"I didn't tell him anything!" she protested. "Ethan, look what he's done. These are marvelous. He wants to make up for the thefts."

The chief didn't even glance toward the easels. She noticed his hand hovering near the belt where he wore a gun. "We can sort this out at the station. Jenni, please move away from Mr. Mendez."

Expressions of uncertainty mingled with resentment clouded Arturo's face. "What kind of game are you two playing? You expect me to believe this wasn't a setup?"

"It wasn't!" Jenni knew the situation could turn deadly if she wasn't careful, yet it infuriated her that Ethan had used her to trap Arturo.

"Please stay out of this," the chief told her. "Mr. Mendez, lie facedown on the floor, right now! Hands over your head!"

He drew the gun. To Jenni, it looked enormous.

"No way!" Despite a nervous quaver, Arturo stood his ground. "I'm not a criminal."

"That's for the court to determine. Get down, now!"

As the young man wavered, the front door burst open and Ben Fellows charged in, revolver gripped in front of him. Jenni cringed as the room filled with shouting, which didn't end until the two officers had shoved Arturo against a wall, cuffed his hands behind his back and patted him down roughly.

"I saw you draw your gun," Ben told the chief. "I was afraid he might jump you."

"I appreciate your help," Ethan said.

Jenni wanted to cry out that Arturo hadn't been about to do anything wrong, but how could she be sure? The captain had only been taking reasonable precautions.

When they spun Arturo around, bitterness burned in his eyes. "Thanks a lot, Doc."

"I didn't do this."

"Yeah? What a coincidence. They happened to stumble on the place while you were here."

Ben, who'd been reporting to the station on his phone, clicked off. "In the car," he snapped at Arturo.

"Yeah, fine. Like I've got a choice," the artist grumbled, and let the captain steer him out.

Only after they'd left did Jenni discover she was trembling. Ethan started to reach out, but one look at her face halted him.

"You can't ignore these!" She pointed at the pictures until he reluctantly turned toward them. "He was trying to make it up. He asked me to go with him and return these to their owners. And he's *not* the one who broke into your mother's house."

"So he says," Ethan muttered, apparently unaffected by the portraits.

"Once Helen told him about the baby, he stopped resenting these families," she insisted. "You can see in the paintings how he's mellowed and matured. If you hadn't come bursting in…"

"You have no idea how volatile this situation was," he answered grimly.

Although he'd put the gun away, Jenni could see the threatening lump it made at his side.

"He wasn't armed!"

"He could have grabbed my gun or taken you hostage," he

replied tightly. "If he'd moved toward either of us, I'd have had to shoot him. You had no business putting Ben and me in this position."

"I didn't put you in any position! I was handling it fine!" To Jenni's embarrassment, she started to cry.

Ethan's hands formed fists at his sides. She could feel how deeply afraid he'd been for her safety. She wanted to forgive him and ask him to forgive her, but she couldn't.

Because of him, she'd shattered Arturo's trust. The young man's future and that of his family might be destroyed forever because his attempt to make good on his mistakes had ended in humiliation and, from his viewpoint, betrayal.

"It's over," Ethan said. "Let it go, Jenni."

"I can't," she told him through a mist.

"At least you don't have to land in jail for him." It sounded like a rueful attempt at humor, but she found nothing funny about the remark.

"That might have hurt less." Her throat clenched until she could hardly breathe. Unable to bear the closeness of the room, Jenni fled.

As she started the car, she suddenly realized that the townspeople might assume, as Arturo had, that she'd cooperated with the police. For them, the whole thing would probably blow over.

But it was only a matter of time before Jenni butted heads with the town's leaders again. If they didn't respect her integrity, if they refused to listen when she had something important to say, she didn't see how she could stay here.

Maybe she'd have to fight the same battles no matter where she went. However, at least they wouldn't feel so personal. Yet leaving Downhome—leaving Ethan—would tear her heart into pieces.

She didn't know what to do.

Chapter Eighteen

For a woman who'd grown up in L.A., Jenni seemed frighteningly naive, Ethan thought as he watched her car jolting away along the drive. She'd apparently had no idea how vulnerable she was, alone out here with a fugitive.

The idea that the man could weasel out of burglary charges by giving back what he'd stolen struck Ethan as preposterous. The law didn't work that way.

He put in a call to Mark. They needed to search the farmhouse properly, although the evidence against Arturo appeared overwhelming.

While waiting for the lieutenant to arrive, Ethan studied the pictures on the easels. In the heat of the moment, he hadn't paid much attention, but now he saw what the young man had done.

He'd used the stolen portraits as inspiration for paintings so energetic they seemed to leap off the canvases. As for the faces, the word that came to mind was *charming,* not an adjective Ethan supposed an artist would appreciate.

So that was what Jenni had been talking about. Arturo's intent wasn't simply to return the photos but to accompany them with his interpretations. Kind of an added bonus for the inconvenience. That didn't make up for the violation the victims had experienced, but it did put the matter in a slightly different light.

The gesture might be enough to persuade a judge to give the young man probation. Still, Arturo had broken into Annette's house the same day he'd extracted Jenni's promise to keep his whereabouts a secret. If anyone had been betrayed, it was her. For heaven's sake, the guy had brought his troubles on his own head.

When the phone rang, Ethan hoped it was her, so they could finally put this business behind them. "Forrest."

"O'Bannon," Mark said tersely. "Chief, we just got a burglary report in the Jackson Park area, a few blocks from your house. Somebody climbed through an open window and stole a DVD player and pair of binoculars from a house."

That tallied with the other thefts reported in that area, Ethan noted. "When did this go down?"

"Twenty, thirty minutes ago," the lieutenant replied.

That ruled out Mendez. So perhaps a second burglar had been at work all along.

"Here's the good part. A neighbor saw a man walking away from the scene carrying a DVD player," Mark went on. "She thought at first that he might be the homeowner's son, but fortunately, she rang the doorbell to make sure. Apparently, the resident had been vacuuming in the living room the whole time."

The noise must have obscured the sounds of the break-in. "Can the witness describe the man?"

"Not only that, she said she's seen him at the high school when she picked up her daughter."

Ethan didn't believe in lucky stars, but he thanked his anyway, for giving him breaks in both of the town's crime sprees. "Show her a yearbook," he said. "Let's nail this sucker."

"You got it."

He clicked off and stood staring at the paintings. After placing Arturo at the apartment behind his mother's house on Wednesday morning, Ethan had been certain he must be the same man who'd broken in later that day.

He no longer felt so sure. But there were still three thefts that Arturo admitted to. At the least, he intended to tell the young man how far the doctor had gone to protect him. Beyond that, Ethan would have to let time work its healing way between him and Jenni—if any of their magic remained.

ON FRIDAY NIGHT, when Jenni phoned Helen to check on her situation, the manicurist declined an offer to help raise bail. "You've done more than enough," she said. "Besides, the court's appointed a lawyer and I'm hoping he can handle it."

They left it at that.

By mid-morning on Saturday, the clinic was packed. People who'd sent their regrets earlier in the week had come in, along with additional sufferers from summer rashes, infected bug bites and farm-related injuries.

Estelle maintained a wary distance, more self-protective than judgmental. Jenni's initial assumption that Ethan had picked up the scent after seeing her leave the clinic yielded to the suspicion that the nurse practitioner had alerted her husband.

She saw no point in holding a grudge. Estelle had presumably acted according to her own moral beliefs, just as Jenni had.

Yvonne was less forgiving of anyone she perceived as a traitor. She virtually ignored Estelle all morning and maintained a cool professional veneer with the rescheduled patients, until one woman asked what was wrong.

While reading a chart outside the examining room, Jenni heard Yvonne say, "We had quite a few appointment changes this week. It inconvenienced the doctor."

"Oh, gosh, I'm sorry," the woman replied. "My car broke down and we had to tow it to Mill Valley. I didn't think it would matter if I rescheduled."

Yvonne's tone warmed immediately. "Well, of course, you couldn't help that."

Perhaps not all the defections had been related to Arturo, Jenni mused. In addition, she was pleased later to observe Yvonne acting friendlier toward Estelle. For the clinic's sake, they ought to let bygones be bygones.

On Saturday night, she hoped Ethan might call or drop by. Staring out her window at the lights of his house, Jenni considered going to see him. Too awkward in front of Nick, she thought.

Something else held her back, as well: a fundamental uneasiness with the cozy scenario she'd created in her mind. What a pretty fantasy it made—the handsome police chief, his precious son and an empty spot where the sweetheart ought to be.

Jenni had dared to imagine herself fitting into that slot, as if her emotional scars and rebellious quirks could be sanded down like the rough surfaces of old furniture. She wanted so badly to have everything she'd missed during her younger years that, for a while, she'd lived in a fool's paradise.

She could still hear Ethan's ragged voice as he stood in her office threatening to lock her up. She didn't blame him. They'd been steering a collision course since the day they met. Now that push had come to shove, she needed to accept as he did the impossibility of continuing.

Her whole body felt heavy. On Saturday night, she couldn't raise enough energy to read through a sewing catalog that had arrived in the mail, let alone pick out patterns.

By Sunday, a restless drive replaced the lethargy. Knowing she was safe from unexpected encounters while most of the population attended church, Jenni went for a jog. She made a loop through Jackson Park, soothed by the now-familiar sight of its greenery, and loped along Heritage Lane past the Lowells' house.

Karen's and Barry's support meant a lot to her. With friends like that, maybe she ought to stay in Downhome if the council decided to retain her, Jenni thought.

She'd have to find a new place to live, of course, and even then, she would inevitably come face-to-face with Ethan on occasion. She pictured him sitting outdoors at Gwen's café, lifting a glass of wine to her in a regretful salute for old times' sake.

Her heart swelling as if it were too large for her chest, she trotted down Tulip Tree Avenue, past the community center and the nursing home. As she crossed the street near the Italian diner, she spotted Pepe Otero descending the steps from his second-floor apartment.

He gave a start when he saw her. He'd been one of the victims of the thefts, Jenni recalled.

She kept on jogging without awaiting his further reaction. With her nerves rubbed raw, she didn't care to absorb any hostility just now.

On The Green, she spotted long tables set up and a few red-white-and-blue streamers draped from trees in preparation for tomorrow's picnic. Although Jenni would be on call, she hoped any emergencies would take her far away from the festive scene. There was nothing like the sight of other people's community spirit to make her feel like a complete outsider.

You have to get over this, she scolded herself silently. Yielding to discouragement seemed counterproductive. She needed to make an objective decision about whether to stay in Downhome if she had the chance.

There was no guarantee she'd blend in better anywhere else. And she genuinely liked this place, Jenni mused as she cut through the park to a curving side street dubbed Grandpa Johnson Way. She swung past the *Gazette* and, beyond it, the Snip 'N' Curl, with its enlarged photos of elegantly coiffed Downhome residents instead of the airbrushed, anorexic models one expected. Next, she passed the K-8 elementary school and Downhome High—Olivia's turf.

A yearning to stay shot through Jenni. Why should she let a broken heart chase her away? Like her father, men had a tendency to leave when the going got rough. So what? She was strong enough to run her own life.

As for the council, if they chose to dump her, Jenni could always fall back on plan B—the Peace Corps. But she hoped she wouldn't have to.

Okay, we're sinking into self-pity again. Get a move on, girl.

She finished her circuit of the town and arrived home, where she showered and changed. Since she wasn't on call that day, she drove to a shopping center in Mill Valley.

Comfortably cloaked in anonymity, she poked through a fabric shop, bought material for a new blouse and toured the home decor emporium next door. An arching floor lamp with a good work light appealed to her, until she remembered that she might be moving. She supposed she could always buy it later.

After dinner at a Greek restaurant, Jenni drove home in the twilight. The cell phone didn't ring once, and when she got to her place there were no messages on her home machine or notes on the door.

Ethan must have reached the same conclusion she had—that they'd shown all the cards in their hands and, in this curious game they were playing, had both lost. It would have happened sooner or later, even without Arturo.

Jenni went to bed convinced that her heart was already half mended. And then, for no reason at all, cried herself to sleep.

A PITIFUL MEWING WOKE HER on Monday morning. With a groan, Jenni cast a bleary glance at the clock. Six-thirty. Way too early to rise on a holiday.

The pathetic noise resumed. Coming fully awake, she realized Boots must be in trouble.

Grumbling about how independent cats were supposed to be, Jenni threw on some jeans and a tank top. Feet shoved into canvas slip-ons, she poked her head outside. The noise halted, then rose to a crescendo. Boots must have heard the door opening and renewed his cries for help.

Jenni thumped downstairs and followed her ears through the garden. In the back, she found the cat caught fast by a thick branch that had jammed beneath its flea collar.

"Aren't you a pathetic sight?" She sat down next to the trapped Boots, whose hackles rose instinctively. "Hey, you're the one who called the doctor."

The cat regarded her suspiciously. When she reached toward the collar, it flinched. "You have to hold still," Jenni soothed.

A thrashing noise nearby made her turn, half expecting to see a neighbor's dog bound into view and complicate an already delicate situation. Instead, Nick pushed through the branches into view.

With his T-shirt backward and his socks mismatched, the boy resembled a ragamuffin. "Boots is over here," Jenni said.

"He sure is loud." Nick plopped down beside her.

The cat's ears perked. It stopped struggling.

"If you pet him, he might let me release the collar," Jenni said. "Don't make any sudden moves or he'll scratch."

"He won't scratch me." Nick reached out to rub the animal behind the ears. "See?"

"If you say so." Moving cautiously, Jenni tugged at the collar buckle, her knuckles grazing the soft fur. A paw came up in protest, but the claws stayed sheathed with what she could have sworn was a major exercise of will by the cat. "You know, I think he's being careful around you."

"Yeah. He's my friend."

Finally, the band fell off and Boots leaped free. Gratefully, he rubbed Nick and then Jenni.

She handed over the offending collar. "You might ask your grandma to buy the breakaway kind next time."

"Okay. Thank you, Jenni."

Nick scooped up the cat. Although it looked heavy, it shifted balance obligingly so he could hold it in place.

They were traversing the yard when Ethan spotted them over the fence. "Nick! There you are!" Uncombed hair flopped over the worried crease on his forehead.

"Feline emergency," she explained, trying to ignore a tug at the sight of him.

"Boots got stuck." Nick trundled forward, the cat draped in his arms.

"Better bring him inside," Ethan said. "It's not wise to leave animals outside on the Fourth of July. The noises scare them."

While the boy trotted around, his father rested one arm atop the fence and regarded Jenni. "Going to the picnic?"

Painfully aware of her disheveled state, she wiped her hands on her jeans. "I wasn't planning to."

"It might feel awkward facing people at first, but that won't last," Ethan advised. His manner seemed kindly yet impersonal.

"I'm not big on crowd scenes."

"Aren't you on duty?" he persisted.

"On call," she corrected. "I'll come if I'm needed."

"You might want to inspect the food," Ethan joked. "At a potluck, there's always the risk of food poisoning."

"All the more reason to stay home." To change the subject, she asked, "How's Arturo?"

"We're releasing him this morning on his own recognizance."

That was better than she'd hoped for. "He and Helen can celebrate. I don't suppose they'll go to the picnic, though."

"You never know."

Jenni felt the chief's intense gaze compelling her to acquiesce. However, she resisted. He hadn't invited her to attend with him, after all. "I'll pass."

Ethan glanced down as his son reached him. "Ready for breakfast?"

"Yes! We're starving." Nick included the cat.

"Don't be a stranger," Ethan told Jenni, and escorted the boy inside.

She stood rooted to the ground, thoughts colliding in her brain. Maybe she ought to call Karen and ask if she could join the Lowells…but she hadn't bought any food to share. Besides, Jenni felt too edgy to deal with the undercurrents at the community celebration.

Still, she kept replaying the conversation with Ethan. Had he been hinting at something? Most likely, she decided, he'd simply been acting civil.

The morning passed slowly. She cut the blouse pieces out of the new rose-colored fabric, then flopped on the couch to read her backlog of medical journals. Her mind drifted frequently.

About noon, the phone rang. She hoped no one had a serious problem. "Dr. Vine."

"It's Gwen Martin—" The woman hesitated.

"Is someone ill?"

"No, just crazy," Gwen said tartly. "Probably me."

"I'm sorry?" Jenni didn't know what to make of the comment.

"Do you have any idea what Ethan's up to?" her caller demanded.

"I'm clueless." But rapidly growing curious, she admitted silently. "What do you mean?"

"I'm standing here in the café watching him and Arturo lug wrapped packages out of the Snip 'N' Curl," Gwen said. "Flat rectangular objects. Sound familiar?"

The photographs. "Yes." Jenni tried to digest the idea that the chief and Arturo appeared to be working together. "What are they doing with them?"

"Taking them on to The Green. I saw Helen and Arturo setting up easels on the stage earlier," she explained. "People are gathering around. It occurred to me you ought to be here."

"That's really kind of you." If Ethan planned to return the pictures in public, why hadn't he mentioned it this morning? Jenni wondered.

"No, it isn't kind," the older woman replied. "It's loony. I've been half in love with that guy for years, although he's way too young for me. But who cares about age these days? The point is, he's not in love with *me*. So I'm giving you a crack at him. I've done some stupid things in my time, mostly involving members of the male persuasion, and I hope this isn't one of them. That's all I'm going to say. You're on your own from here on out."

She clicked off without saying goodbye.

Jenni's heart hammered. She wished she'd finished her new blouse so she could wear it. And that she had wings.

Remembering to grab her medical bag in case of a call, she ran out the door.

Chapter Nineteen

Cars, trucks and motor homes filled every available parking space on Tulip Tree Avenue and Home Boulevard. Swinging into the lot behind the clinic, Jenni saw that vehicles filled it, too. Mercifully, the Reserved for Doctor slots remained empty, perhaps because of the tow-away signs.

As she exited the car, the clamor of shouts, laughter and chatter from half a block off nearly overwhelmed Jenni with raw feelings left from the past. In that moment, she became again a scruffy, unwanted kid who rubbed people the wrong way.

Yet she was Dr. Vine now. In Downhome, people respected her. To most of them, last week's incident must seem like a minor squabble, if they'd heard about it at all.

Besides, she might as well learn the worst, even if she had to do so in public. Leaving her medical bag in the trunk, Jenni cleared the clinic building and caught sight of the festivities.

Red-white-and-blue bunting festooned the trees, augmented by clusters of balloons. The buzz of voices grew louder. When she crossed the street, she felt like she was breaking through an invisible barrier. The wind shifted, bringing the scent of hamburgers on the grill. Jenni ignored the growl of her stomach.

She saw only a few rambunctious toddlers and mothers

lounging around the tables and benches on the park's periphery. Farther in, people seemed to be gathering around a central point, which she assumed was the stage Gwen had mentioned.

As Jenni progressed, she dodged between grizzled farmers, young men in cowboy hats, ladies in housedresses and laughing teenagers. A few greeted her with a "Howdy, Doc," to which she responded with a smile.

A platform suitable for a small band came into view as Jenni drew closer. Instead of musical instruments, a semicircle of easels filled the space.

She recognized the three framed portraits at once. They looked lonely by themselves. Where were Arturo's paintings?

The only familiar person she glimpsed was Helen, weaving in her direction through the crowd. "Dr. Vine!" she called as she approached. "I can't believe they're doing this!"

Before Jenni could learn more, a pair of arm-wrestling preteen boys bumped into her. She stumbled and nearly took Helen down with her.

"Sorry," the boys said, then hustled off.

"Are you all right?" Jenni asked, regaining her balance.

"Oh, sure." The manicurist scarcely seemed to have noticed the interruption. "Would you come meet my family?"

"I'd be honored." Following Helen, she waded back into the throng. Her curiosity would have to wait until they could speak more comfortably.

They stopped by some folks clustered at one side. Helen introduced a middle-aged woman as her mother, Juanita, who ran a catering business. She also presented her father, Pedro, who smiled in friendly fashion from his wheelchair, and her brother, Eduardo, who clerked at the grocery store.

"What's going on?" Jenni asked, indicating the easels. "Is Arturo planning to return them with a flourish?"

"I guess so. It was the chief's idea. He wanted to make it a big production," Helen explained.

Ethan had suggested a public presentation? He hadn't shown so much as a flicker of interest at the farmhouse. The precarious circumstances might account for his delayed reaction, but they didn't enlighten her about his silence on the subject this morning.

Another woman joined them. To Helen, she said, "I want you to understand, I don't blame you for any of this."

"Mrs. Wichita! Thank you." Helen touched her hand. The gesture drew Jenni's attention to the woman's beautifully shaped fingernails. This must be a customer. "I felt terrible about what happened."

Abruptly, Jenni recognized the lady from one of the stolen photographs. A theft victim *and* a customer—perhaps not entirely chosen at random, although in such a small town, coincidences must happen.

"I wish they'd just give the pictures back. I don't know why they're making a big deal about it," the newcomer grumbled. "Oh, by the way, I'll bring those baby things to the salon tomorrow."

"That's so kind of you!"

After the woman left, Helen said, "I wish the others were like her. Willing to forgive Arturo, I mean. But it's a lot to ask."

Ethan took the stage, dressed in a crisp, dark-blue linen suit. The crowd noise muted. Despite his casual manner, there was a commanding air about him that sent a quiver of longing through Jenni.

At the microphone, the chief surveyed the audience briefly before speaking. His gaze didn't sweep far enough to include her, though.

"I guess most of you are aware that the police force has been working overtime—that's just a figure of speech, Mr.

Mayor, so don't worry about the budget," he added with a wink at Archie, who stood beside Olivia. "In the past few days, we've apprehended not one but two suspects in recent theft cases."

Two? The murmur around Jenni reflected her own surprise.

"That's right," Ethan told them. "We have a teenager in custody who's admitted breaking into homes near Jackson Park, including my mom's. I'm afraid I can't release his name because he's underage."

Helen squeezed Jenni's hand in excitement. "I knew it wasn't Arturo!" she whispered.

Jenni wished Ethan had told her the news this morning. She supposed she'd have learned of it soon enough even if Gwen hadn't called, but his decision to exclude her was troubling.

"I can't actually return these photographs without the DA's approval," he informed them, "but I hope the owners don't mind if I display them. Mr. Mendez thought his apology might mean more in context, and I want to make it clear that they're undamaged."

Upon hearing his name, Arturo mounted the stage. With his unruly hair trimmed and his ripped clothes traded for a clean pair of jeans and a pressed shirt, he appeared almost respectable.

He stopped several feet from the mike. Ethan gestured him to move closer, and with some hesitation Arturo did.

"I, uh…" Arturo seemed startled by the sound of his amplified voice, but recovered quickly. "I want to say I'm sorry." He glanced at Ethan and, receiving an encouraging look, continued. "I've been sort of mad at the world for a long time because of problems with my parents and stuff like that. Still, it's no excuse. Everybody's got issues, huh?"

On the faces of his listeners, Jenni noted skepticism mixed with sympathy. At least they were willing to hear him out.

"So, uh, I'm here to apologize for stealing these pictures," Arturo continued. "There was some money in one of the frames, too, and I should have given that back. Now the police are going to do it for me."

He glanced at Ethan uncertainly before adding, "My girlfriend and I—we're going to have a baby. Please don't hold this against Helen, because she didn't know about it. Or against Dr. Vine, either. They both made me feel like my life was worthwhile. From now on, I'm going to try to live up to their expectations."

He stepped back. At first, no one responded. Then a man whose sun-seared face identified him as a farmer jumped up to take the mike. "Well, that's nice, but it doesn't undo what's happened. I question why our police chief is getting all touchy-feely with a crook." He shot Ethan a defiant stare before climbing down.

Jenni became aware of Karen slipping into place beside her. "Uh-oh," her friend said. "Now it starts."

"What starts?"

"Placing blame. Pointing fingers. Ethan's only been around for four years, you know," she said in a low voice. "Some people still think Captain Fellows would have been a better choice."

People muttered in response to the farmer's comments. Some sounded as if they disagreed. However, Jenni saw heads nodding, as well.

Her heart lodged in her throat. She hadn't anticipated that the chief could suffer a backlash. Even if his job weren't imperiled, the situation might hurt his attempts to launch the outreach program he cared about so deeply.

Seemingly unconcerned, he took center stage again. "In case anybody missed it, I'm helping the crook try to atone for what he did. Oh, wait. I think I left something out." He quirked an eyebrow toward Arturo, who remained on one corner of the platform. "Now, what else were we going to do?"

This was pure showmanship, and it was working. An anticipatory hush fell over the crowd.

At that moment, Jenni felt Ethan catch sight of her. Only a flicker of the eyelid revealed it.

Even though she already knew the secret, she waited breathlessly while the artist retrieved a wrapped canvas and handed it to the chief. Taking their time, the two men arranged three packages, one beside each photograph.

"Mrs. Ledbetter was kind enough to agree to inaugurate the unveiling," Ethan said. "She's a bit of a daredevil, because she doesn't know what's under the paper. Elsie?"

"Here I am!" The seventyish woman, aided by a gentleman who must have been her husband, ascended to the platform. "If the chief thinks this is a good idea, it's okay by me!"

With Ethan's help, she ripped the brown paper off the painting next to her family's portrait. Having seen Arturo's work before, Jenni focused on the reactions of those around her.

Confusion. Fascination. Appreciation.

"Mendez made that?" someone called.

"It looks pretty good from here," another voice chimed in.

Tears welled in Mrs. Ledbetter's eyes as she studied the painting. She caught hold of her husband. "It's wonderful. It's so alive. I always wanted a real painting of my family."

"Let's see the other ones!" Mrs. Wichita cried from ground level.

"I thought you'd never ask," Ethan quipped, raising a ripple of laughter.

The next painting drew applause. Mrs. Wichita, who'd gone onstage to unwrap it, swallowed before speaking. "That's lovely."

Pepe didn't wait to be summoned. He hiked onto the platform and yanked the paper off his canvas. When he saw himself with his kids, he let out a whistle.

More applause, along with a few cheers. "Lookin' good, Pepe!" a woman called.

Blushing, the restaurant owner stood his ground. "Thank goodness I didn't have to get my ex-wife airbrushed out of this one!" When the laughter died down, he added, "Arturo, I'll pay you to replace the murals in my restaurant."

"About time you redid that mess," Ethan said into the mike, drawing more laughter.

The young artist shook hands with Pepe. Jenni couldn't hear what they were saying, but it appeared that the offer had been accepted.

"I want to add my two cents' worth." Mrs. Ledbetter stepped forward. "I've been pretty disturbed. Joe and I lost a lot of sleep. We were so shook up, we thought maybe we should sell our house and move to a retirement community."

Arturo ducked his head. "I'm sorry."

"It's like that old play by Mr. William Shakespeare," Elsie replied. "All's well that ends well—for us, anyway. I got an even better picture than I could have paid for, because this young man put real heart into it. So if my vote counts, he's squared the deal, Chief." Pepe and Mrs. Wichita nodded.

Helen blew her nose. "They're such nice people," she told Jenni.

"Amazing," Karen said. "Ethan's a wizard."

Onstage, the chief reclaimed the mike. "This concludes the show-and-tell portion of our program," he joked. "You all have a great Fourth of July now."

Amid clapping, people began to drift off. Some came onstage to examine the pictures, while Arturo answered questions.

Alongside his sister, Barry reached out to shake Jenni's hand. "Fantastic. You proved your point, in spades."

"I did?" In her opinion, Ethan and Arturo deserved the credit for today's success, not her.

"I'm as strong an advocate of punishing criminals as anybody, despite what I've been through," he said. "On the other hand, most of the time you don't have the opportunity to undo the harm that's been caused. But that's what took place here today."

"I hope so," Helen put in.

"I didn't set this up," Jenni explained.

"If it weren't for you, they'd have locked Arturo away and none of this would have happened," said Karen.

Maybe so. Still, Jenni was glad she hadn't had to face the crowd and deal with that farmer's hostility. "Ethan handled most of it."

"There's just one thing wrong with what he did," Barry remarked.

"What's that?"

"His timing."

"He missed the paper's deadline," Karen clarified. "Barry won't be able to run the story for a whole week."

"It's too bad he couldn't reschedule the Fourth of July," Jenni responded dryly.

"I'll make up for it," Barry said cheerfully. "A double-page spread of photos ought to help. Which reminds me, I need to go shoot some close-ups."

Today's performance must have elevated his opinion of Ethan, Jenni noted. She was glad to see that rift mended.

After he left, Rosie, who'd been congratulating Helen, turned to Jenni. "I can't tell you how worried I was! This kind of controversy can put people at one another's throats! But you and the chief sure pulled the irons out of the fire. Speaking of fire, I'm glad you made Helen stop smoking. I'd be proud to give you a free haircut, so stop by anytime."

"Thanks," Jenni said. "I'll be needing one soon."

Olivia and Archie strolled up next. "Look what you did!" the principal exclaimed, and pointed at her own shoes.

No more high heels. "Those look comfortable. And attractive." The sleek pumps with a small wedge heel appealed to Jenni. "I might order some for myself."

"I wasn't keen about the prescription to rub her feet every night," Archie teased. "But it seems to put her in a good mood."

"Use scented oils," Jenni suggested. "That'll put her in an even better mood."

Olivia chuckled.

Her husband got a gleam in his eye. "Thanks, Doc."

After they left, Karen said, "Good going."

"What do you mean?"

"You've got Archie and Rosie in your camp, and it's a safe bet Gwen and Mae Anne will take your side," her friend observed. "That's four out of five council members."

"I guess it is." Jenni released a deep breath. It appeared that she'd won her battles…except for the one that mattered most.

She had no trouble sighting Ethan. He was still onstage, surrounded by a swarm of friends and admirers, with Nick hanging proudly on to his hand.

Jenni was debating whether to join them, when her cell phone rang. It was central dispatch, calling to report that an elderly man was having trouble breathing. His daughter had finally persuaded him to go to the clinic.

"I'll meet them there," Jenni said. "I'm right across the street."

After excusing herself from her companions, she hurried out of the park. She'd prefer to face Ethan alone, anyway.

Glancing back, she saw his broad shoulders above the mass that surrounded him. It seemed as if everyone in town wanted to get close to the police chief.

She didn't blame them.

THE CELEBRATION AT THE GREEN ran well into the night. Jenni dropped by a couple of times to treat minor burns from sparklers and one case involving a firecracker. Fortunately, no serious injuries resulted.

She spotted Ethan a few times, always in a crowd. Plenty of folks stopped to talk to Jenni, as well. Through the general conversation, she caught the underlying message of acceptance.

It came as a relief. She felt the old patterns dissolving: the need to stay on her guard, the sense of being an outsider. Today had changed her in fundamental ways, no matter what happened next.

As she prepared to depart at well past eleven, Jenni decided not to try to speak to the chief. For one thing, she had no doubt tongues would wag if they stepped off by themselves. In any case, she was too bone-tired to conduct a meaningful conversation at this hour.

She slept deeply, barely waking in time to make it to the clinic the next morning. The town lay quiet as she drove; the residents were apparently sleeping off their partying. After opening time, only a handful trickled into the waiting room.

Around noon, Arturo and Helen came in with a gift: the canvas that Jenni had tried to buy the day she first met Arturo. "I love it," she enthused. "I've got the perfect spot for it in my living room. Thank you so much."

Arturo waved away her gratitude. "It's not much compared with what you did. I can't believe you were willing to go to jail for me."

"I made a promise. If my word doesn't mean anything, then I'm not worth much, am I?"

Their eyes met. "You know what gave me the guts to get up in front of the whole town yesterday?" he asked.

"The chief?"

"He's really something, but no. I pretended I was you," Arturo replied. "I just hope I'm tough enough to handle prison."

"I hope you won't have to," she said.

He switched away from the painful subject. "I'm starting to work on Pepe's murals this week. It's cool to think how many people will see them."

"What are you going to paint?" she inquired.

"It'll be a surprise, for the whole town. Maybe for Pepe, too." Mischief glinted in his eyes. Then the couple left arm in arm.

As the women in the office gathered to admire the picture, Patsy seemed wistful. "He really does love her," she said. "It's so sweet."

Afterward, Estelle drew Jenni aside. "I'm glad everything turned out okay. I called Ben when I saw you leave on Friday."

"I figured it out." Jenni pretended to be absorbed in the canvas, unsure how to react to this disclosure.

The nurse practitioner apparently meant to get the whole thing off her chest. "I can't say I regret calling him, but it never occurred to me they'd draw their guns. I didn't mean to put you in danger. Ben felt bad about that, too, especially when he found out Arturo was trying to make restitution."

"I'm not angry." Although less than thrilled to have been turned in by a member of her staff, Jenni preferred to put the situation behind them. "I appreciate your clearing the air."

"Good." Evidently satisfied, Estelle went about her duties.

At home that evening, Jenni found a message on her phone machine from Annette. "In case you're wondering where we are, the three of us are spending the night in Nashville. After all that's happened, Ethan wants Nick to have a complete checkup."

It made sense, considering the boy's episode of low blood sugar. Plus, he ought to be examined before starting school. Still, Jenni wished Ethan had contacted her before leaving. He continued to hold her at arm's length.

Well, of course he did. She hadn't merely stood up for Arturo, she'd challenged the chief's authority in front of the whole town. She just wished he had set the record straight, even if that meant announcing he wanted nothing further to do with her. Instead, she rode an emotional roller coaster, hoping against hope one minute and sinking into dejection the next.

She spent the evening sewing the new blouse. Thanks to her distraction, she stitched one seam crooked, a mistake she hadn't made in years, and had to rip it out, but at last she finished.

Now, if only she had someplace to wear it. Or someone to wear it for.

On Thursday, she thought the day would never end. She finally arrived home to find that the Forrests had returned. Annette reported that the checkup had gone well, but she was too busy unloading purchases from her car and supervising Nick to chat at length. There was no sign of Ethan.

At dinner, Jenni hardly ate a bite of her macaroni and cheese. She spent a while trying to figure out where to place Arturo's painting but could not summon the will to hang it.

By late evening, she could stand the suspense no longer. When she calculated Nick should be in bed, Jenni marched over and tapped on the chief's front door.

For good or ill, she intended to find out where he stood.

Chapter Twenty

When Ethan answered, he wore a striped pajama top over his slacks, as if he'd been interrupted while changing. He greeted Jenni with a quizzical expression. "Hi. What's up?"

It was hardly the welcoming response she'd hoped for. Embarrassment heated her cheeks. "I wondered... How's Nick? Did his doctors make any changes?" Although she'd received a brief report from Annette, she seized on the topic as an icebreaker.

He ushered her inside. "A minor adjustment to the dosage. He's grown more than I realized. They said he's doing extremely well."

"I'm glad to hear it." She indicated his pajama top. "Is that the latest style in Nashville? It suits you."

He gave her a half smile. "I had a long day and I'm planning an even longer one tomorrow, so I thought I'd turn in early."

Jenni's heart sank. Here in Ethan's home, surrounded by sights and scents that reminded her of their lovemaking, she felt their estrangement more keenly than ever. He, however, apparently liked it that way. "I didn't mean to bother you. Sleep well."

A hand on her elbow halted her retreat. "Aren't you going to ask why I'm having a long day tomorrow?"

"Okay." Jenni controlled her tone carefully, afraid she might betray the ache inside. "What's on the agenda, Chief?"

"In the morning, I'm going to take a look at the proposed mall site. Archie asked me to prepare a report on possible law-enforcement impacts."

"Sounds interesting."

"In the afternoon, I plan to call Barry Lowell and give him an item for his front page. After receiving clemency requests from all three victims, the DA has decided not to press charges against Arturo."

Jenni let out a little cry of delight. "That's wonderful!"

"Naturally, I'll wait until the very last minute before deadline just to annoy Barry," Ethan added. "He does his best to poke at me, and I like to return the favor when I can."

Despite the lead weight in her chest, Jenni chuckled. "You devil."

"Then in the evening—" He gave a slight cough. "You've probably figured out by now that I'm the kind of guy who likes to make an occasion of things—plan them out, savor them, even delay them a little to enjoy the anticipation."

"What exactly are you anticipating?"

Instead of answering, he continued. "Whereas you're the kind of woman who barrels right over and confronts some poor slob in his pajamas."

She didn't know whether to laugh or burst into tears. Unable to do either, she simply waited.

Ethan draped both arms lightly over her shoulders so that she and he stood face-to-face. "I've got a refrigerator full of specialty food from Nashville. I hope you don't have anything scheduled for tomorrow night, because I've arranged for a baby-sitter. My mother, of course."

"I think I'm free." Jenni would make sure of it, even if she had to set fire to her calendar.

"Could you come back then? Say, around seven?"

"I don't want to wait," Jenni said. "You've been pushing me away all week."

He tightened his grip. "Does this look like I'm pushing you away?"

She tilted her forehead until it rested against his chest, which rose and fell with his breathing. "You can't fool me. Your heart rate is elevated."

"I'm not trying to fool you." Tenderly, Ethan guided her to the couch and pulled her onto his lap.

They curled into each other, and Jenni forgot everything except the sheer comfort of his presence. As he nuzzled her hair, she experienced something she'd almost ceased to believe could exist for her—a sense of coming home.

Ethan lifted his head. "I wanted to create a special occasion that you'll always remember."

"How about a sneak preview?"

"Well, I could light one of the candles and break out the Middle Eastern food. That's what I bought. I hope you like it."

"That's not all I want a preview of!" she protested.

"Oh?" Ethan queried with mock innocence. "Whatever can you mean?"

"This." Taking his face in her hands, Jenni kissed him. He tasted so good that she did it again.

His hands ran up her back, slipping her deep-rose blouse out of place. On the verge of undoing her bra, Ethan halted. "I'm afraid we might get company." He nodded toward the inner hallway. "My son has an unfortunate tendency to wake up after half an hour and come wandering in search of me."

As urgently as she wanted him, Jenni understood. "We'd better wait until tomorrow. At least we can still talk."

"About what?"

She gave his stomach a mild punch. "You know perfectly well what!"

"You mean the fact that I love you?" He touched her cheek lightly.

Jenni's emotions hovered between ecstasy and disbelief. "You do?"

Ethan drew back far enough for her to see the longing in his gaze. "Honey, I can hardly stand being apart from you."

"You could have fooled me! You've hardly spoken to me all week."

"It's in my nature to stage events for maximum effect," he conceded. "Even when the delay chafes like fury."

"Like your presentation on the Fourth?" she said. "That was quite a piece of showmanship."

"Effective, too." He didn't bother with false modesty.

"You could have warned me. I'd have missed the whole thing if Gwen hadn't called me."

"I had to take that chance." Ethan spoke more soberly now. "Jenni, I didn't help Arturo for your sake. I did it because it was right."

"I know." His statement reminded her of the reason she still didn't quite trust the words *I love you,* even though he'd spoken them aloud. "If you were ready to throw me in the slammer for taking a stand, you certainly weren't going to risk bringing the town's wrath down on your head for my sake."

"Actually, I might have," Ethan corrected. "But if we're going to be a couple, we need to respect each other's territory and each other's sense of duty. And...I hope we're going to be a couple."

"Really?"

"More than anything. I want to be a part of your life— heck, I want to be the center of your life, because you're already the center of mine." He drew her against his shoulder. "I want everything. The ring, the white lace, you name it. I want to hear Nick call you 'Mommy'... Am I going too fast?"

Jenni felt as if the Earth had jolted to a halt. "I love you so much it scares me," she admitted.

"Why does it scare you?"

"I can't do anything halfway," she warned.

"No one's asking you to."

She knew Ethan's sense of honor and his bone-deep integrity. Once he made a commitment, she had nothing to fear—not backpedaling and certainly not abandonment. Getting arrested, maybe, but they'd already survived that issue. It was just hard to absorb that the moment she'd waited for had really, truly come at last.

"There isn't anybody else like you," Jenni went on, unable to stop now that she'd opened the floodgates. "I felt so proud of you, standing up there at the picnic. And I wanted to be with you, for everyone to see us together, to know you loved me. Except I wasn't sure you did. "

Lifting her hand, he kissed her fingertips. "You probably didn't notice the huge crash a few weeks ago. That was me, falling for you. Or possibly my large ego dropping a few notches when I discovered how wrong I'd been."

"You *were* off base," Jenni teased. "Me, rich and spoiled?"

"I knew you were trouble, though," Ethan interjected. "I got that part right."

His teasing tenderness filled her with a desire to tease him back, not with words but with caresses, until they melted together. They shouldn't make love. But if they cuddled any longer, she might not be able to stop.

Besides, she was starving.

"What kind of Middle Eastern food did you buy?" she asked. "You did agree to give me a preview."

"All kinds." Reluctantly, Ethan eased her off his lap. "Let's go see what we can scrounge. But you must pretend to be surprised at dinner tomorrow."

"Okay," Jenni said. "Now, why don't we start with the hummus?"

* * *

NOT BEING ABLE TO TAKE CHARGE of the wedding drove Ethan a little crazy. The truth was, though, that in his exhilaration over marrying Jenni, he'd likely have gone overboard. Flowers outside as well as inside the church, a chorus in the parking lot to greet the arrivals, doves flying—well, that might have been in poor taste, as his mother pointed out one evening when he mentioned his frustration to her.

"Consider yourself lucky that she's letting you handle the reception. And do try to keep it within bounds, dear," she advised.

It hadn't taken long for Jenni and Ethan to tire of living apart, even next door. They'd set the earliest possible date in September, and after that, neither of them got much sleep— not that they'd been getting much before then, either.

Now here he stood, delighted for an excuse to wear a tuxedo and amused by how starched and prickly Archie, the best man, looked in his. Nick, wearing a pint-size version, fidgeted at Ethan's elbow, proudly displaying the ring on a cushion.

As music played, Yvonne paced down the aisle, glowing in her peach-colored gown. Karen followed, beaming as she displayed her maid-of-honor bouquet.

The piano launched into "Here Comes the Bride," and Ethan caught his first heart-stopping view of Jenni in the sleek, off-the-shoulder white creation she'd made. A smile wreathed the face of her mentor, Dr. Susan Leto, as she walked her protégé down the aisle.

Late-afternoon sunlight filtered through a stained-glass window to transform the bride into a walking rainbow. Months ago, Ethan recalled, he'd expected her to decamp for greener pastures. Instead, she'd brought fresh color and joy into his sepia-toned world.

When she took his arm, he got lost in her smile. He barely

heard Ben—officiating in his role as minister—ask who was giving the bride away and Susan answer, "I am."

The ceremony passed in a blur. The only reality was the radiant woman at Ethan's side, and not until he'd slid the ring—brilliant sapphires to match her eyes, since she didn't care for diamonds—onto her finger and made sure she'd become his wife before man and God did he remember the church was full of other people.

When he and Jenni turned, applause swept the chamber. In the front row, he saw his mother and sister wiping their eyes. Then others came into focus: Olivia, Rosie, Estelle, Mae Anne, Amy, Helen and Arturo, Mark and additional off-duty police officers. Ethan regretted that Gwen hadn't been able to attend, but she was attending to the last-minute details of the reception at her café and the planned unveiling of a mural he'd commissioned, with her ready consent.

The wall remained cloaked by a huge drop cloth removed only in the dead of night, when the artist worked. Speculation about what sort of picture Ethan and Arturo had planned had intensified since the completion in August of the Italian diner murals.

One scene showed Pepe and his children picking grapes. Another, on the facing wall, portrayed the family making wine while Pepe's ex-wife, Connie, peered enviously through a window. The owner had been dubious about the latter touch until Barry ran a front-page photo story that made the restaurant a magnet for curious townspeople and visitors.

Gwen claimed to be looking forward to a surge in attendance at the café, as well. But Ethan knew that she, as someone who enjoyed a spectacle almost as much as he did, would have agreed to host the painting for its own sake.

"Let's beat the crowd out of here," he murmured into Jenni's ear. "You don't want soap bubbles flying up your nose, do you?" He'd heard some of their friends planned to salute them outside the church that way, in lieu of tossing the traditional rice.

"Whatever you say, chief," she replied happily.

Catching Jenni with one hand, Nick with the other, he tugged them both down the aisle so fast that Jenni had to grab her hat. Out the double portals they scampered and down to the waiting horse-drawn carriage. Ethan had rejected the ornate Cinderella option in favor of a hansom-cab style, which reminded him of the conveyance an old-time doctor might have driven to pay house calls.

"How darling!" Jenni said as the coachman lowered a set of steps.

"Real horses!" Nick exclaimed.

Behind them, friends poured out. "Don't think you can escape that easily!" Leah Morris called. "We're bringing our bubbles to the reception!"

"I'll have Gwen bar them at the door," Ethan assured his little family as he climbed in beside them.

Jenni laughed. "I can't believe I'm marrying the man I love and we've got so many well-wishers! In L.A., nobody even suggested a farewell party."

"No wonder you left," he said.

"I'm sure glad I did!"

Since the church was only a block and a half from The Green, they didn't get to enjoy their ride for long. On the other hand, had it been a considerable distance, Ethan might have been tempted to hire a helicopter.

They alighted to find the Café Montreal festooned with white bunting. Gwen met them in front, wearing a red-and-white apron that read "Félicitations!"

"You both look great." Her gaze lingered a bit longer on the groom than on the bride.

Jenni didn't appear to mind. "Thank you. You'll always be special to us both."

Gwen's wistfulness yielded to good cheer. "You don't mind if I ogle him occasionally?"

"Not a bit," Jenni said. "I'd think you were strange if you didn't."

Nick ran ahead as they proceeded into the restaurant, which had been closed to the public since lunch. After removing her hat, Jenni fluffed her hair until it haloed her head. To Ethan it seemed she lit up the interior.

The drop cloth still obscured the back wall, he noticed approvingly. Gwen waved to one of the waiters to take it down.

Although he'd approved the concept and seen parts of the mural, Ethan hadn't had a chance to absorb its full impact because Arturo had worked on one section at a time. Now he gripped Jenni's hand in anticipation.

Two employees removed the curtain.

"Oh my!" said Jenni.

"Wow!" Nick chimed in.

"Perfect." It was, in Ethan's opinion, better than presenting a chorus in the parking lot or departing from church in a whirlybird. Much, much better.

Arturo had painted an outdoor café facing a lively street scene populated by *Cirque du Soleil*-style acrobats. Seated at the front table, toasting each other, were the bride and groom, with Gwen hovering behind them wearing a chef's hat and Nick, a tiny waiter in a tux, carrying a tray of pastries.

All the characters bore the faces of local residents. One of Ethan's favorites was a clown recognizable as the dour Beau Johnson. He also loved the youthful Mae Anne seated at a table where she shared an aperitif with an adoring Barry Lowell. That ought to tickle them both.

On the painted street, Archie and Olivia performed cartwheels, their bodies slender and flexible in spangled costumes. Ben Fellows, in tights and a harlequin jacket, held a

hoop for his wife to leap through. If Ben's posture bore a re-
semblance to his assault stance when he'd confronted Arturo
at the farmhouse, Ethan considered that an understandable
touch of artistic license.

Photos of Pepe's mural and the design for this one, along
with slides of Arturo's other work, had persuaded Olivia's
contact in Knoxville to help the young painter obtain an art-
school scholarship and a mural commission and to locate a
gallery willing to show his work. Helen's aunt, who lived
nearby, had found her niece a job in a salon and arranged a
low-rent apartment.

The young pair faced challenges ahead, but they both
showed the right spirit, in Ethan's opinion. The change in Arturo these past two months had been nothing short of re-
markable. And thanks to the murals, which were likely to win
new admirers every day, he and Helen would always be
among friends when they visited Downhome.

"This is fantastic!" Jenni said as she finished walking
along the wall, examining each section. "I could stay here all
day picking out details. Oh, look! There's Arturo and Helen
sitting in the back, holding hands! Ethan, thank you so much."

"It may have started out as my commission, but Arturo insisted on making it his gift," he explained. "He wouldn't let
me pay him. However, I do promise to bring you here for dinner several times a month so you can enjoy it."

"Only several times a month?" Gwen demanded.

"Every week," Ethan corrected.

"Here I am again!" Nick jumped excitedly at a second image of himself playing ball with a group of children. "I'm
famous!"

"You sure are." Jenni crouched to hug her son. "You'll be
the best-known kid in school this fall."

Arturo's insistence on donating his work had forced Ethan
to find a more creative gift. He'd planned to make the an-

nouncement after the guests arrived. For a change, impatience got the better of him. "Also, Dr. Vine, I'm taking you on a tour of France and Italy so you can see for yourself how the real thing compares with Arturo's creations."

"Really?" She straightened, releasing Nick. "Honestly, Ethan? I've always been dying to go!" Another thought occurred to her. "I don't have a passport."

"No hurry." He caught her by the waist. "I figured we'd plan this together."

"Good. I certainly wouldn't like to miss our weekend in Memphis." They were to leave tonight for three days at the legendary Peabody Hotel, where they could watch the daily ritual of ducks waddling off the private elevator from their rooftop home, through the lobby and out to splash in the fountain. Jenni wanted to visit Graceland, while Ethan planned to introduce her to the blues bands on Beale Street.

Behind them, he heard wedding guests arriving. Exclamations of delight filled the air as people spotted the mural. He was relieved to see no sign of the threatened soap bubbles.

"Are we supposed to stand in a receiving line?" Jenni whispered. "I don't know how these things are done." She'd called on Annette's and Karen's help in putting together the ceremony.

"Only if we want to," Ethan said. "And I'd rather just enjoy the party."

"Me, too." Jenni moved forward to greet some new arrivals.

People swirled around, but the only thing Ethan saw was the lively figure at the center of all the attention, the California blonde who'd become a part of Tennessee.

Once upon a time, he recalled, he'd vowed to keep an eye on Dr. Jenni Vine. And he was as good as his word.

He intended, with great pleasure, to keep an eye on her for the rest of his life.

Blaze™

If you loved
The DaVinci Code,
Harlequin Blaze brings you
a continuity with just as many
twists and turns and,
of course, more unexpected
and red-hot romance.

**Get ready for The White Star continuity
coming January 2006.**

This modern-day hunt is like no other....